VAMPIRES NEVER SAY DIE

GLORIA DUKE

sourcebooks
casablanca

Copyright © 2024 by Gloria Duke
Cover and internal design © 2024 by Sourcebooks
Cover design by Stephanie Gafron/Sourcebooks
Cover illustration © Louisa Cannell

Published by Sourcebooks Casablanca, an imprint of Sourcebooks
P.O. Box 4410, Naperville, Illinois 60567-4410
(630) 961-3900
sourcebooks.com

Cataloging-in-Publication Data is on file with the Library of Congress.

Printed and bound in the United States of America.
VP 10 9 8 7 6 5 4 3 2 1

As an aspiring actor, Carrie feels pressure to conform to a certain body type. While her story is ultimately about love and personal empowerment, there are stops along her journey that may be triggering for some.

• • • • •

To anyone who has ever felt powerless. You are so much stronger than you think!

CHAPTER

I

"What can I get you to drink?" I ask.

Nope. Too perky.

"What can I get you to drink?" I ask.

Nope. Too serious.

"What can I get you to drink?" I ask.

"Shouldn't you be asking the customers?" asks Nick, a.k.a. the most annoying guy in Los Angeles and quite possibly the world.

I keep my eyes on the cash register and continue to ring up my sale. "I'm rehearsing," I tell him, not that he even cares. "I have an audition tomorrow. For the role of Bartender."

"Carrie," he says, "you don't need to rehearse. FYI, you *are* a bartender."

That's it. Now I have to look at him.

I'm not short, but he's so tall I need to look up. It's something that's always kind of bugged me, but tonight, for some reason, it bugs me way more than usual. He's standing there in his rumpled black jeans and his wrinkled black tee that he probably just picked up off the floor where he shed them last night. *Wherever* he shed them last night.

"Okay, first of all, I'm *not* a bartender," I tell him. "I'm an actor who *works* as a bartender. And second of all," I continue, "the role isn't just some bartender here at Pete's on Melrose. It's Bartender in a Jennifer Lopez movie. It's only one scene, but it's a pivotal scene, so they won't be able to cut it. It's when J.Lo realizes that she doesn't want a drink at all. And she doesn't want to marry the heart surgeon. Because what she really wants is to follow her own heart and—"

"Heyyy," says Nick, totally bailing on our conversation when he spots a pretty brunette taking a stool at his end of the bar. He walks over to her and leans casually across the counter, and his long, black hair flops seductively over one of his nearly black eyes. With a glance back at me and a smirk that brings out his dimples, he asks her, "What can I get you to drink?"

His delivery is perfect.

I slam the cash drawer closed.

He tries—and fails—to smother his laughter as the woman probably wonders what's so freaking funny.

Most annoying guy in the *world*. Definitely.

· · · · ·

I'm at the taps, pulling a Molson. Nick comes up next to me to get a Sam Adams. He totally crowds me, invading my space with his big, broad shoulders and his stupidly long arms all ridiculously buff with muscles.

I tuck in my elbows and try to ignore them—or rather *him*. I try to ignore *him*.

I go slowly, tilting the mug so the beer runs down along the inside of the glass, pausing periodically to give the foam a chance to dissipate. He just pours and lets the Boston lager slosh over the rim until the head is an acceptable size.

I can't ignore him.

"You're wasting beer," I tell him.

"You're wasting time," he shoots back. "The quicker the service, the better the tips."

As he starts to go, the bare skin of his forearm, the one with the intricate guitar tattoo on its underside, brushes lightly against me.

I gasp, flinching from the contact. Because Nick's skin is freezing. Not just cold. Like absolute *ice*.

I look sharply up at him, and he's staring down at me with an expression I can't quite read. Our eyes lock.

Then he looks past me. "You're wasting beer," he says with an almost imperceptible nod.

I turn, following the direction of his gaze. I see that my hand is still on the tap, and the Molson is overflowing the mug.

"Oh crap!"

Quickly, I let go of the tap, put the glass aside, and reach for a bar rag to clean up the mess.

When I turn back a second or two later—literally two seconds at most—Nick is somehow all the way down at the far end of the bar.

· · · · ·

We're getting a little low on limes, and there aren't any in the bar fridge, so while things are quiet, I head on back to the storeroom to grab a few more to slice.

I pass by the alcove where the restrooms are, and there, in the shadows, I spy Nick and the brunette. Their bodies are joined in an embrace, his face buried deep in her neck.

I stop. Backtrack.

All at once, I have the overwhelming urge to rescue her.

And to…well…*kill* him.

Yup. Kill. As in…uh…*kill*.

Which is ridiculous on so many levels. For starters, it's not as if the woman looks like she needs any rescuing. She's obviously enjoying their little make-out session. Her head is thrown back, and her eyes are glazed over with something like ecstasy.

Something *exactly* like ecstasy.

Gross.

And by the way, it's not as if I give a damn about Nick's love life. It's nothing to me if he wants to hook up with a different woman basically every night of the week. As long as everyone's a willing participant, I really couldn't care less.

Except tonight, inexplicably, I do care. I find that I care very much.

Maybe I've just hit my limit with my coworker's complete and utter lack of professionalism. I mean, the guy *is* on the clock. He's supposed to be working, not canoodling. Plus, we *serve* people here. There's a health code, and this behavior has got to be some kind of a violation or other. Doesn't he have any sense of responsibility at all?

Just then, Nick lifts his eyes, they meet mine, and my vision goes red.

I've always thought "seeing red" was just an expression. A bit of a cliché, really. But for a split second, I'm literally seeing everything through a blood-colored filter.

I blink a few times, figuring something must be wrong with my contact lenses.

Only now, something also seems to be wrong with Nick. He doesn't move. His dark eyes go big and round in surprise. Or could it be…*fear*?

Is he scared I'm going to narc on him to the owner? I wonder. *Worried I'm going to tell Pete about tonight's little on-the-job dalliance?*

I have to give that idea a moment to settle and take root in my brain. More than a moment, if I'm honest.

See, I don't usually find myself in situations like this, where I have the upper hand. More often, I'm at the mercy of others. As an actor, I'm totally dependent on casting directors who barely glance at my headshot or my comp card, deciding in a blink whether I'm pretty enough or thin enough or whatever-they're-looking-for enough to even give me a chance to read for a role. And here at Pete's? Well, night after night, my livelihood is in the hands of customers in various states of inebriation who don't always tip and never bother to stop and consider that their 15 or 20 percent might be the difference between me paying rent on time or not.

But now, for once…

Advantage Carrie?

Hmm…

Having stopped with the deer-in-the-headlights routine, Nick is gently disengaging himself from the brunette. As she stands up straight, her eyes flutter a bit before her gaze lands on me. She doesn't seem at all embarrassed about being discovered like this, although she does raise her hand to cover what looks like a serious hickey blooming on her throat.

Double gross.

"Hey, sweetheart," interrupts a loud, slightly slurred male voice, calling to me from the bar area. "Can I maybe get a little service out here?"

It's my regular Tuesday-night drunk with his regular Tuesday-night BS. The condescension in the guy's tone, in his word choice, makes my insides curdle. Still, it's my job to serve him.

Unless maybe I play this unexpected advantage…

"Break's over," I decide to tell Nick. Like a boss. "Sounds like somebody needs you out front. *Sweetheart.*"

Then, without bothering to wait for his response, I pivot to go.

And it's silly, I know, but as I continue on back to the storeroom, I find that I can't stop grinning. A little swagger makes its way into my step. I swear, I even feel a surge of power coursing through my body. A surge of power that's wildly disproportionate to my teeny-tiny act of assertiveness.

· · · · ·

By the end of my shift, I'm starting to worry that I might be coming down with something. I'm sweaty and flushed and my skin is hot, like I'm spiking a fever. Earlier, when my arm brushed up against Nick's, maybe his skin wasn't so cold after all. Maybe mine was already burning up.

Crap, I think. *I can't be sick for my big audition tomorrow. I just can't be.*

Luckily, it's Nick's night to close. Usually, I offer to stay and help, even though on my late nights, he always has band practice or some other convenient excuse for why he has to rush right off. But tonight? Sorry, dude. I'm out of here. I need to get home, pound some Extra Strength Tylenol, and sleep off whatever this is.

In the back room, I clock out and collect my stuff from my locker. But then, since my Prius is parked out front, I have to go back through the bar area. While I make my way through the maze of empty tables, I see that their chairs are somehow already stacked neatly on top.

Or maybe they were that way before?

I also notice that the soles of my sneakers are squeaking. I look down, and what do you know? The floor is all wet, like it's just been mopped.

That was awfully quick work, I think. Nick isn't usually so efficient. Probably did a slipshod job, just to get it over with, but nope. Not worth dwelling on. Right now, I need to make self-care a priority.

"G'night, Nick," I call over my shoulder. You know, just to be polite.

"You take it easy, Carrie," says Nick. Only the way he says it, it sounds more like a warning than a casual goodbye.

So at the door, I turn. Nick is sitting on the only stool that isn't upended on the bar, getting down to the business of balancing the night's receipts. He's staring at me a little strangely.

From where I'm standing, I can see myself in the mirror that stretches the length of the wall behind the shelves of liquor. But I can't see Nick in the glass.

I squint to try to focus my vision.

Still, as far as I can see, the guy has no reflection whatsoever.

Is it my contacts again? I wonder. *Or some trick of the light? Or is this damn fever maybe starting to mess with my eyesight?*

"What is it?" asks Nick, his dark eyes narrowing at me. "What's wrong?"

I look from Nick to the mirror and then back to Nick. "It's just—" I start to say, but no. It's dumb. Plus, it'll give the guy yet another reason to mock me. I shake my head dismissively. "It's nothing," I say instead. "Nothing at all," I repeat, mostly to convince myself.

Then, turning to the door again, I twist the bolt to release the lock. But as I head out, I can't stop myself from tossing one last glance back at Nick. Still watching me, he raises his eyebrows in question.

"Don't forget to lock up behind me," I mutter.

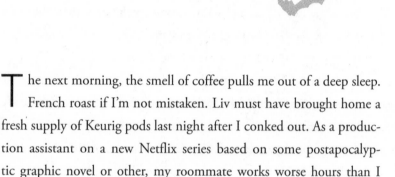

CHAPTER
2

The next morning, the smell of coffee pulls me out of a deep sleep. French roast if I'm not mistaken. Liv must have brought home a fresh supply of Keurig pods last night after I conked out. As a production assistant on a new Netflix series based on some postapocalyptic graphic novel or other, my roommate works worse hours than I do—for equally crappy pay. But as a perk of her job, she can take whatever she wants—within reason, of course—from the show's daily on-site catering spread.

Lying in bed, breathing in the aroma of the strong brew, I realize I feel...*fine*. I'm totally fine. Although the only fever reducer I was able to unearth in our jumbled mess of a medicine cabinet expired about four months ago, it must have done the trick. Thanks to a couple of the outdated Tylenols and a good night's sleep, I don't seem to be sick at all. So bullet dodged. *Yay!*

I reach out and grab my phone from the nightstand. Since I took out my contacts last night, I have to hold it at arm's length to read the time. It's a little after eight.

Okay, I think, putting back the phone. *Rise and shine.*

Still groggy and in need of actual caffeine—not just the scent of it—I throw back the covers, swing my legs out of bed, and haul myself up. But before I stagger my way out to the kitchen to see if Liv was able to snag any hazelnut-flavored pods, I make a pit stop in the bathroom that the two of us share.

I close the door behind me, and out of habit, my sleepy gaze goes immediately to the digital scale. I step on it almost every morning. You know, just to keep things in check. After all, my height and weight are printed on my résumé, kind of like a contract. When I show up for an audition, there are certain expectations. And I don't want to disappoint.

Really, I *can't* disappoint. I mean, body acceptance at any size might be a growing thing on social media, but it hasn't exactly caught fire in Hollywood. Oh sure, there are the Aidy Bryants and the Gabourey Sidibes who've managed to break through. But make no mistake: they're the exception, not the rule. Despite all the talk about diversity in casting, there's still a definite size bias. So for someone like me, who's just starting out? The pressure to be thin—and to stay thin—is real.

So I measure all my food portions. Track calories on a phone app. Go running at least four times a week. Drink lots of water. And keep regular tabs on my weight.

But all that said, there's really no reason to weigh myself now. Yesterday's number was right on target. And nothing I've eaten or drunk in the last twenty-four hours would have moved the needle significantly one way or the other.

Besides, I admit it, the number on the scale tends to affect my attitude. If I had a different career goal, I wouldn't care. I really wouldn't. But as an aspiring actor? It's sad but true: when my weight goes down, my mood goes up—and vice versa. And today of all days, I really don't want to risk anything bringing me down. I need to stay positive if I'm going to book this J.Lo movie.

Still, I keep eyeing the scale.

And finally, I can't stop myself. I give in. I step on it.

I stare at my feet, waiting for the numbers to—

What?!

I squint down in disbelief. Am I still asleep, dreaming? Or more accurately, having a nightmare?

I must not be seeing correctly. Only, I'm farsighted, and the numbers are far enough away to be pretty darn clear, even without my contacts.

It must be a mistake.

So I step off the scale. Wait for the screen to reset to zero. Step back on, and…

Impossible!

Absolutely wide awake now, I step off again. Inhale deeply. Exhale slowly. Tell myself not to lose it.

Okay. One more time.

I pick up the scale and put it down in a different spot on the hexagon-tile floor. Place one foot on it, ever so carefully. Then the other. Hold my breath.

Aaand…

Same result.

Somehow, since yesterday morning, I have gained twenty-four pounds. *Twenty. Four. Freaking. Pounds.*

"*Nooo!*"

Barely a moment later, there's a knock on the bathroom door.

"Carrie?" calls Liv's voice, full of concern. "Are you okay in there?"

"No," I say, still looking down in horror at the digital screen. The numbers are gone but definitely not forgotten.

Maybe the scale is broken, I think. *Or needs new batteries. Or—*

Just then, the door flings open, and my roomie comes charging in like some kind of a rescue brigade in Hello Kitty pajamas and fuzzy Uggs. But when she sees me, her petite, wiry figure stops cold. Behind the tortoiseshell frames of her glasses, her brown eyes widen. Her brown skin pales. Her mouth gapes open. Even her high, dark ponytail seems to reel back in surprise.

"Dios mio," says Liv, her voice barely above a whisper.

Crap, I think. *The scale* isn't *broken*.

"Can you retain twenty-four pounds of water?" I ask. I can hear the desperation in my tone. "And how can I get rid of it before my four o'clock audition?"

Instinctively, my hand goes to my stomach, only it doesn't feel bloated. It feels…*hard?*

"Carrie," says Liv, still gawping at me. "You're…*ripped*."

I crinkle my brow at her in confusion. "What?"

She raises her arm in slow motion, like one of the postapocalyptic zombies on the show she works on, and points at me. "M-muscles," she stammers.

"*What?*" I repeat.

Only Liv seems to be out of words. She just gawks at me in silence.

Suddenly, my throat feels tight, and it's hard to breathe. My heart is pounding. I look down, but without my contacts, I can't really get a good view of myself. So I shove past Liv and head back into my bedroom. I pause at my nightstand and root around in the top drawer for my glasses. Then, putting them on, I make a beeline for the full-length mirror that stands in the corner.

I peer at my reflection, and okay, I recognize what I see from the neck up. Shoulder-length blond hair with sideswept bangs. Light blue eyes behind the lenses of my black cat's-eye frames. Fair complexion. Nearly invisible lashes and brows. Slightly crooked nose and a downturned mouth.

Only from the neck down? All that looks even a little bit familiar are the white tank top and pink-striped boxer shorts that I wore to bed last night.

My chest is *huge*, straining against my tank, stretching the cotton to its absolute limit, except it's not my barely A cups that have gotten bigger. It's the muscles beneath them.

And it doesn't stop there. My shoulders are at least twice the size they were last night. The arms that extend from them have the kind of chiseled definition that should have taken ages to sculpt in a gym. And the thighs poking out from the leg holes of my boxers? They're rock hard and screaming with power.

No joke, it's as if I stuck my head through the hole in one of those carnival cutouts, like my head is sitting on top of a painted caricature of a muscle-bound figure.

Slowly, I look down at the body that's my body but…*not*. I stretch out one of my wildly buff arms, then bend it at the elbow, flexing. I watch—in shock or awe or I-don't-even-know-what—as my newly developed biceps swells, bulging even more.

I feel a gentle touch on my back, startling me.

Liv. I didn't hear her follow me into the bedroom or walk up beside me. My eyes find hers in the mirror, and I see my own fear and disbelief reflected back at me.

"Do you see what I see?" I ask.

"I see you," she says, "but, like, supersized."

I gulp. "What in the actual hell is going on here?" I ask. "How is this even possible?"

"Have you visited any experimental labs lately?" she asks.

"What?"

"Maybe you were exposed to radiation?" she suggests with a small shrug.

"*What?*"

"Well, I don't know," she says. "Did you check for spider bites?"

"Liv," I say. "We're in Santa Monica, not the Spider-Verse."

Her dark brows shoot up over the frames of her glasses. "Are you sure?"

Honestly? I'm not. I'm not sure about anything right now, least of all how I could have gone to bed on the skinny side and woken up the next morning looking like a female bodybuilder, with over twenty additional pounds of muscle.

"Can you shoot webs out of your wrists?" asks Liv.

"Stop," I say. "Of course not."

"No, seriously," says Liv. "Did you try?"

"Of course not."

We're both silent for a moment.

"Maybe you should try," Liv says quietly.

I want to tell her that she's being irrational, that the combination of her aspiring writer-director brain and her PA gig on the zombie show must have distorted her perspective on reality. Except in the reality I used to know, a person's body couldn't completely transform overnight. No matter what those online pop-up ads claimed.

So what have I got to lose? Tentatively, I extend the arm I was flexing. Then I give my wrist a flick.

Nothing.

To be perfectly frank, I'm not sure if I feel relief or disappointment. I mean, on the one hand, I guess we can safely cross "Spider-Girl" off the list. But on the other hand, what else is even *on* the freaking list?

"No," says Liv. "You have to really try." She lifts her gaze to the corner of my bedroom ceiling and gestures with her head. "Aim up there. And concentrate."

I roll my eyes at her.

"Go on," she urges me. "You're an actor. Act. Act like you have superpowers."

I see what she's doing. I know Liv is just trying to stay grounded by grasping at bits and pieces of pop culture, desperately seeking an explanation for what we both know is inexplicable.

I'm about to protest, only it's not as if I have any better ideas. Or any other ideas at all for that matter. Plus, I figure if I try to act like a superhero, it'll at least keep me from acting like someone who's on the verge of having a panic attack.

And I am. On the verge of having the mother of all panic attacks.

Obviously, I am freaking the freak out about this new comic-book-caliber build of mine that defies all known rules of the natural world. But it's more than just that. A ton more.

On my frame, twenty-four pounds—even if it's muscle—is a lot. Probably enough to make some of my slimmer-fitting clothes not fit me anymore. Definitely enough to make my go-to audition outfit of dark skinny jeans and a tailored white blouse not fit me anymore. And maybe even enough to make the role I'm hoping to land this afternoon not fit me any—

Nope. I can't go there right now. I just can't.

So instead, I stuff down my rising anxiety, and ridiculous as it is, I do what Liv suggests. I stretch my arm up toward the crown molding.

I close my eyes. Breathe. Focus.

I try to get my inner superhero on.

And strange as it sounds, I really do feel power flooding through my body. It's the same kind of surge I thought I felt last night when I told Nick to get back to work—only multiplied by about a thousand.

I open my eyes, take aim, and—

"Fire!" screams Liv.

Because all of a sudden—and against all conceivable logic—that's what's launching out of me. Instead of casting spiderwebs, I am casting flames. In an arc. In the shape of a sword. Somehow, I am actually standing here brandishing a blade made entirely of…*fire*.

My roomie runs from the room, but I just stay where I am, unable to move, too stunned by the spectacle I'm seeing.

I can feel the nuclear heat. I mean, I'm holding it in my hand, for crying out loud! But somehow, I also seem to be immune to the blaze. I don't get burned.

Holy crap! I think. *I'm a human blowtorch.*

Just then, the fire that's emanating from me—*me!*—laps at the edge of one of the blue linen curtains, and I learn in a flash that, unlike me, the fabric is *not* immune. The drapes start to smolder.

The smoke alarm above the door goes off.

The earsplitting noise startles me, and that does it. Just as suddenly as the mysterious flaming sword appeared, it disappears.

Meanwhile, Liv returns with the fire extinguisher from our kitchen in tow. She points it at me. Before I can find my voice, she releases the pin and squirts, covering my right arm in a powdery white substance.

"No!" I shout at her above the blare of the smoke alarm. "Not me! The curtains! Get the curtains!"

Liv blinks at me. It takes a moment or two before it registers that I'm not on fire anymore, but the window treatment sure is. Then she nods, redirects her aim, and sprays again.

While she tackles that, I run over to the opposite corner of the room, where there's a wooden chair. Quickly, I shove the laundry basket of dirty clothes off its woven seat and drag the chair over to the doorway. Then I climb up on top of it, stand on my tiptoes, and reach for the alarm. After fumbling with the device for a few seconds, I finally manage to turn the damn thing off.

Quiet settles over the bedroom.

My ears are still ringing, but at least I can hear myself think again. Too bad I don't know what *to* think.

I look back over at my roommate. I'm a little surprised she hasn't run for the Hollywood hills by now, but then, I guess I really shouldn't be. Since I found Olivia Sanchez on an apartment share website when I first moved to Los Angeles a couple of years ago, she's been there for me through one awkward breakup, too many tanked auditions, and the inevitable weekly BS with my family on Zoom. She may have started out as someone to split the rent with, but she's become so much more. She's become one of my best friends.

Still, what's going on here is a lot, even for a bestie.

But despite her small stature, Liv can be a lot too.

Slowly, she lowers the fire extinguisher. She's effectively put out the blaze, but the curtains are scorched, burned half away, and the wall by the window is singed. Irrefutable evidence that this really happened.

"So…uh…that really just happened?" I ask anyway, to make sure. My voice, like the rest of me, is shaking as I climb down off the chair and collapse into it.

My friend turns to me, wide-eyed, and nods. "Yeah," she says. Her voice is wavering too. "That really just happened."

"How did my life turn into some kind of a third-rate action-fantasy?" I ask.

"Nothing third-rate about it," says Liv. "Your special effects are seriously top notch."

"Except we're not in a movie," I say. "And there's no green screen. How can this all be real?"

She scrunches her face up and thinks for a beat. "You're a really good actor?" she suggests with a weak smile, trying, I think, to lighten the mood.

"Thanks, but nobody's that good," I say. "Meryl Streep's not that good."

"Demonic possession?" she tries.

"I really hope that's a joke," I say.

"Me too," she says in a squeaky-high voice that betrays her own anxiety.

Then we both fall mute.

The power I felt surging through my body has ebbed. Now, I just feel tired. Drained. Burned out—literally, I guess you could say.

I slump down farther in the chair. I know I should probably be having a no-holds-barred emotional meltdown at this point, but I simply haven't got the energy. I'm too wiped out to even bother brushing the white residue off my arm.

Maybe I'm in shock?

I played someone in shock once, when I got work as a background player on an episode of *The Rookie*. I spent a whole day of filming sitting in the back of an ambulance looking catatonic, wrapped in a blanket.

Maybe I should go and get a blanket?

"Why do you need a blanket?" asks Liv. "Are you cold?"

I realize I said that out loud. I shake my head. "Never mind," I tell her.

I'm at a total loss. I don't know what to do, and I can tell Liv doesn't either. But we have to do *something*. Don't we?

"Carrie," says Liv. "Don't worry. It'll be okay. We'll figure this out."

But will we? After all, this isn't exactly the type of problem you can google, like *how do I get rid of red wine stains?* Or *how do I know if it's poison ivy?*

How do I stop my suddenly buff bod from spontaneously combusting?

Do we phone a doctor? The fire department? Some real-life Ghostbusters?

Clearly, we need some kind of help.

"Okay," I say decisively after a bit. "Okay." I get up from the chair to go get my phone. "I think it's time for us to make a 911 call."

CHAPTER
3

We make the call for help. And in less than half an hour—the blink of an eye, considering morning rush hour traffic in LA—help shows up at the door.

While Liv and I are still wearing our pj's, Heather Mancini arrives from her place in West Hollywood fully styled, made-up, and coiffed. Of course. Even back when we worked together at Pete's, she dressed for the job she wanted—and eventually landed. She left the bar about a year ago to work full-time as a wardrobe assistant on a big network procedural crime drama.

This morning, her long, brown hair with blond highlights is curled into perfect beach waves. Bronzer gives her flawless skin a natural-looking glow. And her curvy, statuesque figure is draped in flowy, wide-leg pants and a boho-style blouse expertly French tucked. From the looks of it, the job she wants next is seaside resort goddess queen.

Heather gets a glimpse of me and my newly pumped-up physique, and the skin beneath her carefully applied bronzer turns a ghostly white. "Shit," she says. "You weren't kidding, were you?"

• • • • •

"I don't understand," says Heather a few minutes later.

The three of us are standing together in my bedroom. Once my other bestie got past the initial shock of seeing me in all my muscle-bound glory, Liv and I brought her in here to show her the fire damage.

"She was trying to make spiderwebs," Liv starts to explain.

"Spiderwebs?" asks Heather.

"But instead," continues Liv, "she made fire."

"I don't understand," says Heather.

"It was like a whatchamacallit," says Liv. "A katana? Like in *Kill Bill*? A samurai-type sword? Except completely made out of flames. One minute, nothing. Then—*poof!* Inferno."

"I don't understand," repeats Heather.

"That makes three of us," I say.

Liv looks across Heather to me. "You have to show her."

"What?" I shake my head violently and wave my hands in a gesture of absolute freaking refusal. "Oh no. No way. We were lucky I didn't burn the place down the first time."

"But now we know what to expect," says Liv. She somehow manages to sound reasonable in the middle of all this. "We can take the necessary precautions."

· · · · ·

A couple of minutes after that, we're all crowded into the bathroom.

"See?" Liv says to me. "You can stand in the shower stall and…you know…*manifest*. Then if things get out of control, I can reach in and turn on the water. Instant sprinkler system."

I frown doubtfully. "I don't know about this."

Liv jerks her thumb toward Heather. "If she's going to help," she says, "she needs to *see* it."

I look at Heather. Clearly, she knows something wicked strange is going on here. I mean, the overnight change in my body is real. Ditto the state of my bedroom. So it's not as if she thinks we're lying to her.

But still, I can tell she's skeptical. Who wouldn't be?

I sigh. Liv's right. If I want Heather's help, I need to show her the extent of the...*problem*.

"Okay, fine," I say to Liv. "But if we don't get our security deposit back when we eventually move out of here, don't blame me."

Still clothed, I pull the glass door open. I step into the stall, leaving the door ajar. I face the showerhead.

"Just like before," coaches Liv. "Aim and concentrate."

But this time, it's different. I'm nervous and afraid, and not just for the obvious reason. Not just because I could quite possibly torch our apartment and the three of us along with it. It's ridiculous, I know, but I'm actually a little scared of disappointing my friends, of not living up to their expectations.

I feel the same kind of fluttering in my gut, the same kind of wobbliness in my knees, the same kind of wooziness in my head that I feel right before pretty much every audition. It's like, even though I know I can do it, I suddenly start to doubt myself. Can you say performance anxiety?

"Carrie?" Liv prods gently.

Right, I think. *Concentrate.*

So same as last time, I stretch out my arm. Focus. Aim at the ceiling of the shower stall, and—

"Holy fucking shit," says Heather. Her face is like a surprise emoji as she stares at the mysterious sword of fire that I have, for the second time this morning, somehow conjured into being.

Liv dives for the faucet.

The shower rains down on me. Oddly, though, the water doesn't douse the flame. But it drenches me and fogs up my glasses, so I lose my concentration—and *bam!* Once again, the fiery blade vanishes.

As Liv turns off the water, I remove my glasses and push my dripping bangs out of my eyes. And I can't help thinking that, not for the first time after a performance, I've ended up all wet.

. . . . .

Once I towel off, pop in a fresh pair of contacts, and change into some sweats, I join my two friends in the kitchen. I try not to think too much about how the normally loose pants and shirt are now hugging my figure, fitting much snugger than usual. I've got bigger issues after all.

Liv hands me a cup of coffee. Hazelnut, with a splash of oat milk. Just the way I like it.

"Thanks," I say with a small smile. I take a sip. With everything that's happened this morning, I don't really need the caffeine to wake up anymore. But the taste and the smell of it are at least a comfort.

Heather is already seated at the island with a mug of the French roast. Liv grabs her own steaming mug and hops on a stool. I sit too.

At first, no one says anything.

"Avenging angel?" says Liv, breaking the silence.

"Stop it," says Heather. "We need to look at this logically."

And just like that, I start to crack.

"Logically?" I ask. The pitch of my voice goes up so many octaves I'm surprised it's still audible to the human ear, surprised every dog in the neighborhood doesn't come running. "*Logically?* I woke up with giant bodybuilder muscles and I'm a walking cigarette lighter. How do you look at that *logically?*"

"Okay, okay," says Heather. "Calm down. You just said it. You *woke up* like this. Right? So what happened yesterday?"

I shake my head. "Nothing," I say. "I mean, nothing out of the ordinary. Nothing that would have caused *this*." As if there's anything that could have caused *this*.

"Walk us through it anyway," says Heather. "And start from the beginning. On *Robbery-Homicide Division*, the writers always have the characters look at the timeline leading up to the incident to figure out what happened."

"Telekinetic fire starter?" says Liv.

Heather shoots Liv an annoyed look.

"What?" says Liv. "Clearly, there's a lot more going on in this world than we know." She shrugs. "Plus, on *Dystopia Now*, the writers just make shit up."

Heather pulls a face at Liv, then turns back to me. "Yesterday," she says. "Tell us, what did you do?"

I take a deep breath and try to pull myself back together. It's good we called Heather. Maybe this rational, step-by-step, recreate-the-timeline approach of hers will actually get us somewhere.

"It was a totally average day," I say. "I got up. Had my usual break-fast. A cup of plain nonfat yogurt and a cup of fruit. Went for a run down by the beach. Showered. And then I just ran some errands."

"What errands?" asks Heather.

I take another sip of the coffee and think back. "I picked up the dry cleaning," I say. "Then I had to go to my agent's office to get my audition sides because they weren't allowed to email them. I swear, the production company is treating this J.Lo script like a classified document. I even had to sign a nondisclosure agreement." I shake my head. "Anyway, afterward, I stopped and got gas. Grabbed a salad, dressing on the side. Then I just came home and ate and prepped for the audition until it was time to leave for my shift at Pete's."

"What happened at Pete's?" asks Heather.

"I mean, it was Tuesday, so it was a pretty slow night," I say. "I was working with Nick."

"Nick?" asks Liv.

"Nick Stokes," explains Heather. "He took over my job when I left the bar. I trained him. Cute wannabe rock star."

"He's not cute," I mutter.

"Oh, he's cute," says Heather with a knowing nod. "*Very* cute. Some might even say hot."

"Please," I say. "He's not cute and he's not hot. Mostly, he's just a ginormous pain in my ass."

As Heather and Liv exchange a look, I realize how angry I sound.

Then I remember how angry I *felt*. At Nick.

"And oh my God, the guy was getting on my nerves even more than usual last night," I say. "First, he totally made fun of me for having an audition to play a bartender."

"Well, that is kind of funny," says Liv.

"And then," I continue, getting pissed off all over again, "I caught him making out with one of the customers when he should have been working. I mean, who does that?" My fury dials up another notch. "I'll tell you who does that. *Nick*. Nick does that." And suddenly, just like it did the night before, my vision changes, and it's as if I'm looking at the world through a blood-colored haze. "I swear, I could have killed him."

"Did you catch that?" asks Liv.

"Sure did," says Heather.

As my eyesight clears and settles back to normal, I see my two besties staring at me with a mix of apprehension and concern. And now I'm pretty sure that this seeing-red thing has nothing to do with my contacts. "What?" I ask, even though I don't think I want to know the answer. "What is it?"

"Your eyes," says Liv. "They just did this freaky flashy thing."

"While you were talking about wanting to kill Nick," adds Heather.

"Maybe you're a Terminator sent from the future to eliminate this Nick guy," says Liv. "Before he becomes the leader of the human resistance against artificially intelligent overlords."

"She's not from the future," says Heather. "She's from Philadelphia."

"And Nick couldn't lead anything," I grumble. "He wouldn't even want to. He's a total slacker."

Heather studies me, her eyes becoming little green slits. "You know, you really do have an awful lot of hostility toward Nick," she says.

Okay. That's it. Time for a new topic.

"Why are we even talking about Nick?" I ask. "None of this has anything to do with Nick."

"I don't know about that," says Heather. "It seems like the guy might be some kind of a trigger for you. I mean, he certainly gets you all hot and bothered."

"Do you like him or something?" asks Liv.

"What?" The question hits me like a sucker punch to the jaw, knocking me a little off my balance. "No. Of course I don't like him," I say when I recover. "I already told you. He irritates the crap out of me."

"And you said he irritated you even more than usual last night," says Heather, still poking at the sore spot that is Nick. "What else was different between the two of you?"

I sigh, frustrated that she won't let this subject go and move on. I'm about to say that nothing was different, that Nick was just his typical everyday super annoying self. But then I start to recall all the curious little details. Like how his skin felt cold as ice when we accidentally touched. And how he seemed to move with lightning-fast speed when I wasn't looking. And how he didn't appear to cast a reflection in the mirror behind the bar.

I tell all this to my friends.

"Nick's a vampire!" exclaims Liv. "And you're a…a…*a vampire slayer!*"

Liv raises her mug in triumph and smiles at Heather and me, quite satisfied with this latest deduction. Then she takes a big gulp of her coffee.

Heather frowns and rolls her eyes, unconvinced.

I'm equally dubious, mostly because vampires and vampire slayers don't really exist. But also, I remember something else. "No, I think it was just me imagining things," I say. "Because of the fever."

"Fever?" asks Heather.

I nod. "I thought I was getting sick," I say. "But then I came home, went to bed…" I let my voice trail off, thinking.

"And you woke up like *this*," says Heather, finishing my thought. "Well, that's something real at least. A clue maybe."

"But what does it mean?" I ask.

"You were accidentally dosed with a top secret military drug that creates flame-throwing super soldiers?" suggests Liv.

Heather and I turn to her. I hate to admit it, but so far, that's the first explanation that seems even remotely plausible.

Just then, Heather's cell phone *pings*.

She glances down at the screen and sighs. "Shit," she says. "I need to get to work. I have to do a wardrobe fitting." Her eyes dart between me and Liv. "Is everything going to be okay here?"

"Absolutely," says Liv. "*Dystopia* has a night shoot today, and I'm late PA. I'm not scheduled to work until after dinner. I can stay with Carrie until then."

"Good," says Heather with a nod. "I can swing by on my way home tonight."

"Uh, excuse me," I say. "I appreciate the concern and all, but I don't need tag-team babysitters. And besides, I have an audition in Beverly Hills at four."

Liv and Heather look at me like I've completely lost my mind.

"Carrie," says Heather. "Be serious. You can't go to your audition like this."

"You mean because of the extra bulk?" I ask. My voice cracks with anxiety on the last word.

"Oh my God, I'm not talking about the extra *bulk*," says Heather. She gestures at her plus-size figure. "As if *I* would ever be critical of a little extra bulk. I'm talking about the weapon of mass destruction that you seem to be able to call up at will."

"Think about it," adds Liv. "What if you accidentally go all CGI on the casting director? It could be a huge catastrophe. You could end up in Quantico or Area 51 or something."

So far, even if I do say so myself, I think I've been doing a pretty good job of keeping my cool in the middle of this whole supernatural shit show. But at the prospect of missing a chance at what could be my big break? That's it. I start to unravel like a cheap freaking sweater.

"No," I say. I get up and start pacing around. "No, no, no, no, no. I can't be a no-show. I just can't be. I've been trying to get in front of this casting director for months. *Months.* If I cancel now, I may never get another shot. And you know how it is." I stop pacing and look at my friends, who are also in the early phases of their Hollywood careers, still paying their dues. "You both know how this business works. My *agent* got me this appointment. If I blow it off, she'll think I'm not serious about acting. She could stop submitting me for roles. Drop me as a client. I mean, we all know there's basically an endless supply of hopefuls out there who are exactly my type, who would be more than happy to take my spot on her roster. And then, after two years of busting my butt, I'll be right back where I started. I'll be back to mass mailings and open cattle calls and doing student films for free. And crossing my fingers that something will somehow pay off. And I'm already twenty-four," I add. "Almost twenty-five. In Hollywood years, that's practically ancient. I already look too old to go up for the teen parts."

I pause to catch my breath. My body is shaking. I'm on the edge of hysterics, but I'm also more resolute than I've ever been in my life. "So I don't care," I tell my friends. "I don't care if I'm shooting fire out of my arms or my eyes or my ass, goddammit. I am not flaking on this audition."

CHAPTER
4

I calm down, Heather leaves, and my flaming sword doesn't make any encore appearances for the rest of the morning. I don't know what the rules are that govern its comings and goings, but it does seem like I need to intentionally call the thing up somehow. I talk it through with Liv for a while, and we decide—okay, *I* decide, despite her serious misgivings—that as long as I don't deliberately try to summon the fiery blade, I should be okay to go to my casting session. Probably. Hopefully.

Before I know it, it's time to get ready.

I manage to shower and dry my hair without incident. Then, with my supersize body wrapped in my oversize bathrobe, I gaze wistfully at my fresh-from-the-dry-cleaners audition outfit hanging on the back of my bedroom door. Against my better judgment, I decide to give it a shot.

Just as I feared, I am barely able to get the narrow legs of my dark skinny jeans past my newly muscular thighs. Barely able to get the sleeves of my fitted white blouse over my suddenly massive shoulders, barely able to button its buttons across my broadened chest. When I finally squeeze myself into the ensemble and check the mirror, I'm a dead ringer for She-Hulk, about to explode right out of my clothing. If only I were reading for a Marvel movie.

My heart sinks. What am I going to do?

"Liv?" I call, hoping she can help me solve my wardrobe problem.

Moments later, she comes bursting through my doorway, fire extinguisher at the ready.

"Whoa!" I say, stepping back and holding my hands up. "Relax. This time, it's just a fashion emergency."

As if to punctuate my statement, I hear my shoulder seam rip.

· · · · ·

Liv and I go through my closet together, searching for some options to accommodate my brawny new body. I try on a few different outfits, my friend snaps photos, and we text them all over to Heather for her professional opinion. After expressing the same grave reservations as my roommate, she reluctantly gives her stamp of approval to a pair of stretchy black leggings and a loose, long-sleeved black sweater.

"You look good," says Liv when I present myself for one last wardrobe check. And even though I know she's still worried for me, she gives me a nod and a supportive smile before I head on out the door. "Vaya con Dios," she calls after me.

· · · · ·

As I walk into the casting office, clutching a manila envelope containing a few extra headshots and résumés, my step is a little unsteady. Obviously, I'm still reeling from this morning's…*rude awakening*. But that's not the only thing that's got me feeling off.

I fidget with the bottom of my sweater, wishing I was wearing my customary jeans and blouse. The former go-to audition ensemble was fashionable without being distracting. It showed the contours of my body without being too sexy. I liked to think it helped people concentrate on my performance, not my appearance. And that helped me to concentrate too.

But now I just feel like I'm hiding something. Probably because, well, I *am* hiding something—or trying to hide something anyway. Twenty-four extra pounds of something to be exact.

Which kind of puts me at cross-purposes here. Acting—good acting—is about revealing, not concealing. It's about tapping into your true emotions to create something real. Not pulling off some big lie.

Firmly telling myself that I'm not a big liar, I give my name to the receptionist at the front desk.

· · · · ·

At my level, walking into an audition is always a little bit surreal. You show up, you sign in, and then you sit in a room or a hallway or wherever to wait your turn with a bunch of other women who all essentially look like *you*. Oh sure, they may have different hair colors. Different eye colors. Different skin tones. But everybody is pretty much your age. Your size. Your…*look*. Like cookies all cut in the same shape from the same batch of dough but with slight variations in the frosting.

Then, if you're me, while you sit there, you start to play the comparison game. You look around at all the different versions of yourself, and you start to wonder if they're somehow better versions. More castable versions. Instead of thinking like the actor you are, you fall into the trap of starting to think like the casting director you desperately want to please.

Determined not to fall into that trap today, I tighten my grasp on my manila envelope and follow the hand-lettered signs to a long, nondescript hallway lined with gray metal folding chairs. The only unoccupied seats are at the far end of the hall, so before I can sit down, I have to parade past a half dozen other candidates waiting to read for the same role.

While I walk down the center of the corridor, my eyes dart to my right and my left, assessing my competition out of habit. They're all in their twenties. All girl-next-door types. All pretty but in a basic kind of a way, a way that won't pull focus from the lead—in this case, J.Lo. And like a string of paper dolls, they're all the same size and shape.

It's surreal, but not in the usual way. Not in the everybody-looks-like-my-sister-from-another-mister kind of way.

I continue on down the hallway, and my posture sags. My shoulders slump. As I size up my rivals, it's not that I worry I won't measure up to them. This time, I'm absolutely certain I don't.

Out of nowhere, that old song from *Sesame Street* pops into my head: *One of these things is not like the others, one of these things just doesn't belong...*

And it's true. With this bigger, buffer body of mine, I don't belong in this casting pool anymore.

Self-consciously, I take a seat. I cross my arms and legs, desperately trying to take up as little space as possible, but it's no use. I may be able to produce a sword made out of freaking fire, but I'm not able to shape-shift back to my former shape.

I peer up the aisle at the other women. I don't want to sabotage myself, but I can't help thinking that I could give the best performance of my life right now, and it simply won't matter. Obviously, I'm not what the casting team is looking for. I'm not what they've got in mind. Not anymore. I may have these new muscles, this new power, but in this moment, I'm feeling more powerless than ever.

It's definitely not the best head space to be in just before an audition. I should be psyching myself up, not psyching myself out. I should be getting ready to take the stage and own it.

As the other actors start to get called in one by one, I try to give myself a major attitude adjustment. I can't let this kind of negative thinking drag me down. I've got to be so good that I make them see the role differently. So good that they can only see *me* in this role. No matter what I look like.

I close my eyes, shutting out my surroundings. I breathe in. I breathe out. And then I try to visualize myself nailing this part, giving the perfect read.

What can I get you to drink? I think.

Except, it's not my delivery I hear in my head, dammit. It's Nick's.

And now I see Nick in my head too. I see his mocking look and his mocking grin and his mocking goddamn dimples, and my anger at him begins to simmer all over again. I can only imagine the incredible amounts of shit he'll give me if I don't land this gig. I'll never hear the end of it. The bartender who couldn't even get cast as a bar—

"Carrie Adams?"

Hearing my name, I open my eyes, and I notice that the corner of the manila envelope I'm holding is starting to burn.

I jump to my feet, drop the envelope, and stomp on it with the toe of my black suede bootie before it can fully ignite. Still, the scent of smoke drifts up from the floor. And now everyone is staring down the hallway at me, watching me curiously.

I break out in a cold sweat. If my name had been called even one second later, the whole place could be up in flames—and my budding career along with it.

What in the actual hell was I even thinking? Liv and Heather were right, of course. I should have just made up some excuse and cancelled.

It's fight-or-flight time for sure, and every cell of my body wants to pull an Usain Bolt and run straight on out of here. Except I've already made one scene. Probably best not to make another. Not unless I want to end up on the Do Not Cast list in perpetuity.

Trying to stitch together the frayed edges of my nerves, I commit to seeing this audition through. I leave the singed envelope where it is on the floor. Then, knees trembling, I walk to the head of the hall, where a curly-haired assistant stands waiting. While I approach her, she frowns disapprovingly at me.

"There's no smoking in here," she scolds me.

As I follow her back, I try to look on the bright side. She just thinks I was sneaking a cig, not performing my fiery new party trick.

· · · · ·

A minute or two later, I'm standing in front of three people seated on a couch. In the middle sits an older woman with long salt-and-pepper hair wearing a linen maxi dress and lots of handcrafted, southwestern-type jewelry. I'm pretty sure she's the casting director I've been dying to meet. To her right sits a younger woman who seems to be trying to copy her style but on an entry-level, H&M-clearance-rack budget. And on her left is a guy who looks too young to be here, his khakis and blue cotton button-down reading more like a uniform for a private high school than the office-casual attire I assume it is.

When I entered, they all gave me a quick once-over and muttered some mildly friendly greeting or other.

Not one of them introduced themselves. And not one of them has said anything since. They all seem much more interested in the water bottles on the coffee table in front of them than in me.

I try to pretend that this incredibly awkward situation isn't awkward at all. I plant my feet firmly, resisting the urge to shift my weight self-consciously from one black bootie to the other.

The assistant who led me in walks over to a camcorder set up on a tripod behind the couch. She presses the Record button. "Look straight into the camera, and say your name and your agency, please," she tells me.

Aaand here we go.

I take a deep breath and try to compose myself. Stare at the red light. Smile. "Carrie Adams," I say. "The Rebecca Sloane Agency."

I can still pull this off, I think. *I've got this. I'm not going to shoot fire. Nope. I'm going to* be *fire.*

"Turn to the left, please," the assistant says.

At that, my stomach lurches. This is always my least favorite part. The 360-degree view. They don't ask for it every time, but when they do, it's demeaning, demoralizing, and like so much of the audition process, it has nothing to do with whether you can actually play the role you're here to read for.

On a normal day, the request would make me uncomfortable. But today? As I turn and show my profile, exposing my newly sprouted bulges and swells to scrutiny from yet another angle, my discomfort hits an all-time high.

"And to the back."

I turn my back to the room. It's like I can feel everyone's eyes on me, assessing me, judging me. But then again, who am I kidding? I'd be lucky if they were surveying me so closely. In truth, they're probably not even paying attention. If I read things correctly, they dismissed me as soon as I walked through the office doorway.

And to be honest? I don't really blame them. Even I can see how they wouldn't want the audience wondering if the bartender moonlights as a professional wrestler while J.Lo is having her big on-screen rom-com epiphany.

"And to the right."

I turn to the side and show my other profile. Now my gut is all butterflies, my legs are wet noodles, and my head is a little wonky, like a giant helium balloon.

"And back around to the front."

I face the room again, and I'm afraid I might pass out. Or vomit. I try to stay focused on the little red light.

"Now we'll get to it," says the assistant. "I'll read you in."

Staring at the camera, I see the trio on the sofa in my periphery looking bored and indifferent, like they're all trying not to be the first one to yawn. But I remember how much I want this job, what a great opportunity it would be. I mean, I could be in a scene with Jennifer Lopez. *Jennifer freaking Lopez!*

So I'm not going to give up just yet. I can still surprise these people, still get them to wake up and take notice.

At least that's what I tell myself.

"Ready whenever you are," I tell the assistant.

"'Interior bar, night,'" she says, beginning to read the scene with absolutely no inflection whatsoever. It's like she's going out of her way to just mumble and drone her way through the words. "'Visibly upset, Lulu takes a seat at the bar.'"

And this right here is the biggest problem with auditions—or, I guess I should say, *my* biggest problem with auditions. They're not about acting. Acting is about being present and connecting in a real way with another player. It's about living truthfully, just under imaginary circumstances. But auditioning? That's about performing on cue, like you're a trained circus animal. You're expected to be real—and to make the people watching you feel something *real*—all while the assistant reads the rest of the script like she couldn't care less about any of it. Hardly the ideal scene partner.

"'The bartender spots her,'" continues the assistant with the same flat delivery, "'and crosses over.'"

I know that's my cue, but for a moment, I blank. I can't think of my first line.

But I know it. I know I know it. Dammit, it's right on the tip of my—

"What can I get you to drink?" I blurt out.

Nope. Too…awful.

And just like that, any last shred of hope I was hanging on to slips away, and I feel like I'm plummeting into a deep, dark abyss.

The assistant goes on to read J.Lo's follow-up line with the same lack of passion so I can complete the scene. But really, there's no point. In my heart, I know without a doubt that this audition is already over.

· · · · ·

"Oh no!" says Liv over my hybrid's Bluetooth connection. I made a three-way call to her and Heather to fill them in as soon as I got back in the car.

"Oh *yes*," I say, steering my Prius onto Melrose. "I choked. I totally blew it. I tried, but after I almost incinerated myself in the waiting area, I couldn't get it together. The whole thing was just a big, flaming-hot turd of a disaster."

"But you're okay?" asks Heather. "Everybody's okay?"

"Yeah, everybody's okay," I say. "I guess the one saving grace is that nobody had to pull the fire alarm." I sigh. "You were both right. I should have called in sick."

To their credit, neither of my friends says, "I told you so." But their momentary silence on the other end of my car speaker says enough.

"Well, come home now," says Liv after a beat. "We can order in dinner before I have to leave for work. Thai, maybe? My treat."

"Thanks, but I can't," I say. "I have a shift at Pete's."

"Carrie," says Heather, her voice heavy with misgiving.

"I know what you're going to say," I say, cutting her off before she can say it. "But I need to go in."

"Are you kidding?" says Heather. "After what just happened at the audition—"

"*Especially* after what just happened at the audition," I say. "I've got to go to work."

"If it's about money," begins Heather.

"It's not about money," I say quickly. "It's about…uh…"

I hesitate. What I'm about to say isn't going to make any sense to them. It barely makes any sense to me. But sense isn't really factoring into things right now.

"It's about Nick," I confess.

"Aha!" says Liv. "So you do like him."

"What? No!" I say. "Jeez, how many times do I need to tell you? I can't stand the guy."

"Tomato, to-*mah*-to," Liv says in a teasing tone.

"No, listen," I say. "When we were all talking this morning? Well, Heather, I think you might've been onto something. Nick really might be the trigger for what's going on with me. It fits. I mean, I was thinking about him earlier, when my eyes…uh…"

"Did that freaky flashy thing?" Liv supplies.

"Right," I say. I'm almost at Pete's. I spot a car pulling out of a parking spot halfway up the block, so I put my signal on and slow to a stop. "And I was thinking about him again when I almost set my headshots on fire."

"You think about him an awful lot," says Liv. "For somebody you can't stand."

"Cut it out," I say. "It's not like that. I just think he's part of this somehow. So I need to see him. And talk to him."

What I don't tell my friends is that I don't just need to talk to Nick. Since I left the audition, it's like I've been running on automatic pilot. I've got this uncontrollable urge to go and confront my coworker, to face off with him. I feel as if something inside me is compelling me, pushing me into his path. Honestly? I don't think I could stay away from the bar tonight if I tried.

"Are you sure talking to this Nick guy is a good idea?" asks Liv. "Can you trust him with this?"

"I don't know," I say. "But I don't think I have a choice."

"Well, please be careful," says Heather. "With what you tell him. And what you show him."

"I will," I say as I pull into the empty parking space. "I promise."

"And make sure you know where all the fire exits are," says Liv.

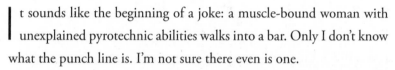

CHAPTER

5

I t sounds like the beginning of a joke: a muscle-bound woman with unexplained pyrotechnic abilities walks into a bar. Only I don't know what the punch line is. I'm not sure there even is one.

I step into Pete's. The place is about halfway filled with patrons sipping drinks and munching on bowls of complimentary pretzels and peanuts. Based on the number of guidebooks on the tops of tables and shopping bags tucked underneath, I'd say most of the current customers are tourists. Pete's is written up in a bunch of the LA visitors' guides as "a refreshingly downscale drinking establishment in the heart of the upscale Melrose shopping and dining district," so we get a lot of out-of-towners dropping by. The rest appear to be locals taking advantage of the happy hour specials.

"Hiya, Carrie," calls Sara from behind the bar. A thirtysomething single mom, she works the afternoon shift while her kids are in school. She starts to go back to wiping down the bar counter, but then she does a double take. "Cute outfit," she says.

But her body language and tone seem to be saying something else. Maybe she's just wondering why I'm not wearing my usual work attire of jeans and a T-shirt. Or maybe she's struggling to put her finger on why I look noticeably bigger than I did the last time she saw me, around this same time yesterday.

Either way, I'm not going to worry about it right now. Nope. I've got something else on my mind.

"Is Nick here yet?" I ask.

I don't really need to ask though. I know he's not here, and not just because the guy has never once had the initiative to show up early for a shift. No, it's more like I can *sense* he's not here.

"Not yet," confirms Sara.

But I know he's on his way. Strange as it is, I can totally sense that too.

· · · · ·

A little later, I'm helping Sara out behind the bar, refilling the bowls of snacks, when the door swings open. I look up to see Nick's broad-shouldered frame filling the doorway, and suddenly, a wave of absolute loathing washes over me. Admittedly, it's not as if I'm ever exactly jumping for joy at the sight of the guy. But this? This is way more than any ordinary dislike. What I'm rocking right now is an epic, good-versus-evil kind of bone-deep hatred. Like Nick is a blight on the face of humanity, and I must be the one to remove him. Eradicate him. Freaking destroy him.

Nick's eyes find mine, and once again, my field of vision becomes saturated in a bloodred fog.

I want to launch myself over the bar counter, conjure my fiery blade, and cut Nick down right where he stands. Although "want" doesn't even come close to expressing what I feel. The urge to attack my fellow bartender is all-consuming and irresistible.

But I do resist it. *Just.*

Because there's something holding me back that's a teensy bit stronger. I'm acutely aware of all the people around me, talking and laughing and getting tipsy on four-dollar drafts and house wine, and I know I can't get them caught in the middle of this—whatever *this* even is. As compelled as I am to assault Nick, I'm compelled to protect them more.

My vision clears.

Nick hasn't moved. He's still staring at me from the doorway. But the atmosphere between us prickles with a volatile energy, and I know there's something between us that's bigger than us both, that's building to some kind of an inevitable clash.

And I can tell he knows it too. He nods, indicating the back of the bar. Then his lean figure, clad tonight in worn Levis and a black Guns N' Roses tee, strides through the main room, strolls past me, and heads for the rear exit.

"Can you cover here alone for a few?" I ask Sara.

But I don't bother waiting for her to answer. Like a moth to a flame, I follow after Nick.

· · · · ·

Darkness has fallen completely by now, and the moon has slipped behind a cloud. The alley in back of Pete's, devoid of lighting, is inky black, but I don't need light to find Nick. It's as if Google Maps has been downloaded into my brain, and Nick is my destination.

We stand in the middle of the alleyway, facing each other but keeping our distance. The whole scene has the vibe of an old-school western. We're like two rival gunslingers sizing each other up, about to draw pistols and aim.

"What do you know about all this?" I demand, cutting straight to the chase. I don't see any reason to be coy. "What in the actual hell is going on with me?"

At first, Nick doesn't say anything. He just shoves his big hands deep into the pockets of his jeans and transfers his weight from one black Converse high-top to the other.

"Before I answer that," he says finally, "I think you need to know what's going on with *me*."

"Really?" I ask. "You're going to make this about *you*?"

This is just so typical. Once again, Nick has absolutely no freaking consideration for anyone but himself.

My anger flares, my vision goes red, and incredibly, my eyes illuminate the space between Nick and me. The light emanating from my gaze cuts through the darkness like twin headlights. It glints off the silver chain hanging from Nick's belt and makes the barbell piercing in his eyebrow sparkle. Now I understand what my friends must have witnessed earlier. But unlike Liv and Heather, Nick doesn't look the least bit shocked by the light show.

"Carrie," he says slowly, "I'm a vampire."

It makes absolutely no sense, yet somehow, it makes perfect sense. This morning, when Liv said the same exact thing, I dismissed it as pure fiction. Because it *is* pure fiction—or I thought it was. But in this moment, it's like I can feel the truth of the statement vibrating through every inch of my body.

"Vampire," I whisper.

"I was turned this past weekend," he says. "And I thought I knew what I was getting into. But as it turns out, there were things I didn't know."

"Your skin is cold," I say as I recall what I told my besties. "You're unnaturally fast. And you don't have a reflection."

He nods. "I expected all that," he says. "But something happened that I didn't expect. Something no one warned me about. Not until after."

"Me," I say. I don't know why I say it or what it means. But again, I feel the *truth* of it. "No one warned you about *me*."

Nick nods again. "Your skin is hot," he says. "Your body is strong. And you can produce a weapon made of fire."

"But how do you even know that?" I ask. "How do you *know*?"

He takes one of his hands out of his pocket and runs it through his long, black hair with a sigh. "Here's what I was told," he says. "When a new vampire is created, the universe sometimes seeks…*balance*."

"*Balance*?" I ask.

He nods at me once again. "If somebody becomes a vampire, there's always a chance that somebody else will become, well, a vampire slayer."

"Vampire slayer," I repeat softly.

"And if that happens," Nick adds, "the 'somebody else' is always somebody the vampire already knows. And it's always somebody…" He takes a moment, seeming to search for the right words. "Somebody who's not exactly a friend" is where he ends up.

I try to get my mind around what he's telling me, only it's like my mind isn't completely under my control anymore. It's as if some other force is starting to creep through me and take over.

"Carrie," Nick says, "you're a vampire slayer."

The idea lands in my head, but it's a crash landing at best. I mean, I believe what he's telling me. I do. But how can it be true? How is it possible that one of the wild theories that Liv was throwing around earlier today actually hit the bull's-eye?

"So let me get this straight," I say. At this point, I'm not just struggling with the absurdity of what he's telling me. I'm seriously fighting to stay coherent, to maintain command of my own body, of my own brain. "You decided to turn into some kind of a real-life Count Dracula. And because I'm not your goddamn BFF, I changed too?"

He looks a little pained. He opens his mouth—to try to explain maybe? Or to apologize? But I don't want to hear it. Dammit, I won't hear it. I am absolutely freaking furious.

I look at Nick, and just like last night, I want to kill him. *Kill* him. But this time, I know *exactly* why. "Because of you, I blew my big audition!" I scream at him. "Because of you, I lost the J.Lo movie!"

That's it. I can't contain myself any longer. I just can't.

In a flash, fire explodes from me, and I'm wielding that blazing sword. The flame of my blade lights up the dark alley. And now I can see that Nick has fangs.

Fangs, I think. *Holy crap! He* is *a vampire.*

And suddenly, that's all I can see. I'm not looking at my coworker anymore, the slacker who kind of rubs me the wrong way. Nope. I only see my enemy. A bloodsucker who must die. And I must be the one to take him down.

I unleash my fury and swing at Nick, fire streaking in an arc through the dark. But I'm no swashbuckler, and Nick is too fast for me. He moves out of the way before I can strike him, and my sword just slices through empty air.

I sense him behind me, so I spin. Swing again. But again, he evades my blade.

Now he's on top of the dumpster. And he's saying something, saying my name I think, but it barely even registers. All I can hear is the voice inside my head. The voice that's urging me on, telling me to *slay*.

Instinctively, I bend my knees. I push off the ground, and before

I know what's happening, I'm doing a pretty convincing Simone Biles imitation. My body launches up with a twist and a flip and—*thunk!*—I stick the landing on the dumpster lid right in front of Nick.

Slay, says the voice echoing through my skull. *Slay!*

So I take another stab at it. At *him*.

But Nick jumps out of the line of my fire, back down to the alley. And I miss again.

Driven by a force I still don't understand, I go after him. Relinquishing the high ground, I leap down from my perch atop the dumpster and square off with him once more.

"Carrie!"

Even though Nick is standing right in front of me, his shout sounds muffled. It's as if his voice is traveling to me through an invisible wall.

"Carrie!" he repeats more forcefully. And that's when the wall between us begins to crack.

Regardless, I draw my sword hand back, preparing to attack again.

"*Carrie!*" he screams. "Will you quit being so uptight for once? You need to chill and rein this shit in."

Just then, something in my brain clicks, and I surface. The light shining from my eyes dims. The fire wanes. And I'm me again. Fully me.

"Did you just call me uptight?" I demand.

For a moment, Nick just stares at me. Then, as the moon emerges from behind the cloud bank, he tosses his head back and laughs. The moonlight makes the piercing in his eyebrow glimmer.

"Well, it got your attention, didn't it?" he asks, still grinning.

I can see that Nick's fangs, like my blade, have also receded.

I smile back despite myself. Despite my *uptight* self.

"Uh, hello?"

The voice startles us both. In unison, we turn toward the back door to Pete's. Sara is poking her head out, surveying us curiously.

"Are you two about done out here?" she asks. "I need to get home and feed my kids."

Immediately, I feel a twinge of guilt for leaving her on her own to deal with the happy hour crowd. I kind of welcome the guilt though. It helps to reinforce that I am, in fact, still *me*. The conscientious worker. Not the angry vampire slayer. For now, at least, my rage at Nick switches to the back burner.

"Sorry," I tell her. "We'll be right in."

Sara gives me and Nick another speculative look. Then she nods and disappears inside.

I start to go after her. But before I reach the door, Nick taps me lightly on the shoulder. Even through my sweater, I can feel his unnaturally cold touch.

"We still need to talk," he says. "There's more you need to know."

CHAPTER
6

"Y ou have got to be shitting me," says Heather. She dropped into Pete's on her way home from work, after the happy hour crowd had thinned down. "You mean one of Liv's screwy ideas was actually right on the money?"

"Yup," I say with a nod. I pour her a generous glass of the house rosé, which I'm guessing she could use right about now. Since she arrived to check in on me and grabbed a seat at my end of the bar, I've been quietly filling her in on the latest...*developments*.

"Jesus," she says under her breath. She picks up the wineglass and takes a big gulp while I stick the bottle back in the fridge. I notice that her hand is trembling slightly. "You know, if I hadn't actually seen your...uh..."

"Magical, flaming, vampire-slaying sword?" I suggest with raised eyebrows.

"Yeah," says Heather. "That."

"I know," I say, shaking my head. "I wouldn't believe it either. I mean, even after the whole vampire-versus-slayer death match we had out back, I'm still having a hard time getting my head around it. But I'm telling you, it's the absolute, honest-to-God, cross-my-heart truth."

Heather takes another big swallow of her wine, and her gaze slides down to the other end of the bar. Nick's end of the bar. Since he and I came in from the alleyway, we've been avoiding each other as best we can, considering we have to share the same space. And the same cash register. And the same beer taps. If working alongside Nick was annoying before, it's now nearly unbearable. Luckily, the presence of the customers—the *human* customers—helps me keep a chain on my wrath.

But it also raises a question. A question that won't stop nagging at me until I ask it out loud.

"Heather," I say in a small voice, "do you think I'm still...*human*?"

She turns back to me, surprised. "What?"

"If I'm a vampire slayer, does that mean I'm not human anymore?"

"Honey," says Heather, "of course you're still human. You're still *you*."

I frown. "I don't know about that," I say. "When I was fighting with Nick, it was like I wasn't me. I was all weird instincts and homicidal rage." I lean closer and lower my voice. "I tried to *kill* him, Heather. For real."

"But you didn't, babe," she says. She reaches across the bar and gives my hand a quick, firm squeeze. And just like that, her trepidation is gone, and she's back to being my unshakable, rock-solid, no-BS friend again. "And you won't."

"I was so angry though," I tell her. An involuntary shudder runs through me at the thought.

It's not as if I never get angry. But usually, I don't express my anger. Not in the moment like that anyway. Instead, I suppress it. In Hollywood, it's just the way it is, the way it has to be. I can't go ballistic every time my agent doesn't return my calls or every time a casting director says no. I need them more than they need me. So if I want my career to go anywhere, I have to suck it up, smile, and try to go along to get along.

Although, okay, suppressing my anger isn't just a career thing. It's also kind of a *me* thing.

"Anger is human," says Heather. "It's a normal human emotion."

"I guess," I say.

Except it's not normal for *me*. I've always had trouble expressing my anger. Or expressing any strong emotions that could potentially stir up conflict. I guess you could say I'm a hopeless people pleaser. If I were a bus, my route would run straight up and down the path of least resistance.

But all that suppressed emotion doesn't just evaporate. It has to go somewhere. So since high school, I've been channeling it into my acting. That's really what drew me to the craft in the first place—well, that and growing up watching the Disney Channel, memorizing every episode of *Wizards of Waverly Place*, and wanting to be Selena Gomez. But childhood fantasies aside, being an actor gives me a way to release all the negative things I'm feeling, just in a positive way.

But what happened out back in the alley? That wasn't acting. Nope. It was more like something was acting *through* me. And in retrospect, unleashing at Nick the way I did feels wrong.

Except it also feels kind of…*good*?

Possibly a little too good.

Which is bad.

Isn't it?

Uggghhh!

Okay, so maybe I am still human. Maybe this jumble of contradic-tory emotions I've got going on just reaffirms my humanity. Still, it's like something inside me has been uncorked. And I'm not sure I can put the genie back in the bottle.

I'm not sure I even want to.

"But I'm still angry, you know?" I tell Heather. "I'm so angry at Nick right now. I mean, I've got this strange new body and these strange new powers and these strange new urges, and it turns out they're all because of him. All because he was too freaking lazy to get all his facts straight before he went over to the undead side."

"Well, it's not *all* because of him."

"What?" Now it's my turn to look surprised. "What are you talking about?"

"Carrie," says Heather, "face it. You've had a stick up your butt about Nick ever since he started working here."

"That's not true," I say.

"It is true," she says. "And it sounds like this happened because you two can't play nice together, so you're at least partly to blame. You could have tried to work out your differences."

"There was never anything to work out," I say with a shrug. "I just don't like the guy."

Heather peers down the bar again. "Well, I think you may be the only one," she says with a toss of her head in Nick's direction.

I turn, and I see what she means. Nick is basically holding court, chatting up a couple of young women drinking bottles of Corona Light. They seem to be hanging on his every word.

"Vampire, huh?" says Heather.

"Fangs and all," I say.

I want to accuse him of using some kind of vampire magic on the women. But the fact is he's always had an uncanny knack for charming the customers. Especially female customers. If I had even half his appeal, I swear I wouldn't have to work as a bartender anymore. If I could command an audience like that, I'd be writing my freaking Oscar acceptance speech by now.

"So which one of them do you think he wants to *fang*?" Heather asks, still watching Nick.

I shoot her a look. I don't know if it's the wine or what, but it seems to me that she's gotten awfully comfortable awfully quick with this supernatural situation.

She looks back at me, all innocence. "What? That's what vampires do, right? They use their fangs to bite people. And drink their blood."

I guess they do. I haven't exactly had time to consider all the gory little details.

Only now that I'm thinking about it, I start to think back to last night. I remember catching Nick with that brunette, necking by the restrooms. And I have to wonder…

Was he really necking with her? Or was he maybe just extremely interested in her neck? Was that really a hickey she tried to hide? Or was it some other kind of mark?

Was Nick actually…*drinking* on the job?

I shudder again.

"So now, in addition to the sexy musician thing," continues Heather, "he's also got the sexy vampire thing going on." She sighs. "As if the guy needed any help in the sexy department." She takes another sip of the rosé.

"No comment," I say.

Heather grins. "Oh, come on," she teases. "You wouldn't let him bite you?"

I feel my slayer start to rise. "No," I mutter. "No, I would not."

"Whoa," says Heather. "Down, girl."

I realize my vision temporarily went scarlet.

I blink a couple of times. "I'm okay," I assure her. "For now anyway. But Nick says there's still more he needs to tell me. And honestly? I'm not sure how much more of this I can take."

"You'll be fine," says Heather with a confidence I wish I had. "You know, you're a lot stronger than you think you are. Even without all these new vampire-slaying muscles."

My friend smiles kindly at me. After a beat, I smile back. Then, gradually, we both let our gazes drift back to Nick.

Heather catches his eye, and he grins and nods in recognition.

"Try not to kill him, huh?" she says to me as she gives him a little wave back. "Anyone with dimples that epic deserves immortal life."

· · · · ·

It's my night to close up. Heather offers to stick around, but I know she has to be on set early the next morning, so I send her home. I tell her I'll talk to her tomorrow, and I lock the door behind her.

Then it's just me and Nick.

I start to stack the chairs on the tabletops so I can mop up, and for once, Nick actually stays and helps. We work together in silence for a bit, sticking to opposite sides of the room, circling each other but careful to always keep a couple of tables between us.

"It was nice to see Heather again," says Nick tentatively, breaking our silence. "She's good people."

"She is," I agree.

"So you told her?" he asks. He raises an eyebrow, the one with the piercing. "About…uh…"

"I told her what you told me," I say. "And what happened between us in the alley. Is that a problem?"

Nick hesitates a moment, then shakes his head. "Probably not," he says. "It's not like she's going to take the story public or anything, right?"

"Who would believe it if she did?"

"I don't know," says Nick. "People seem to believe a lot of bizarre things these days."

He lifts another chair. One of the legs catches at the bottom of his T-shirt and hikes it up, briefly flashing a few inches of smooth, flat stomach before the tee drops back into place.

My body heat rises—with slayer anger, I'm sure. Not attraction. Nope. *Definitely* not attraction.

Tomato, to-mah-*to*, Liv would say. I can almost hear her singsong voice in my head.

Whatever.

"You said there was more I needed to know," I say, trying to regain some self-possession. "And I have questions. Like, if I were to say to you, 'What can I get you to drink?' would you say beer? Or…uh…*blood*?"

Nick shrugs those big shoulders of his. "Both," he offers. "Either."

"So you drink blood?" I ask.

"I'm a vampire."

"I know, but—"

"Carrie," he says. "I'm a vampire."

I swallow. "Right." I stack the last chair on my side of the room, and Nick does the same on his. "So that woman I saw you with last night—"

"Was a mistake," he says, abruptly cutting me off.

"A mistake?" I ask. "A mistake *how*?" My focus sharpens, my body goes rigid, and the smoldering within me is unquestionably slayer rage. No tomato, to-*mah*-to about it.

Nick sighs and walks over to his end of the bar. "Easy there, slayer," he says, reading my reaction. "I promise you, the woman is still very much alive and well."

I cross over to my end of the bar. "But you…uh…*drank* from her?" I ask. "You drank her blood?"

"Quentin and Zach sent her over," he says.

"Quentin and Zach?"

"My bandmates," he says. "We play music together. But as of this past weekend, we're also literally a band of vampires."

"So the guys in your band are vampires too," I say, trying to keep the details organized.

"They turned me. Well, Zach turned me," says Nick. "He turned Quentin too, but that was a really long time ago. The two of them have been a couple for over a hundred years."

"So I guess vampires really are immortal?" I ask.

"Vampires never say die," he says with a grin that coaxes those epic dimples out of hiding. "That is, assuming nothing kills us."

Like me, I think.

So far, it sounds like the truth about vampires is lining right up with the fiction.

Nick starts stacking barstools from his end of the bar, and I start stacking from mine.

"So *how* exactly did Zach turn you?" I ask. "If you don't mind me asking."

"Actually, it was kind of cool," he says. "We went down into the tunnels—"

"You mean the subway tunnels?" Although I've never used it, I know there's a very limited subway system in LA. Nothing like the ones back east though.

Nick shakes his head. "No, there are actually all these abandoned service tunnels running underneath Los Angeles. I guess they were used for smuggling during Prohibition. And as passageways to the basements of the speakeasies." He waves it off. "Anyway, Zach and Quentin and a few other vampire witnesses gathered together down there for the blood exchange—"

"Blood exchange?" I ask, interrupting.

"Zach drank from me, then I drank from Zach," he explains. "That's what initiated the change."

I'm almost sorry I asked. I try to suppress my wince of revulsion.

To be honest, I'm not even good with scary movies. I actually turned down work as a background player on Liv's zombie show because even though I know it's all makeup and special effects, the idea of having to live in that world was just a little too intense for me. How on earth am I going to live in *this* world?

"Then it was pretty much lights-out for me," Nick continues calmly, like he's recounting the highlights of last night's baseball game. "But when I woke up the next night, I was a vampire. And I signed"—he makes air quotes and lowers the pitch of his voice. "—*The Book*."

"The Book?" I ask.

He nods. "It's like this ancient book that all the vampires have to sign after they're made. In their…uh…*blood*."

My stomach roils a little at that. I can't help it. An antique tome filled with countless centuries' worth of bloody autographs? Gross.

"Arlo from the Vampire Council flew it in special from New York," adds Nick. "In a private jet."

"Wait, wait, wait," I say. I do my best to get a handle on my squeamishness. I've got to pay attention to this stuff after all. "The Vampire Council? What's that?"

"Apparently," says Nick, "it's this governing body made up of the oldest vampires. The American chapter is headquartered in New York City. They kind of lay down the law for the rest of us."

"You have *laws*?" I ask.

"Not many. From what I understand, it's kind of like Fight Club," he says. "The first rule of Vampire Club is you don't talk about Vampire Club." He looks at me and raises his brow again. "So I'd really appreciate it if you and Heather could keep this on the down-low. Okay?"

I nod slowly. My mind, however, is racing. "So you woke up, you signed *The Book*, and then what?"

He smiles a little sheepishly. "Then we had a big party. With cake."

I pause, taking a break from the stools while I digest this. On the plus side, I don't feel queasy or repulsed anymore. But on the minus side, I'm starting to feel…well, not jealous exactly, but…jealous adjacent maybe? I mean, what in the actual hell? He gets some legally sanctioned, by-The-Book ceremony? With a reception? And cake? Meanwhile, I just wake up to the worst surprise party ever and almost set my apartment on fire.

"You okay?" asks Nick.

"Peachy," I snap. But then I check my bitterness. I resume stacking barstools, and my mind circles back to what we were discussing before we took this conversational detour down into the tunnels. "And the woman?" I ask. "The one you drank from last night?"

Nick sighs, like he doesn't want to go there. But then he grudgingly says, "Her name is Jess. She's kind of a Dracula's Army groupie."

"Dracula's Army?" I ask.

"That's the name of our band," he says with a smile. "It's an inside joke."

I don't smile back. "Okay," I say, knitting my brow. "So this woman.

Jess. Is she a groupie because she likes the music? Or because she likes the…uh…uh…" I'm not sure how to phrase it, so I just gesture in the vicinity of my own neck.

"Both?" Nick offers again. "Either?"

"Huh," I say, pondering this. I have to say, it's hard for me to believe that anyone would enjoy being a vampire's blood donor. Different strokes, I guess. And at least it confirms that things between them were consensual.

Nick and I keep on upending the barstools, working our way closer and closer to each other.

"Anyway," says Nick, "she offered to feed me, and I accepted. Only I didn't realize how…how…*personal* it would be."

Suddenly, I recall the look of straight-up rapture that shone in the woman's eyes while she was with Nick. And I feel…well, again, I'm not exactly sure how I feel. I've got a whole soup of emotions simmering inside me—some of them mine, some of them my slayer's.

"I mean, I barely know Jess," continues Nick. "And I'm not really interested in getting to know her any better. So even though she was totally on board, the casual intimacy of it all just didn't sit right with me." He shakes his head. "So I won't be doing that again."

Now my inner slayer feels a little confused. Cheated, in a way. This doesn't sound like the bloodsucking human predator that my alter ego is so hell-bent on destroying.

And admittedly, *I* feel confused too. This definitely doesn't sound like the emotionally shallow player that I've come to know and dislike. Given the way Nick flirts with the customers, I've always assumed that casual intimacy was totally up his alley.

"But you need human blood to survive, don't you?" I ask him.

"Yes, but Zach has connections at a local blood bank," he says. "So I'll be fine. Thanks for the concern though," he adds with a grin.

"My concern isn't about you," I grumble.

"Riiight," he says. "You're all about protecting humans from us big bad bloodsuckers."

Finally, Nick and I meet in the middle. We pick up the last two stools and plunk them onto the bar in unison.

I turn to face him. Eye level with his broad chest, I can just make out the outline of what must be well-developed pecs beneath his Guns N' Roses T-shirt. This close, I notice that the graphic on the tee shows the cover of the band's debut, *Appetite for Destruction*. I wonder if that's some kind of an inside joke too.

I also wonder what he looks like without the shirt.

When I realize I've been staring at his chest a little too long, I make my gaze rise up to meet his. "Your secret's safe with me," I say. "I won't talk about Vampire Club. Is that all you wanted to tell me?"

"Actually, no," he says. His dark eyes peer down at me with seriousness. "I still need to warn you about something."

CHAPTER

7

N ick goes behind the bar, grabs a bottle of Maker's Mark and a couple of glasses, and pours two shots. Then he slides one across the counter to me.

Now, I'm not much of a drinker. Alcohol is nothing but empty calories. Plus, it dries out your skin. Not exactly an aspiring screen actor's friend. So unless it's a girls' night with Liv and Heather or a special occasion, I mostly stick with water.

But tonight's already been something of an occasion. And looking at Nick, I have the strong feeling it's about to get even more...*special*. So I pick up the glass.

"Cheers," says Nick.

"Cheers," I return.

Nick knocks back the whole shot, but I just take a sip. The bourbon is sweet and smooth and leaves me with a warm feeling inside. But I don't let myself relax into the warmth. I think I'm going to need to stay alert and keep my wits about me.

"So what is it that you need to warn me about?" I ask.

Nick puts his hands flat on the bar and leans forward, and I can't help noticing how the tendons beneath his guitar tattoo ripple as they tense. "Here's the deal," he says. "Before I became a vampire—before I even knew Quentin and Zach were vampires, back when we were just playing music together—I kind of complained to them about this woman who was always on my case."

Waiting for him to continue, I don't say anything. But after a few moments, his brows shoot up, and he gives me a pointed look.

"Me?" I ask. "You were talking about me?"

"Who else would I be talking about?"

"I'm not always on your case."

"Oh no?" he asks, challenging. He stands up straight and puts his hands on his hips. "Nick, break's over," he says in a high-pitched, whiny voice that I guess is supposed to be me, although from my perspective, his acting is way over the top. "Nick, don't forget to lock up. Nick, you're wasting beer."

"Well, you *were* wasting beer," I say. "You're *always* wasting beer. If you would just tilt the mug so the beer pours down along the inside of the glass…" I see that Nick is smirking at me, and I realize I'm kind of proving his point, so I don't bother finishing my sentence. And I drop my hands, which yes, have somehow made their way onto my hips.

Annoyed, I pick up the tumbler of Maker's Mark again. This time, I take a bigger swallow.

"So now my bandmates are suspicious of you," says Nick. "They know that if my making triggered a new slayer, it has to be you."

"Why does it have to be me?" I ask.

"Because the slayer is always someone the vampire doesn't get along with," he says. "And I get along with pretty much everybody else."

"You do not," I say.

"Sure I do," he says with a shrug.

"That's impossible," I say, even though I've seen the way he is with the customers. "No one gets along with everyone."

"Seriously?" he says. "You're even going to get on my case about this?"

I scowl at him. Then—screw it—I pick up the bourbon and drain the glass.

"Okay," I say. "For the sake of argument, let's say your vampire buddies figure out that I'm the new slayer in town. What's the big deal? Then they'll just know to stay away from me."

"No," says Nick.

"No?"

He shakes his head. "It doesn't work like that, Carrie," he says. "Think about it. As long as you're out there, every vampire in Los Angeles is in danger. I mean, you did just try to kill me in the alleyway."

"Sorry," I say—a little belatedly, I know. "But it wasn't about you, exactly. And I wasn't me, exactly. There are all these unnatural urges…"

"I know," Nick says, nodding. "I get it, believe me. I know all about unnatural urges."

I guess he would, considering the new addition to his personal drink menu.

"It was like I had no control," I hear myself confess to him.

"I know," he says. There's real empathy in his voice. "But, Carrie? You need to get control. Fast."

Nick picks up the bottle and refills our glasses. And that pretty much tells me that I'm not going to like where this conversation is going.

"The thing is," he says, "Quentin and Zach are going to be watching you. And if they see what you are? Well, they'll take action to eliminate you before you can eliminate us."

My slayer perks up at that. I do too.

"Hold on," I say. "Are you saying they'll kill me?"

"Yes."

"*Kill* me?"

"'Fraid so."

"As in…"

"They're great guys," he says. "But they're not really guys, you know? They're vampires. *Old* vampires. And the way they see it, when it comes to your kind, it's slay or be slain."

What?

"And it's not just them," says Nick. "Arlo from the Vampire Council is still here. And apparently, he's not going back to New York until the slayer question is…uh…*resolved*. One way or another."

That's it. Rage explodes in me. It's slayer rage—but Carrie rage too.

"You have got to be freaking kidding me!" I shout. "First, you make a choice that turns my whole life upside down. And now you're saying I could lose my life altogether?"

"Carrie…"

Bloodred mist clouds my vision.

"Carrie!"

Nick's fangs have reappeared, and before I know it, I'm wielding my sword of fire again.

"Carrie, stop!" shouts Nick. "You could burn down Pete's!"

I could burn down Pete's.

He's right. I could. With the wooden tables and chairs, bar and barstools—not to mention all the alcohol? The place could go up like a tinderbox.

I feel my flaming blade waver.

"You don't want to burn down Pete's!" he shouts.

I don't want to burn down Pete's.

He's right again. I don't. I may want to burn his goddamn vampire ass to the ground, but I don't want to destroy my employer's livelihood. Or destroy my own livelihood, for that matter. Right now, with no potential acting gig in the offing, I can't exactly afford to do a slay job at my day job.

My fiery weapon retreats. My vision returns to normal. And even though there's been no battle, I kind of feel defeated. Not to go feeling all sorry for myself or anything, but why am I the one who's always got to be reining things in? Goddammit, it's like these superpowers are making me more vulnerable than ever.

"You suck," I tell Nick. "You know that? You totally, totally suck."

"I do," he says with an amused grin. His fangs have retracted, I notice. I guess they must pop out as some reaction to my slayer form. Just like my blazing sword seems to show up in response to him.

He pushes the second shot of bourbon a little closer to me. But I don't need more alcohol. What I need is…

Well, actually, I'm not sure what I need.

"So what am I supposed to do?" I ask. "Obviously, I'm *not* in control. So if Dracula's Army is watching me, eventually they're going to see what I am."

"Maybe not," says Nick. "I have an idea, if you're game."

I eye him warily, through the legs of the stools stacked between us. "Go on," I say. "I'm listening."

"We work on it together," he says. "I'll help you to restrain your slayer and get control."

All at once, I realize that's exactly what I need. Help. Except…

"How can you help me?" I ask. "You're a vampire. You're what sets me off and makes me want to slay."

"But I also managed to get through to you and make you stop," he counters. "Out back in the alley. And then again just now."

I think about this for a moment. I guess he's not wrong.

"We can have, like, nightly training sessions," says Nick. "I can try to provoke you, and you can try to hold your shit together."

"Sounds like a typical shift at Pete's," I mutter.

He laughs at that. After a beat, I reluctantly smile back.

"And I suppose they'd have to be *night* sessions?" I ask.

He points at himself. "Vampire," he says. "So yes."

"Right."

Once again, vampire mythology holds true.

Just then, it occurs to me that there's all this well-known lore about vampires but virtually nothing about vampire slayers. I know that Nick can't go out in the sunlight, but I know nothing about myself. Or my *new* self, I should say. I mean, I didn't even know what I was until he told me. And suddenly, it all just seems so...*unfair*.

"You all right?" asks Nick, crashing the private little pity party I've got brewing.

"Fine," I say. "I'm fine." I'm not fine, of course. Not even close. But goddammit, I'm not going to start crying to him about it. "So you were saying...?"

He eyes me for a long beat before he continues.

"A week from tonight," he says finally, "Dracula's Army has a gig at the Whisky on Sunset."

"That's impressive," I say, a little thrown. For one thing, I'd always figured that if Nick's stupid garage band ever managed to score a gig, it'd be at some unknown little hole-in-the-wall, not at one of LA's most historic music venues. And for another thing, well…I just don't see what the band's show at Whisky a Go Go next Wednesday night has to do with my current predicament. "Congratulations."

"Arlo will be there. Along with a bunch of other vampires," says Nick. "I'm thinking you should come too."

"What?" I ask. "You *want* to get me killed?"

"No, listen," he says. "That's what we'll be training for. What *you'll* be training for. I'll put you on the VIP list, and you can come backstage. You can meet Quentin and Zach and Arlo and the others. And when they see you *not* making with the slayer rage around all that undead energy, they'll think you didn't turn. They'll think you're just an ordinary human. They won't have any reason to kill you, so they'll leave you alone. And Arlo can go back to New York and report that no slayer was created during the making of"—he gestures at himself with both thumbs—"this vampire. Problem solved."

Nick looks at me like he's just handed me a gift and he's waiting to see if I like it.

I don't want to seem ungrateful. Certainly, I appreciate the gesture. But I can't overlook the obvious flaws here.

First off, this plan involves the two of us spending the next week together. And it's bad enough just working the bar with Nick. But hanging out afterward? And on our nights off? We'll be lucky if we don't kill each other. Literally.

And even if I can learn to put my slayer on a leash around Nick, who knows what'll happen in a room filled with other vampires? This has the potential to end badly. Really badly.

"What if it doesn't work?" I ask. "What if I can't get control?"

Nick shrugs. "Then you're no worse off than you are right now," he says. "And neither are any of us."

That's the second time he's said *us*, I notice. Because he's a vampire. He's one of them.

"But why even help me?" I ask. "Won't your bandmates be pissed if they learn you're consorting with the enemy."

"If we pull this off," he says, "they'll never have to know."

"But you could get hurt," I say.

"I could get hurt anyway," he says with a wry smile. "I can deal."

"But why risk it?" I ask. "You don't even like me."

Nick starts to say something, but then he hesitates. He stares down at his drink, frowning. The silence stretches out to a point where it starts to get awkward.

Finally, he peers back up at me.

"It's like you said," he says carefully. "I chose to become a vampire. But you didn't choose this. You didn't choose to be a slayer. You're in this mess because of me. So I feel like I owe you. I just want to make things right."

Not for the first time tonight, Nick surprises me. It's not like him to step up and take responsibility this way. Or at least I didn't think it was like him.

"So what do you say?" he asks. He picks up his glass and raises it to me. "Frenemies?"

I start to think about it, but really, what is there even to think about? If what Nick is saying is true, I'm in some pretty deep shit here, and he might be throwing me the one and only rope to help me climb my way out.

Plus, the damage is done. I'm a slayer now, and it doesn't seem like there's any way to change that. So if I'm ever going to have the career I want—the *life* I want—I need to learn how to control these new impulses. I can't continue to live with the fear, day in and day out, that

I might become an accidental arsonist. Auditions are stressful enough without the added worry that I might burn the freaking casting office down.

So I raise my glass and clink it against Nick's. "Frenemies."

"Oh, and, Carrie?"

I stop with the glass halfway to my lips. "Yeah?"

He gives me a contrite smile that accentuates those dimples again. "I really am sorry you don't get to be J.Lo's bartender."

. . . . .

About an hour later, keys and cell phone in hand, I'm walking back to my car. It's not even midnight, but the street is deserted. It's one of the things I've had to get used to since I moved to LA.

In Philadelphia, where I grew up, and in New York City, where I went to college, there's foot traffic at all hours. Even late at night, you always find people walking home, walking to the bus stop or the subway station, or sometimes just walking for the hell of it. But nobody walks in LA. It's too spread out. Everyone drives everywhere. The only place anyone walks to is their car. So once the shops and the bars and the restaurants close, the streets are a virtual ghost town.

But as the heels of my booties pound the pavement of Melrose Avenue and my footsteps echo eerily through the darkness, I don't really feel afraid. After all, I've got pepper spray on my key chain and 911 on speed dial. And I guess I've got a flaming blade of supernatural destruction at my beck and call too. So I'm good.

Or am I?

Continuing along to my Prius, I feel *something* that makes my muscles tense. The back of my neck starts to prickle. My slayer radar goes on full alert.

Someone is definitely watching me. Someone not human. And not Nick.

I know it as surely as I know my own name. A vampire is observing me from somewhere in the shadows. If I had any doubts about what Nick just told me, they evaporate at once into the balmy night air. Dracula's Army is on the lookout.

I'm not exactly thrilled to realize that one of Nick's blood-drinking bandmates is spying on me. But my inner slayer is absolutely livid about it. Anger starts to gather like a ball of fire in my gut, but I know I can't let that fire explode. I can't show what I am. Not after Nick's warning. Not unless I want to provoke a supernatural fight to the finish. A fight that might well finish me.

So like a nauseous person trying to make it to the bathroom before getting sick, I try to make it to my car before my eyes flash and my flaming blade materializes, outing me to my enemies. I pick up my pace, but I try not to run. I don't want to arouse any suspicions.

The fire in my belly is gaining strength though. That now-familiar bloodred haze is teasing the periphery of my field of vision. I'm right on the verge of being completely overwhelmed by a murderous hatred for this vampire voyeur.

But it's only half a block to the car. Only half a block to go. I just need to keep my slayer in check for a little while longer.

To combat the rising wave of hate, I try to concentrate on all the things that I like. I think of my girls, Liv and Heather. Hazelnut coffee with a splash of oat milk. The way Nick's eyebrow piercing glimmers in the moonlight.

The way Nick's eyebrow piercing glimmers in the moonlight?

Why on earth am I thinking about that?

My slayer is just as thrown as I am. But as it turns out, that's a good thing. The confusion is a distraction, and the fire inside me starts to dim. Just a few feet from my Prius now, I press the unlock button on my key fob. With a *chirp-chirp*, the headlights blink on. I quickly open the driver's side, climb inside, and pull the door closed after me.

In the relative safety of my car, I lean back in my seat, close my eyes, and let out a breath that I didn't realize I was holding. I send my feelers out into the dark night, but I don't sense anything. I don't think I have an undead observer anymore. For now, at least, I seem to be alone.

I open my eyes, toss my stuff onto the passenger seat, and punch the hybrid's start button. As the engine rumbles to life, I buckle up. To keep from thinking too much about vampire assassins lying in wait— or vampire bartenders with silver piercings in their brows—I turn on the radio and crank up the volume.

"A-Punk" by Vampire Weekend blares out at me. The universe, it seems, has a sense of humor.

I hit the gas and begin the drive home. But even the loud, frenetic music can't keep me from wondering what my own upcoming vampire weekend will be like. Well, vampire *week*, really.

Sounds like a promo on the Discovery Channel.

Except, incredibly, this upcoming week of vampire games isn't some must-see ratings grabber of a reality show. How in the actual hell did *this* become my reality?

CHAPTER

8

Thursday. It's 9:00 a.m. here in Los Angeles, noon back east. Time for the Adams family weekly touch base.

It's Adams with one D, not two. My parents are Grace and Alex, not Morticia and Gomez. And my sister? She's Teri, not Wednesday. But my family can be scary in their own special way.

I grab a seat at the kitchen island and open my laptop. Before I dial into Zoom, I test my webcam. I take care to adjust the framing so that I'm only visible from the neck up. I don't need any questions about my mysterious new physique. God knows there will be questions enough that I won't know how to answer. I also check the background, making sure there's nothing showing behind me that anyone can criticize. When I'm as ready as I'll ever be, I click the meeting link.

"Carrie!" says my mother once I'm connected. Her image, like a thirty-years-older version of me, fills my computer screen. The similarity between us ends there though. She's in her office, I see, in front of a carefully curated backdrop that displays the two books she's authored on estate planning. And she's already frowning at me in disapproval. "We were all just wondering what could have happened to you."

I glance at the clock in the corner of my screen. It's literally two minutes past the scheduled start time. But as I was told over and over again growing up, "Early is on time. On time is late. And late is unacceptable." And once you have that little glimpse into my childhood, I guess it doesn't take a PhD in psychology to figure out the roots of my extreme people-pleasing tendencies.

Teri scoffs, and her image replaces my mother's in the prime position on my laptop screen. One year younger than me, she has our mother's light eyes and our father's dark hair. "Well, when all you do is lounge around at the beach all day," she says, stretched out on the sofa in the town house she shares with two other students, "I guess it's easy to lose track of time."

"I don't lounge around all day," I say. "And by the way, it's still morning here. And I work nights."

"You're on mute," says my father.

Of course I am. Which, honestly, is just as well. As his judgmental expression stares out at me, I know my protests would only fall on deaf ears anyway. So I turn on my grid view, turn on my audio, and turn on my big, bright smile. "How is everybody?" I ask.

"Apparently, your sister is doing quite well up there in Cambridge," says my mother.

"Oh really?" I do my best to look and sound interested. "So catch me up. What's going on?"

"I made editor of the law review," Teri announces.

"That's awesome," I say.

"*Awesome?*" my sister says, her voice dripping with sarcasm. "Seriously? Now you even sound like a beach bum."

My smile tightens. "Well," I say, "I'm just glad to hear all the money Mom and Dad are spending on your tuition isn't going to waste."

"Carrie," says my mother in an admonishing tone. "You know

we're happy to pay for your sister to go to Harvard. Just like we'll be happy to pay for your tuition. Wherever and whenever you decide to go to law school."

Here we go again, I think.

Despite everything I've told them to the contrary, my parents still stubbornly believe that my acting aspirations are just a phase and that one day, like my sister, I'll be following in their footsteps.

Grace Gordon Adams Esq. is a professor of estate law at the University of Pennsylvania Carey Law School. Alexander Adams Esq. is a name partner at one of the top law firms in Philadelphia. And I'm pretty sure they both leveraged every connection they had to get Teresa Adams into Harvard Law. Not to be petty, but her LSAT scores weren't exactly Ivy League. They weren't even as good as mine, although in retrospect, I wish I'd never taken the damn exam at all.

I sat for the Law School Admission Test to please my parents. Of course. I'd hoped it would get them off my back for a little while so I could pursue my own career path in peace. Except now, it's the thing that they cling to, the thing that makes them think I'll eventually get the acting bug out of my system and switch over to *their* path. The only correct path.

They don't understand that I'm not like them. I've got zero interest in being an attorney. I'm kind of the black sheep of the family in that regard, although to me, it's always felt more like I'm the *only* sheep in a family full of wolves.

While the rest of the Adamses love a good argument—or rather love *winning* a good argument—I don't. Disagreement doesn't energize me. It flat out exhausts me.

Still, I have to at least make the effort to set them straight. Again.

"I'm not going to law school," I say for about the millionth time. "I don't want to be a lawyer."

I know I'm not on mute anymore, but I can tell from the expressions on my parents' faces that I might as well be.

"Sweetheart, we just worry about you," says my mother. "This gap year of yours has already stretched into more than two. We don't want you to wake up one day and realize your whole life has passed you by."

"My life isn't passing me by," I say. "I'm living it. Every day."

"So let's hear about it then," says my father. "Didn't you say you had some kind of an audition or something this week?"

The question sounds perfectly innocent—offhand, even—but I'm not fooled. After all, Dad didn't get all the degrees and awards I can see hanging on his office wall behind him for nothing. One of Philly's most prominent trial attorneys, my father is a master at luring witnesses into a false sense of security by asking them seemingly innocuous questions, then trapping them with their own words. So I tread carefully.

"I did have an audition," I say.

"And did you get the part?" he asks.

I use every acting trick in the book to not visibly grimace as I recall just how badly I botched things up. "I haven't heard from my agent yet," I tell him. Not a lie. Nope. If I were under oath right now, I would not technically be committing perjury.

"But it would be good news if you got this part?" he asks.

"Of course."

"And bad news if you didn't?"

"I guess, but—"

"And in general," he persists, "wouldn't you agree that people are more eager to share good news?"

"Uh—"

"And less eager to share bad?"

"Oh, for the love of God, stop," says my sister. "We all know she didn't get the part. She *never* gets the part. The only job she's ever going to land out there in LA is bartender at that dump on Melrose."

"Pete's," I mumble. "It's called Pete's."

"Well, I have some news for you, Carrie," says my mother. "And for what it's worth, I'm *very* eager to share it. I was talking to Jonathan the other day, and—"

"Wait, Jonathan?" I ask, interrupting her. "You mean *my ex*, Jonathan?"

"According to him, you two are just taking a break," says my mother.

I close my eyes and sigh. It's true, I may have led him to believe that—partly to spare his feelings, yes, but also partly to spare myself the difficult conversation. I just kind of figured that with him on the East Coast and me on the West, he'd find someone else soon enough. And that would be the end of that.

I open my eyes again. "Mom," I say, "why are you even talking to him?"

"He's one of my students," she says. "I think I'm allowed to talk to my own student."

Right. I forgot. Jonathan goes to Penn Law now.

"But isn't that unethical?" I ask, continuing to protest nonetheless. "Like a conflict of interests or something?"

"Maybe go to law school before you start throwing those terms around," says Teri smugly.

"Anyway," says my mother, "he's going to be in Los Angeles this weekend. For a wedding."

"So?" I ask.

"He's going stag," says my mother. "He's not seeing anyone else. He doesn't even have a plus-one."

"So?" I repeat, even though I know *exactly* where this is headed.

"So you could go with him," says my mother.

"And why would I want to do that?" I ask.

"To fix this, Carrie," says my mother. "You can still fix this."

"There's nothing to fix," I say.

"But he's perfect for you," says my mother.

"No," I say. "He's perfect for *you*."

"Are you seeing someone else?" asks my mother.

Nick, I think immediately. Not that I'm seeing him. Nope. Definitely not. But with our new arrangement and all, I will be spending a lot of time with him.

"I'm busy this weekend," I say. "Working," I add.

"Wonderful!" says my mother. "I'll tell Jonathan to drop by the bar when he gets to town."

I'm about to object, but really, what's even the point? She's just going to do whatever she wants to do anyway. Like she always does.

"Fine," I mutter. Caving. Like *I* always do. "Whatever."

· · · · ·

By 9:45 a.m. my time, my father has to leave for court, my mother has a staff meeting to get to, and my sister has a class, so the cross-examination is officially adjourned until next week. With a sigh of relief, I close my laptop.

A moment later, Liv's bedroom door opens, and my roommate's sleepy face appears, peeking out around the doorjamb. She puts her glasses on, and her heavy-lidded gaze finds me. "All clear?" she asks.

I remember that she had a night shoot last night, and she still wasn't home when I went to bed a little after one.

"Sorry," I say with an apologetic smile. "Did I wake you?"

She shakes her head and pads over to the kitchen, the soles of her fuzzy Uggs slapping against the floor. Today, she's wearing the jammies with the lemons and limes all over them. She makes straight for the Keurig machine. "Coffee?" she asks.

"No thanks," I say. "I caffeine loaded before the inquisition."

Liv nods knowingly as she pops a French roast pod into the brewer and presses the start button. As the machine hisses and gurgles, she says, "Be grateful your family is three thousand miles away. I have to defend my choices to my parents in person. Over Sunday brunch. And last time, my dad made huevos rancheros with marshmallow Peeps." She winces at the memory. "He saw somebody do it on *Guy's Grocery Games*. I think he forgot that using the Peeps was a challenge, not a recommendation."

I give her a sympathetic smile. "At least you're not still day-jobbing it as a bartender," I say. "At least you're actually working on a show."

"I suppose." The Keurig sputters, spitting out the last of Liv's coffee. She grabs the mug and joins me at the island, sitting down next to me. "But mostly, I just make Starbucks runs for people with the jobs I wish I had."

"You'll get there," I tell her.

"And when I do," she says decisively, "I will never ever yell at the PA because my half-caf skinny vanilla soy latte tastes like it might have been made with almond milk."

With that, Liv proceeds to drink her French roast. And me? I just slip into my standard weekly post-Zoom funk.

"Hey," says Liv after a moment. She gives my shoulder a gentle bump with hers. "You'll get there too, chica."

I nod, although honestly, it's more in appreciation than agreement. I doubt myself and my career prospects all the time. Thank God for supportive friends like my roomie. God knows I don't get any support from my family. Never did.

Not even when I first started acting, back in high school. Most parents would have been proud that their daughter—a first-year—beat out all the older kids to land the lead role of Katherina in the fall production of *The Taming of the Shrew*. But my parents? They just questioned why I was wasting my time doing theater instead of debate.

And of course, I couldn't tell them why. I couldn't tell them that acting in general—and playing Shakespeare's feisty heroine specifically—gave me the outlet I needed to express all the anger I was constantly feeling toward *them*. I was super pissed at them the day of the tryouts, which no doubt gave me the competitive edge. They'd just grounded me—*grounded me!*—for having the audacity to dye my own hair pink. They saw it as a calculated move to sabotage the upcoming photo shoot for the Adams family Christmas card. As if I even thought that way. As if I thought like them.

No, the pink hair was just me trying something new. Except, in the Adams family, you didn't try new things. You simply toed the line.

"You know what's really annoying though?" I tell Liv after we've been sitting together in silence for a while. "My mom and my dad and my sister all think I can't act for crap. But I put on an act with them all the time. And I'm so good at it, they don't even seem to know I'm acting. Or else they just don't care."

"Maybe the time has come to quit acting."

I look at my roommate sharply.

"With *them*," she clarifies. "Maybe the time has come to quit acting with your family."

"Maybe," I say doubtfully.

"When my parents start asking me the tough questions," says Liv, "I just tell them that George Lucas went to USC film school, same as me. And before he made a gazillion dollars with *Star Wars*, he was a PA. Same as me."

"Is that really true?" I ask.

"Straight white cis male?" says Liv. "Please. He graduated and started a production company with Francis Ford Coppola. But my parents have a dental practice in Long Beach. What do they know about Hollywood?"

"My parents are lawyers," I say. "They would fact-check. Or else they'd have their underlings check for them."

"Look," says Liv, "I know you want to make your parents happy. But you can't always please everybody."

"Unless you're Nick, apparently," I mumble.

"What?"

"Nothing," I say.

Liv continues to caffeinate while I continue to ruminate.

"The thing is," says Liv after a bit, "it's okay to do what makes *you* happy. And it's okay to stand up for yourself. Even to your parents."

"Maybe I can get my slayer to do it for me," I say. "After all, people say that lawyers are bloodsuckers. Right?"

Liv just stares at me in confusion. That's when I realize that because I crashed before she got home from work, I haven't had a chance to fill her in on last night, and she hasn't had enough coffee to remember to ask. So I bring her up to speed. I tell her about my supernatural showdown with Nick in the alley out behind Pete's. I explain that my coworker is a vampire and that his transformation apparently turned me into a vampire slayer. And then I drop the final bomb about how

I'm going to be working together with my new frenemy to learn how to hide what I am so that his undead bandmates don't freaking kill me.

"So I was right?" squeaks Liv excitedly. "Nick's a vampire. And you're a vampire slayer!"

"Did you miss the part about my life being in danger?" I ask.

"Sorry," she says. "But it sounds like you've got Nick on your side, right? And he has a plan to keep you safe."

"I guess," I say with a shrug.

"Don't worry," says Liv. "In the screenplay version of your story, this whole slay-or-be-slain thing would just be the external conflict that brings you two together and helps you work out your differences."

I smile. I know her well enough to know she's just trying to make me feel better in her own way. "Yeah," I say. "Except this isn't a screenplay."

"But it totally could be," she says with a sparkle in her eyes. "Once you train your slayer and convince the vampires you're not a threat, and you and Nick fall madly in love and have babies with magical cross-species superpowers, I call dibs on the movie rights." She grins. "It'll be my *Star Wars*."

"Me and Nick?" I shake my head. "Oh no. Nope. No way. That wouldn't even happen in a galaxy far, far away."

"*Bar Wars!*" she tells me, and okay, I have to laugh at that. "I'm going to call it *Bar Wars!*"

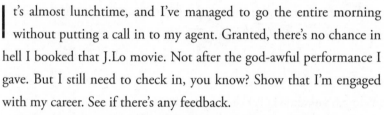

CHAPTER
9

It's almost lunchtime, and I've managed to go the entire morning without putting a call in to my agent. Granted, there's no chance in hell I booked that J.Lo movie. Not after the god-awful performance I gave. But I still need to check in, you know? Show that I'm engaged with my career. See if there's any feedback.

Hopefully, it'll just be a *no*. Not a *no, and*. Like *no, and does your client have a nicotine problem?* Or *no, and has your client gained some weight recently?* Or *no, and by the way, your client can't act for crap, so please don't submit her to us for any role ever again.*

But before I make the call, I decide to go for a run. I figure the repetitive motion, the rhythmic pounding of my feet, one in front of the other, will help me clear my head and get my thoughts in order. Help me sort out what I want to say. Plus, as an extra added bonus, it'll be a good way to procrastinate doing something I really don't want to do in the first place.

I cover up in joggers and a long-sleeved tee. This time, I'm not hiding my body because I have an audition, because I feel pressure to conform to a certain physical type. And in broad daylight like this, I know there's no chance of any vampires seeing my muscles and surmising what I am. Also, it's not as if I think I look bad. I mean, if I saw a stranger on the street who was this physically fit, I'd probably be impressed.

But that's the thing. I look like a stranger. I don't look like *me*. I'm not entirely at ease with this buff slayer build, so I'm not exactly ready to bare it all to the world. But I guess I need to start getting comfortable, and taking this new body out for a spin seems like a good way to start.

I call a quick goodbye to Liv, who's typing away at her computer in some kind of the-muse-has-struck, the-artist-is-in, the-creative-juices-are-flowing frenzy, and I head out of our apartment. Our place is on Fourth Street, near Rose Avenue. The building is mid-century modern, but not in the trendy hip way that you see on a lot of home improvement shows. No, our rental complex is more of a worst-of-the-1960s eyesore, maintained over the years to keep it habitable, sure, but never with the intent to restore any of its former architectural charm. If it ever had any, that is.

I turn down Rose and walk toward the beach, past the eerie but iconic thirty-foot-tall *Ballerina Clown* sculpture that looms over the CVS at the corner of Main and Rose. Although the public art piece installed in the late 1980s is something of a tourist draw, I barely even notice it anymore. Over the last couple of years, it's become an ordinary part of my everyday neighborhood landscape.

But today, it's like I see it—really see it—for the first time. I'm struck by the uneasy tension between its lithe ballerina body, dressed in a pink tutu and red toe shoes, and its oversize, sad-clown head. And suddenly, I feel a rush of affinity for it.

I know exactly how that damn sculpture feels. I understand what it's like when two opposite forces are forced to share the same body that way. I swear, that thing is like a bigger-than-life reflection of my own new duality.

But hey, if it's managed to survive all this time? Maybe I can too.

• • • • •

I keep going west until I reach the running/walking/biking path. As I start to stretch, I contemplate my course. Technically, Liv and I reside in Santa Monica, but we're just on the border of Venice. Right takes me deeper into Santa Monica, toward the amusement pier. Left takes me into Venice, along the lively, funky oceanfront walk. I flip a mental coin, and I choose right.

I take off up the beach at an easy jog. I feel the warmth of the sun shining down on my face, the cool ocean breeze blowing through my hair. I can taste the salty air on my lips. And I get the surge of satisfaction that always comes from the simple act of moving my limbs and exercising my body.

I push a little harder.

At this pace, I usually start to break a sweat. And considering how *overdressed* I am today? Well, I'm pretty sure I'll be drenched in no time. But somehow, I stay dry. It's as if I'm not exerting any effort at all, like I'm enclosed in my own personal climate-controlled bubble.

I push harder.

And it's *no sweat*—both literally and figuratively. My heartbeat stays steady, and my breathing remains even. Like Nick pointed out last night, my body is *strong*.

So I push myself even harder.

Now, I run regularly, but I'm no athlete. Mostly, I do it because I need a budget-friendly way to burn calories and stay in shape, and running outside is free. But today, as I hit a pace I've never hit before, I actually *feel* free. I feel powerful. I feel like I can do anything.

I can *do anything*, I think.

I can get a handle on this whole slayer thing.

I can keep what I am hidden from Dracula's Army.

And yes, goddammit, I can even call my agent and have an honest conversation with her about my stalled acting career.

As I approach Santa Monica Pier, I squint against the sunlight gleaming off the spokes of the big Ferris wheel. Once I get a little closer, I can hear the music streaming out from the arcade. Adjusting my stride to match the beat, I loop back around to begin the return leg of my run. On the way back, I rehearse what I want to say to my agent.

"I'm tired of being typecast," I say into the wind.

Nope. Too whiny.

"I need you to put me up for a wider variety of roles," I say.

Nope. Too demanding.

"Let's discuss where we see my career going," I say.

Yup. Better. Much better.

"When it comes to submissions," I say, "maybe we can start thinking less about whether I can *look* the part and more about whether I can *play* the part."

Yes!

"I'm all in here," I say. "And I need to know that you're all in too."

YASSS!

I enter the homestretch of my run, and I don't want to drag my feet on this any longer. I pick up my pace.

• • • • •

By the time I get back to the apartment, I'm totally pumped for some real talk. I find my phone, open my contacts, and dial my agent.

"The Rebecca Sloane Agency," says the assistant.

"Hi, Kevin," I say. "May I speak with Rebecca, please? It's Carrie Adams."

"Hold, please."

There's a click and a short silence on the other end of the line. Then, "Sorry," says Kevin after he clicks back in. "She's not available. I'll tell her you called."

I open my mouth to protest, but before I can even say anything, the line goes dead.

I deflate. Despite my new physical prowess, that I-can-do-anything feeling is quickly replaced with my usual sense of frustration and helplessness. Apparently, even with my new vampire-slaying powers, I'm still no match for the freaking entry-level Hollywood gatekeepers.

That night, I arrive for my shift at Pete's, and—surprise, surprise!—Nick is already working the bar, not running late for a change. And Heather—*my* Heather—is perched on a stool down at Nick's end, engaged with him in animated conversation.

I have to say, I don't like it. I don't like seeing the two of them together this way. I mean, Nick is a vampire, Heather is human, and as a slayer—I can't help it—I'm hardwired to disapprove. Oh sure, maybe Nick hasn't hurt anybody yet. And okay, maybe it doesn't look like he means my friend any harm at the moment. But try telling that to my new alter ego.

Also, as silly as it is, I guess I feel a little bit betrayed. Even though I don't doubt Heather's friendship for a minute, I'm not big on her becoming the newest member of the Nick Stokes fan club.

Heather spots me and gives me a big smile. I just nod, frowning, and head into the back area to stow my stuff and clock in.

When I return, my bestie has relocated and is now occupying the corner stool at my end of the bar.

"*Bloody* Mary?" I ask, skeptically eyeing the telltale concoction of tomato juice and garnish in her tall, condensation-beaded glass.

She shrugs and grins. "I thought it was funny."

"Hmph."

"Sorry," she says. "Just trying to lighten things up." Her expression gets serious. "I talked to Liv. And if I had a lethal band of vampires after my ass, I'd be grumpy too."

"I'm not grumpy," I say, a little defensive.

Heather scrutinizes me, raising her perfectly groomed eyebrows. "Jealous then?" she asks.

"Jealous?" I ask. "Why would I be jealous?"

"Oh, I don't know," she says in a mildly teasing tone. "Maybe because I was talking to your boyfriend?"

I'm about to respond when a guy in a Dodgers cap steps up to the bar and signals to me. I just shoot Heather a dirty look and cross over to him. "What'll it be?" I ask.

"Let me get two Bud Lights and a chardonnay."

I get the drinks and ring up the sale. Then I go back to my friend. "For the record, I am not jealous," I tell her. "And Nick is not my boyfriend."

"Oh. Okay. Good to know," she says. She sips her Bloody Mary. "So where are you and Nick going tonight on your date?"

I gasp in outrage. "What exactly did Liv tell you? Because Nick and I do not have a date tonight. We have a...a...a *training session*."

"Yeah, yeah. I heard all about the *training sessions*," she says. "But if you ask me, it's pretty clear why Nick came up with that particular plan to save your slayer butt. He wants to spend time with you."

"Don't be ridiculous," I say. "Why would he want to spend time with me?"

"Get a clue, Sherlock Holmes," says Heather. "The dude likes you."

For a moment, I'm totally speechless.

"Uh, excuse me?" says a female voice.

I turn and see that a couple of women have grabbed stools at the bar a few seats over from Heather. Thursdays are usually busy nights, and it looks like tonight will be no exception. So I put my conversation with my friend on pause again while I go over to take their order.

As I fix their drinks, I try to sort through my own complex cocktail of emotions. But trying to separate my human feelings about Nick from my supernatural impulses is like trying to separate the vodka from the vermouth in my shaker. I simply can't do it.

I can, however, distinguish truth from straight-up fantasy.

"You're wrong, you know," I tell Heather after I serve the women their martinis. "Nick doesn't like me. He's only helping me because he feels responsible for my situation. He told me as much."

"If you say so," she says. But she sounds as if she's just humoring me.

And now for some reason, I'm the one who can't drop the subject of Nick.

"I mean, if the guy likes me," I say, "then why would he go out of his way to annoy me every chance he gets?"

"Since you don't wear pigtails," says Heather, "he can't pull them." She shrugs. "He has to get your attention somehow."

I shake my head. "It's *not* a date," I insist.

"Fine," says Heather. "It's not a date. But when it is, do me a favor and consult me on what to wear. Because that 'fit you're rocking right now is seriously fugly."

I look down, and okay, I really can't disagree with her on that. But my wardrobe options have become pretty limited. Once I eliminated the clothes that don't fit me anymore and the clothes that would expose my new muscles to prying vampire eyes, there wasn't a lot left to choose from. I landed on black yoga pants topped with an old denim button-down of my ex's that I found at the back of my closet. Admittedly, not my best look.

"Point taken," I say. "But I have things I need to keep under wraps. You know?"

"No excuse," says Heather. "I'm keeping Bella Drake's pregnancy under wraps at work, and she doesn't look like a walking fashion don't."

"Bella Drake is pregnant?" I ask. The popular star plays the tough but idealistic ADA Helen Moore on *Robbery-Homicide Division*.

Heather nods. "It's all very hush-hush for now, but she's planning to leave the show at the end of the season." My friend does a quick scan of the room. Then, leaning in closer across the bar, she motions for me to do the same. I duck my head. "That means they're looking to cast a new ADA," she says quietly. "And they'll be introducing her on the season finale."

"Really?" I whisper back, my interest piqued.

"Really," says Heather. "And they haven't filled the part yet. They're not sure what they're looking for, so they've been seeing all types."

"*Really?*" I repeat.

The gears in my head start to spin. A role like that—a regular on an established hit series—would be the gig of a lifetime for an aspiring actor like me. And having grown up around lawyers, I just know I could play the part.

But Bella Drake is a stunning redhead with legs for days. She absolutely exudes star quality. Not girl-next-door quality. Or third-lead quality. Or background-player quality. Or whatever quality it is that I'm projecting these days.

But if they're really seeing all types…

"I'm not even supposed to know she's leaving," says Heather, "so

I can't recommend you for the role. But you could get your agent to submit you."

And that's when I realize she still hasn't called me back.

· · · · ·

It's last call at the bar. A few diehards order one more for the road, but most of the patrons settle up and head out. As long as the place was packed with customers, my inner slayer was content to sit back and let me do my job, but now that the crowd has dispersed, I'm much more aware of my supernatural side. And we're both more aware of Nick.

As I catch his eye, I realize we've barely had any contact tonight. Consciously or not, I guess we've both been tiptoeing around each other, careful not to incite a confrontation.

But now, I walk toward the center of the bar. He meets me halfway, by the register. Eye level with his chest, I notice that tonight's band tee has a Grateful Dead graphic on it. I wonder if it's another inside joke… or just a shirt that happened to be clean.

"Are we still on for tonight?" I ask.

He nods, shrugs. "Sure."

But I'm picking up on some weird energy. Not so much weird vampire energy. Weird *Nick* energy.

"Did you change your mind?" I ask.

"Why would I change my mind?" he shoots back.

"I don't know."

"Did *you* change *your* mind?" he asks.

"Why would *I* change *my* mind?"

"You tell me."

There's a palpable tension between us, but it's not coming from our preternatural rivalry. It's coming from…*us*. But what else is new?

"I'm in," I say. "But can you maybe quit trying to pick a fight with me until the rest of the customers leave?"

"Fine," he says.

"Fine," I return.

"Fine," he repeats.

And I'm tempted to give the last call bell another ring as we both turn and go back to our respective corners.

Heather was wrong. This is definitely *not* a date.

While we close up Pete's, Nick and I do manage to agree on one thing. If we're going to provoke my slayer, we'll need to do it someplace where the only thing I can set fire to is…well…*him*.

At the thought of that, I get a sick feeling in my stomach. "You don't have to do this, you know," I say.

"I told you," he says. "I can handle it."

"But what if *I* can't?" I ask. "What if the urges are too strong for me to contain?" I start to feel the same kind of jitters I normally feel before an audition, only worse. Way worse. If I flub a line reading, nobody actually dies.

"That's your slayer talking," says Nick. "You need to show her who's boss." He grins and cue the dimples. "Just treat her the way you usually treat me."

Despite my nerves, I smile back.

I suggest using the alley out back again as our training ground. But it turns out Nick lives not far from me, in Venice. I never knew that before. I guess there are a lot of things I don't know about my coworker. But anyway, after a brief discussion, we decide to take our cars home and regroup down at the beach.

I park on Main Street, in full view of the *Ballerina Clown*. As I lock up my Prius, there's no one around, but I get the creepy feeling that I'm being watched. Only it doesn't feel the way it did last night. It doesn't feel like a vampire is stalking me. And my slayer seems totally unconcerned. So I dismiss my own uneasiness. I figure I'm just imagining things.

I walk west on Rose, and just as I reach the beach path, I spy Nick standing on the sand, down by the water. Waiting for me.

Now, my slayer sits up and pays attention. Out here in the open, without the potential for injury to people or property, there's nothing to keep her reined in.

Nothing except me.

Trying to maintain that restraint, I take a careful step out onto the beach.

"So how are we going to do this?" I ask, raising my voice so it carries across the distance, so Nick can hear me over the crash of the waves behind him.

"You don't have to yell at me," he says.

"I wasn't yelling at you," I yell. But then I lower my voice to a more normal level. "I just want to know what the plan is here."

He shrugs. "I thought we'd play it by ear," he says.

Typical, I think.

"So you don't have a plan?" I ask.

He shrugs his big shoulders again. "There's not exactly a handbook for this kind of thing," he says. "How are you feeling right now?"

"Like I want to kill you," I say.

"Because of the slayer thing?" he asks. "Or because of the no-plan thing?"

"Both?" I offer, borrowing his words from last night. "Either?"

He laughs. After a moment, I do too.

"Okay, here's an idea," Nick says. "Why don't you try to walk toward me? And when you feel like you're starting to lose control, stop and try to get a grip."

It doesn't sound like much of a plan to me, but considering I don't have an alternate suggestion, I nod.

I take another tentative step forward. My Nikes sink into the sand with a soft *crunch*.

"How do you feel now?" he asks.

It's almost like we're playing some supernatural version of red light, green light or Simon says or something.

"Honestly?" I ask. "I feel a little silly."

"Better than homicidal," he says.

"Don't get too comfy," I warn him. "I still want to kill you."

I take another step. My vision briefly flashes red, reminding me that this really is no game.

"Easy there, slayer," says Nick. "Easy does it."

"It might help if you distract me," I say.

"Distract you how?" he asks.

Unconsciously, my eyes drift down to his chest.

"Carrie?"

Okay. It's time to stop and try to get a grip—and not just on my slayer. "So what's with the T-shirt?" I ask.

"What do you mean?" he asks.

"Grateful Dead?" I step cautiously closer.

"Good band," he says.

"So that's it?" I ask. "You don't have a secret death wish or anything?"

He frowns at me. "Why would you ask me that?"

I step a little closer. "Because you're playing with fire here," I say. "Literally."

"If I had a death wish," he says, "I wouldn't have signed up for immortal life." He grins at me. "Sometimes a band tee is just a band tee."

After a beat, I smile back, step closer. There's about six feet of beach separating Nick and me.

"So what's with *your* shirt?" he asks. There's a strange undertone to his voice. I feel the same weird vibe I was getting from him back at the bar.

I tug at the denim button-down, a little self-conscious. "What do you mean?" I ask.

"Is that your boyfriend's shirt?" he asks.

I blink, a little taken aback. "My *ex*-boyfriend's, actually," I say after a moment. "How would you know that?"

"For one thing," he says, "it buttons to the right, so it's a man's shirt. And for another thing, I...uh...I can smell him on it."

I blink again. "I'm sorry," I say. "You can *smell* him on it?"

He shrugs. "Vampires have a more highly developed sense of smell," he says.

"B-but I've washed it since the last time he wore it," I say.

"I know," he says. "I can smell the laundry detergent. And the dryer sheet too. Lavender."

Well, this is news.

I grab the collar and give it a quick sniff. I swear, I don't smell a thing.

I look back at Nick. He's eyeing me strangely.

"You know, sometimes the shirt you borrowed from your ex and forgot to give back is just the shirt you borrowed from your ex and forgot to give back," I say. "It's not like I'm wearing it to remember him or anything. It's not like I'm carrying a torch."

He raises his eyebrows at me.

"Okay, okay, bad choice of words," I say. "I guess, these days, I am kind of carrying a torch. But not for *him*. Definitely not."

He nods. "Okay," he says. "If you say so."

"I do."

I take another step forward. And another. Nick and I are about four feet apart now. My slayer is on alert but not on attack—mostly, I think, because we're both still trying to digest this latest revelation.

"So you can really smell my ex?" I ask Nick.

"Yes."

"So can you…uh…smell *me*?" I ask.

He hesitates. "Yes."

"What do I smell like?"

He gazes at me for what seems like a long time. "Sunshine," he says softly.

Sunshine?

It's as if the word floats across the space between us and strokes my cheek, gently caressing my skin. It makes me melt inside a little. Maybe more than a little.

"Sunshine?" I ask out loud. My voice is soft too.

"Yes."

This word of his is also like a physical touch. But it seems to touch me in other places, more intimate places. It sends a rush of heat spreading through me that has nothing to do with my slayer and everything to do with the way that Nick is looking at me right now.

"B-but you're a vampire," I somehow manage to say. "Sunshine can kill you."

With a sigh, he runs a hand through his shaggy, dark hair and scratches at the back of his neck. In the moonlight, I get a glimpse of his well-developed biceps and the guitar tattoo on the underside of his forearm. "Yeah," he says. "I guess it can."

I move a little closer. We're near enough now that I have to look up at him. But for once, I don't mind looking up. Actually, I have to admit, the view is kind of nice. The moonlight is reflecting off the barbell piercing in his eyebrow again, making the silver balls glitter like diamonds. Out of nowhere, I think of the expression *diamond in the rough*.

Is that what Nick is?

Or is he, as my slayer thinks, a bloodsucking predator who must freaking die?

Tomato, to-*mah*-to?

"How do you feel now?" Nick asks.

"Like I want to kill you," I say. "But…*not*."

The truth is I'm not sure if I've ever felt more confused in my whole life. It's like there's a big-screen-blockbuster-worthy battle raging inside me. I've got my human side fighting with my slayer side. I've got all these preconceptions about Nick facing off against the very different picture of the guy that seems to be emerging. And I've got my urge to attack him wrestling with my desire to *attack* him…but in another way entirely.

"Progress," he says.

"Progress," I echo.

I step closer. We're not touching, but we could be. Oh, we definitely could be. We could be doing a lot of things here, in the dark, on this empty beach.

"So are all your senses jacked up?" I ask, just to say something. "Not just smell?"

"Not just smell," he says.

"Hearing too?"

He nods. "Hearing too."

"Is that why you told me I didn't have to yell at you?" I ask.

He smiles and shrugs. "But you also didn't have to yell at me."

I smile back.

And then it's like we're having a moment. As in…*a moment.*

That's when something occurs to me. My smile fades, and I get a slightly nauseous feeling in my gut. "So earlier, back at the bar… Did you hear my conversation with Heather?" I ask.

His smile fades too, morphing into a frown. "I try not to eavesdrop," he says. "But I can't always help it. This is all new to me too and, well, I'm not always in control either."

"So you heard—"

"It's not a date," he says. "Got it."

But there's a note of challenge in his voice. He stands his ground, not moving away from me, like he's silently daring me to back off.

I don't. I stay exactly where I am, feet planted in the sand, just inches separating the two of us.

He doesn't look away, and neither do I. And suddenly I don't feel confused at all.

"Nick," I whisper. I say his name like it's a prayer and a confession and an invitation all rolled into one little syllable.

In answer, he starts to close the short gap between our bodies, between our lips. He moves slowly though, so slowly it's almost as if he's not moving at all. I wonder briefly if it's because he's unsure of my slayer or unsure of me. But after what seems like a lifetime—like an immortal lifetime—his mouth is hovering over mine, so close I can feel his breath.

I shiver with anticipation, and—

Nick abruptly pulls back. Looks around.

"What's wrong?" I ask. "What is it?"

"Someone's here," he says.

I do my own quick sweep of our surroundings. I don't see anyone, but I know what he means. I have the same sensation of being watched that I had when I got out of my car earlier. I consult my inner slayer, but it doesn't feel like an enemy is watching. Not an immortal one anyway.

"I'm not picking up on any vampires," I say.

"It's not a vampire," says Nick.

"Maybe it's just someone out for a late-night swim?" I suggest.

Nick shakes his head. "I don't think so."

Honestly? I don't either.

Then, somewhere near the start of the Venice beach walk, fire suddenly shoots into the air. At first, I think it must be some kids playing with fireworks. But the fire extends way, way up and over in an arc, streaking straight across the night sky like a rocket. I peer up at the fiery trail as it blazes through the heavens until it fades off into the distance.

"What in the actual hell was that?" I ask, my voice a little awestruck. I'm still staring where the light vanished.

Nick pauses a moment, brows knit together, before he gives me his one-word reply. "Slayer."

CHAPTER
12

I take a step back from Nick and regard him a little suspiciously. The sexual tension between us evaporates, and another kind of tension springs up in its place. "You mean there are other slayers out there?" I demand.

He shrugs.

"Other slayers like me?"

"Apparently."

"And slayers can *fly*?" I demand.

"Apparently."

"*Apparently?*"

My alter ego is getting angry, and so am I, goddammit. All this time, I realize, I've trusted Nick, trusted everything he's told me. But now, I have to wonder...

Has he been holding out on me? And have I been too naive to see it?

"Carrie, I've been a vampire for, like, two minutes," Nick says. He holds his hands out in a gesture of helplessness. "I've told you all I know, but I'm not exactly an expert on any of this. I'm still learning too."

I want to believe him, but I'm not sure I can. And I'm not sure how much longer I can contain my slayer rage.

In fact, the only thing that I am absolutely certain about is that I cannot stand here with this vampire even one second longer. I need to go, or else I'm going to completely lose my—

Just then, my flaming sword appears. But this time, I don't aim it at Nick. Intuitively, I know to point it overhead, at the sky.

Fueled by my intent, the fiery arc of the blade extends up and up and up, pulling me along with it—but no, that's not quite right. I'm not just along for the ride here. I'm in the driver's seat. It's as if I *am* the fire. I *am* the sword.

For once, my slayer and I don't feel like separate entities, like awkward roommates occupying the same body, battling for control. We are somehow one and the same.

I glance down, and it seems both impossible and completely inevitable that I am levitating high above Nick. Then, suspended in midair—*suspended in midair!*—I peer inland. I can see all of Los Angeles County, all the way to the Hollywood sign.

It's…*breathtaking.*

But this isn't a sightseeing tour. And I'm not up here to enjoy the view.

I want to get out of here.

I want to go home, I think.

It seems like it should take more than that, more than just my own resolve. Like I should need ruby slippers or a magic carpet or some ancient incantation to embark on this kind of mystical travel. But somehow, my intention is enough.

Bending to my will, the blazing ribbon of fire curls into an arch. And then, well, it's not like I'm flying exactly. It's more like I'm surfing. Like I'm riding a wave of flames, coasting over the palm trees, over the rooftops. Only I'm not just riding the wave wherever it decides to go.

The fire is an extension of me, and I'm steering it exactly where I want it to take me.

As I glide homeward, floating through the night sky, I feel this indescribable rush of power—indescribable not just because it's beyond words but also because it's simply beyond *me*.

I zip through the atmosphere, and my neighborhood slips by in a blur. Soon—too soon, to be honest—I find myself homing in on my building on Fourth.

My landing isn't perfect, but it's dead-on accurate. With a thud and a bit of a forward stumble, I find myself right at my doorstep.

Wow.

I mean, just...*wow*!

On solid ground again, I stand at my front door, trying to wrap my head around what just happened. What I just *made* happen. It takes some time before it even occurs to me to go inside.

When I finally dig out my keys, something compels me to look over my shoulder. Across the street, illuminated by a hazy circle of light, I spy Nick leaning against a lamppost. He must have used his vampire superspeed to follow me.

He gives me a tentative wave. After a moment, I bite my lower lip and nod back.

I turn and unlock the door to let myself in, and I can't decide what's more surprising: me catching a lift home on a fiery tsunami of my own making, or Nick watching over me until I'm safely inside.

· · · · ·

"So wait. You can fly?" asks Heather.

"Like, it's-a-bird, it's-a-plane, no-it's-Carrie-Adams-vampire-slayer *fly*?" asks Liv.

"Not exactly like Superman," I say. "But…*yeah*."

"Why didn't you tell us before we drove up here?" asks Liv. "We could have saved the gas money."

When Heather, Liv, and I realized we all had Friday afternoon off, we decided to drive up the Pacific Coast Highway together and hit our favorite taco stand for lunch. With Heather at the wheel and Liv riding shotgun, I sat in the back and spent the road trip up to Malibu filling my besties in on everything that went down last night. And now that we've gotten our orders and grabbed a spot at one of the sun-bleached picnic tables overlooking the ocean, the two of them won't stop badgering me with questions.

"I don't know if the I-can-fly thing works like an Uber," I say. "I'm not sure if I can take passengers. Honestly? I'm still not clear on how any of this slayer stuff works."

"Now for the really important question," says Heather. I assume she's going to ask me about the existence of the other vampire slayer, someone who might actually possess the answers that I lack. But instead, Heather just grins and asks, "So? *Was* it a date?"

The question makes me a little annoyed, and for once, I don't suppress what I'm feeling. "It was me trying to learn control so Nick's vampire bandmates don't find out I'm a slayer and kill me," I snap. "Or have you forgotten about that?"

Heather blinks, a little surprised by my outburst. Then she reaches over and gives my arm a pat. "No one's forgotten about that, babe," she says quietly.

"It's just hard to talk about," adds Liv. "It's hard to even think about."

"But if you want to talk about it…" says Heather.

And just like that, my annoyance disappears. Deep down, I know my friends are every bit as freaked out about all this as I am. And while normally I want to discuss and analyze everything with them, this time, I decide to pass. "No," I say, shaking my head. "Let's not go there. Not today anyway. I think I'd rather you just grill me about my current relationship status with Nick."

"Okay!" says Liv, jumping right back on that train. "So tell us. How did things vibe last night? Did it feel like a date? Or not?"

I frown. A best-of/worst-of highlight reel of the previous night is playing in my mind, and I don't know how to respond. To give me some extra time to formulate a reply, I take a quick bite of my chicken taco. I chew it slowly, thinking, while my friends eye me expectantly.

"I don't know," I say finally after I swallow. "I mean, at first, it definitely wasn't a date. But then it did kind of start to feel like one. Except then it turned into a *bad* date. And then..." I let the sentence drop off as I remember the sight of Nick making sure I got home okay, even after I got mad at him and made my dramatic exit. "I don't know," I say on a sigh.

"What about tonight?" asks Liv.

"I don't know," I say, shrugging.

"Do you want it to be a date?" asks Heather.

"I don't know."

"*Ehhhnt*," says Liv, making a sound like a game show buzzer. "Wrong answer."

I look from one of my friends to the other. "You know, you two armchair matchmakers are totally ignoring the real headline from last night. There's another vampire slayer out there. Someone who could maybe help me."

"I thought Nick was going to help you," says Heather.

"I thought so too," I say. "But he clearly doesn't know a lot more than I do about the whole slayer thing. And I'm not sure if he's being completely straight with me about what little he does know."

Liv uses one of the paper napkins from the stack in the middle of our table to wipe a drip of salsa off her chin. "You really think Nick could be lying to you?" she asks.

"Not lying, exactly. It's just…" I shrug in confusion.

Chewing on that, the three of us eat in silence, and for a little while, I just let myself enjoy the awesome street tacos and the gorgeous coastal view and the bright sunshine that means no vampires are currently watching me.

"Okay, new topic," announces Heather. "Did you talk to your agent? About the open role on *Robbery-Homicide Division*?"

"There's an open role on *Robbery-Homicide*?" asks Liv.

Heather nods. "Bella Drake is leaving."

Liv turns to me. "Carrie!" she says excitedly. "That would be the perfect way to get your family off your back. You wouldn't be a lawyer, but you'd be playing one on TV!"

"Yeah," I say, not quite matching her enthusiasm. "It would be perfect. If I could actually get the part."

"So did you talk to your agent about it?" asks Heather again.

I squirm a little on the picnic bench. "Not yet."

"*Not yet?*" asks Heather. "Wake up, Sleeping Beauty. They're seeing people *now*."

I squirm a bit more.

I want the part. Of course I want the part. Who wouldn't? But I just know my agent will say that I'm not right for it, that I don't have the right look. If I can even get through to talk to her about it at all.

"Carrie," says Liv sternly. "You are a badass vampire slayer. You can summon fire, and you can defy gravity. I'm pretty sure you can tell your agent to do her job and pitch you for this role."

"Yeah," I say. "But first, I'd have to get her on the line."

"So call now," says Heather.

"What?"

"You heard me," she says. "Get out your phone and call now."

"B-but it's lunchtime," I stammer.

"So?" asks Liv.

"She's probably at lunch."

"Well, I'm sure she has her phone with her," says Heather. "Just like you do." And before I can stop her, she plucks my mobile out of the side pocket of my leggings and thrusts it in front of me. "Call. Now."

I glance over at Liv for help, but the serious set of her jaw tells me that she's taking Heather's side on this one. In my heart, though, I know they're both totally on *my* side. They're both Team Carrie all the way, just wanting me to succeed. And right now, I guess the one who's mostly standing in the way of my potential success is *me*.

I take my phone back from Heather and take a deep breath.

"You've got this, chica," says Liv with an encouraging smile and a nod that makes her ponytail bounce up and down.

After a beat, I nod back. And dial.

One ring. Two rings. Three—

"The Rebecca Sloane Agency."

"Kevin, hi," I say as my eyes dart between Heather and Liv. "It's Carrie Adams again. May I speak with Rebecca, please? It's—it's important."

My personal cheering section pantomimes all kinds of positive reinforcement.

"Hold, please," says Kevin.

I hear the familiar *click* on the other end of the line. But as I brace for the assistant to come back with his usual brush-off, I remember that feeling I had last night as I flew—literally *flew*—across the sky. That feeling of complete and utter control, of being able to take the reins and direct my own path forward.

As the phone clicks again, something else clicks. Last night, it wasn't just a feeling. I didn't just *feel* in control. I *was* in control. Because I *took* control.

"Sorry," says Kevin, launching into what I've come to recognize as his standard reply. "She's not avail—"

"Kevin," I interrupt before he can finish the sentence and hang up on me. "We both know you have her on the line. And usually I don't push. But this time, like I said, it's important." I don't sound angry exactly. I sound like I'm *controlling* my anger. "I need to speak to Rebecca about a casting opportunity," I continue firmly. "And I need you to make that happen."

Nothing.

I don't move. I don't breathe. I don't dare. Then—

"Hold again, please."

In the silence that follows, I get up from my seat at the picnic table and walk off a bit. Standing close to the edge of the beachside cliff, I keep my back to my friends and stare out over the waves. God knows I appreciate their support, but I really don't want to be having this conversation in front of an audience. I need some privacy so I can concentrate on—

"It was a no," says my agent in a clipped, slightly annoyed tone as soon as she comes on the line. No chitchat. Not even a hello.

It takes me a moment to realize she's talking about Wednesday's audition.

"I-I figured," I say. "But I'm not calling about—"

"Have you gained weight?" she asks.

Crap, I think. *So it wasn't just a* no. *It was a* no, and.

"I've put on a little muscle," I mumble.

"If you gain weight, it's going to limit your options," she says. "And I won't be able to help you."

Any other day, I would have accepted this, but today, it really kind of bothers me. It seems like *she's* the one limiting my options.

"I've put on a little *muscle*," I repeat more forcefully.

"Well, I don't have anything else for you right now," she says.

"But I do," I say quickly, before she can disconnect. "I have some inside information. Bella Drake is leaving *Robbery-Homicide Division*, and they're casting a new ADA to take her place."

"You're not a Bella Drake type," she says.

"They're seeing all types," I say.

"You're not a series lead type," she says.

I recall all the things I wanted to say to her, all those lines I practiced yesterday, when I was running. When I felt powerful. I try to call up some of that power now.

"Maybe we can start thinking less about whether I can *look* the part," I say, "and more about whether I can *play* the part." I pause. "I know lawyers," I tell her. "And I know I can play this part."

"You're not—"

"Instead of focusing on what I'm *not*," I say, interrupting, "maybe we can focus on what I *am*. I am all in, Rebecca. I am. And I need to know that you're all in too."

And for once, however this turns out, I feel like I gave it my best performance.

. . . . .

I walk back over to the picnic table as I finish the call.

"Okay," I say. "Thank you. 'Bye."

I hang up and look at my girlfriend posse.

"Well?" asks Liv. "Did you talk to her?"

"What did she say?" asks Heather.

I milk the suspense a little before I break out in a big grin. "She'll reach out and see if she can get me in to read next week."

From the outbreak of excitement that ensues, you'd think I'd actually landed the role instead of merely convincing my agent to try to get me a slot to audition for it. But as my friends know, in this business, you have to celebrate every win, no matter how small.

I reach down to pick up my bottle of water and raise it up in a toast. "Here's to pushy friends," I say.

"Pushy friends!" echo Heather and Liv in unison as they enthusiastically bump their plastic water bottles against mine.

We all drink. Then I swing my legs over the picnic bench and sit back down at the table.

"So that's one problem down," says Heather as I settle in next to her. "One more to go."

I look at her, thinking about all the twists and turns my life has taken in the past few days. "Just one?" I ask sarcastically.

"Well, one that I know how to solve anyway." Heather tugs at the arm of the faded, old, oversize Barnard College sweatshirt that I'm wearing today to conceal my biceps and triceps and other supernaturally buffed-up 'ceps. "We have got to do something about your wardrobe," she says. "Just in case tonight's training session *is* a date."

CHAPTER
13

That night, Nick and I arrive for work at the same time. As I walk down Melrose from my car to the bar, I spot him ambling toward me, approaching from the opposite direction. Tonight, he's wearing jeans, a plain white tee, a slouchy gray cardigan, and an expression that's full of uncertainty, as if he's trying to figure out where we stand with each other.

I know the feeling.

"Hey," he says tentatively when we come together outside Pete's.

"Hey," I return.

"You look nice," he says.

I readjust the ensemble that Heather selected for me: boyfriend jeans loose enough to camouflage my supermuscular thighs, rolled up at the ankle; a sheer white blouse drapey enough to disguise my upper-body bulk, French tucked to define my waist; and platform sandals to add some height. Heather also insisted that I put on some lip gloss, mascara, and brow pencil to complete the look.

"Thanks," I say, suddenly pleased that my friend forced me to make the effort. "And I'm sorry for ditching you last night."

"Well, I'm sorry for...uh..." He thinks a beat. "...everything?"

I smile. "I'm not sure you need to be sorry for *everything*," I tease. "I mean, there must be something going on in the world that's not your fault."

"You're too kind," says Nick with a sardonic grin. But he seems to relax a little.

I do too.

He pulls the door open. "After you," he says with a sweeping gesture, ushering me inside.

To any random observer, we probably look like two people meeting for a date, just getting to know each other. Not coworkers who also happen to be supernatural foes, trying to avoid killing each other.

As I enter the bar and Nick follows me in, I wonder if it's possible for both things to be true.

· · · · ·

Friday night is usually our busiest time at Pete's, and the place is already pretty crowded. Nick and I dive into action as soon as we arrive.

While I'm tending my end of the bar and he's tending his, we don't have a ton of time to chat. But through quick exchanges at the beer taps and by the cash register, we agree that we're on for later tonight and that we'll hit the beach together again to…*train*.

"Carrie?" I hear a male voice say above the bar noise.

I hold up a finger without looking to see who it is. "Be right with you," I say as I clear a pair of empty bar glasses and slide a couple their check. Then I turn in the direction of the voice. "What would you like?"

"For starters, how about a hello?" says a guy with short, dark-blond hair and tanned skin. My first glance at his preppy getup of khaki shorts, a white oxford, and loafers makes me wonder if he just stepped out of a Tommy Hilfiger ad or something. But after a moment, I realize he actually stepped out of my past.

"J-Jonathan," I say, blinking at him in surprise.

There was a time when I would have been thrilled to see him, when the sight of him strolling across the Barnard College campus set my whole body on fire.

But now...

"Wh-what are you doing here?" I ask.

His bright white smile falters a bit. "Your mother said to stop by," he says. "She said you'd be expecting me."

Crap.

With everything else going on, I totally forgot what my mom told me on our last Zoom call. I forgot that my ex was coming to town and that she was going to tell him to drop by the bar. And now, goddammit, here he is. And I've got no one to blame but myself.

Why did I let her bully me like that? Why didn't I stick to my guns and make her understand that Jonathan and I are a long freaking way from that perfect-for-each-other couple she imagines us to be?

The two of us started dating the summer before we both left home for college. He was lifeguarding at the country club pool where my sister and I were spending most of our afternoons, and yes, okay, I may have faked a cramp while I was swimming to get a chance to meet him. A girl had to keep her acting skills sharp after all.

I lost my virginity to Jonathan Vanderbilt that Fourth of July, our sweaty eighteen-year-old bodies tangled together in the pool's storage shed while fireworks *literally* exploded above us in the midsummer night sky. At the time, it seemed like fate that he was headed for Columbia University in the fall while I'd be attending its nearby sister school, Barnard. And since I'd be matriculating at a women's college, where meeting guys wouldn't necessarily be so easy, I was happy to take up residence in my first-year dorm room that August already having a boyfriend I could see on a fairly regular basis, just a subway ride away.

But over the next four years, he became more and more entrenched in the preppy, elitist, frat-boy culture, and I threw myself into my school's liberal, artsy, theatrical community. By the time we both graduated, other than our schooling and our privileged family backgrounds, we didn't really have a lot in common anymore.

We still don't.

"I'm sorry," I tell him from behind the bar. "But I can't talk right now. We're too busy."

I have to talk to him though—talk straight to him—at some point. I know I do.

"I can wait around for a while," Jonathan offers.

Involuntarily, I glance down the bar at Nick, who seems to be occupied with a customer, before I respond. "Tonight's just not a good time."

Following the direction of my quick gaze, Jonathan frowns. His light eyes are clouded over when he turns back to me. "Okay, then how about tomorrow?" he asks, smiling hopefully. "I have to go to my cousin's wedding, but it doesn't start until six. I'm free all day. Maybe we could get together?"

Tomorrow, I think. *Yup. I'll set him straight tomorrow.*

"Sure," I say. "Let's talk then. I'll text you a time and a place we can meet."

"Great," he says. "So I'll—"

"Uh, hello?" interrupts a loud, impatient voice. "Are you just gonna gab all night, or can we maybe get some beer over here?"

I peer down the bar at the displeased patron. Then I look back at Jonathan. "Sorry," I say helplessly. "I really do have to get back to work."

Before Jonathan can say anything else, I make my escape. I've never been so happy to wait on someone I know full well isn't going to tip me.

"Sorry about that," I tell the customer with a smile. "What can I get you?"

"Pitcher of Miller Lite."

"Coming right up."

While I'm grabbing an empty pitcher, I spot the back of Jonathan's dark-blond head disappearing out the door, and I breathe a sigh of relief.

As I head for the taps, I see Nick is already there. With a sudden sinking feeling in my gut, I remember that he has those dialed-up vampire senses. The way his nostrils are flaring, I can tell he must have *recognized* my ex. And the way he's looking at me? I can also tell he must have just overheard everything.

Double crap.

Once again, just when Nick and I seem to be making some headway toward each other, we hit another roadblock.

I take a deep inhale and step up next to him.

"It's not what you think," I say proactively as I start to fill up the pitcher.

"That was the guy whose shirt you were wearing yesterday?" asks Nick.

"Well, yes."

"And he thought you were expecting him tonight?"

"Yes, but—"

"And you just made plans to see him tomorrow?"

I hesitate. "Yes."

"Then it's exactly what I think." he says.

It occurs to me that Nick's interrogation skills are almost on par with my dad's.

I try to come up with a response, but it's like Nick can't get away from me fast enough—not without using his supernatural superspeed and revealing what he is to the whole bar anyway.

For the next few hours, the vampire proceeds to give me the *very* cold shoulder.

· · · · ·

There's about half an hour to go before closing. The crowd has peaked and is finally starting to drop off as we coast toward last call. I'm opening a fresh bottle of cabernet when I get that feeling. The same feeling I had when I was walking to my car, just after Nick informed me what I was. The feeling of being observed by a vampire.

I peer down the bar at Nick. He's still playing the ignore-the-crap-out-of-Carrie game, mixing up something in a cocktail shaker, not even looking my way. But I already knew it wasn't him watching me. The energy I'm picking up on feels stronger. More powerful. More... *vampire-y*. Like, if Nick is a scotch and soda made with the shitty house stuff, this other presence is a double shot of the top-shelf single malt.

Trying to keep my slayer in check, I pour two glasses of the cab and plunk them down in front of my customers. Then I turn to ring up the sale.

While my back is turned, I hear a smooth male voice with a hint of an accent rise above the chatter. "When you get a chance, love, can you pour me one of those too?"

The words are benign enough, but the intent behind them, I

know, is deadly. Because every fiber of my body is telling me that the man who just spoke them isn't a man at all.

Vampire, I think.

"Be with you in a sec," I say, tossing the words over my shoulder without turning around.

Has Dracula's Army grown impatient with simply spying on me from the shadows? Has one of them come here to the bar, invading my space to try to suss out what I am?

Quentin? I wonder. *Or Zach?*

My slayer doesn't care about his identity though. She doesn't care *who* he is, only *what* he is. She wants to attack this new arrival, big-time. But she has to get through me first.

Controlling my slayer rage around Nick is challenging, for sure. Challenging but doable. Probably because there are other factors at play. For one thing, he's my coworker. Has been for a while. I knew him before he became a vampire. And while I didn't particularly like him all that much back then, I certainly didn't want to *kill* him.

And for another thing, now that I'm spending more time with Nick and actually getting to know him? I'm starting to question a lot of the assumptions I made about him. Turns out he may not be the guy I thought he was. Or the vampire my slayer expects him to be. My feelings about him are *complicated*, to say the least.

However, with the blood drinker standing behind me, there are no such complications. We have no history, and there is no gray area. Everything is simply black and white. He's a vampire, and I'm a slayer, and right now, even the presence of the human bar patrons isn't doing a whole hell of a lot to keep my impulse to attack in check. To my supernatural side, he's a danger to every person in this bar, and it's my job to eliminate that danger.

Red clouds loom, ready to eclipse my vision. Fire gathers in my core like a storm, preparing to rain down on my enemy. I honestly don't know if I'll be able to stop this tempest of fury building within me from exploding out of me.

But on a sheer survival level, I know I *must* stop it. I can't let this vampire know what I am.

Taking my time at the register, I cast another brief look down the bar, but Nick is still ignoring me, concentrating all his attention on splitting the pink-tinted contents of his stainless-steel shaker between two martini glasses.

Looks like I'm on my own here.

If I dally any longer at the cash register, it will start to look suspicious, so I complete the sale. As I walk over to my previous customers to hand them their bill, I give the newcomer a sidelong glance. Appearing to be in his twenties, he's wearing the kind of retro-1970s ensemble that, up until now, I thought only Lenny Kravitz could pull off successfully. He's tall, dark, and *very* undead.

My body goes taut. As I reach for a wineglass to pour his drink, I feel my temperature rising fast. Too fast. I give everything I have to drive back my slayer, but I'm not sure it will be enough.

The intense heat pulsing from my skin heats up the glass, and I feel it start to crack in my—

"Ow, crap!"

The glass shatters in my hand, cutting a neat slice in the pad of my index finger as the broken shards fall with a clatter to the floor. A few drops of blood bead on my fingertip.

Nick's head snaps toward me, and all of a sudden, he's not so intent on garnishing the two cosmopolitans he just poured. With the scent of my blood in the air, it seems he can't ignore me any longer.

Realizing this, the undead Lenny Kravitz wannabe stops homing in on me and shifts his attention to Nick.

"Nicholas!" he calls out affably, like he's just spotted him. But I can detect an undertone of concern in his voice.

I watch him move quickly and purposefully down to the other end of the bar, and I wonder...

Did I just stumble into a way out of this screaming-hot mess of a situation?

The vampire I assume is part of Dracula's Army clasps Nick's hand across the bar, subtly angling him away from me, distracting him from my blood. Evidently, preventing Nick from revealing his true nature to the crowd is more important than provoking me to reveal mine. First rule of Vampire Club, I guess.

I figure I should take the win and make my getaway.

I grab a clean bar rag and wrap it around my hand. "Be right back," I call, already heading out from behind the counter. "Need to go take care of this. Health regulations and all."

· · · · ·

About twenty minutes later, I hear a knock on the restroom door.

"Carrie?" comes Nick's voice. "You okay in there?"

Physically, I'm fine. The cut from the wineglass was pretty minor, really. Within a couple of minutes, I found what I needed in the first aid kit under the sink, disinfected my wound, and stuck a Band-Aid on it.

Paranormally, I'm fine too. The self-inflicted injury distracted my inner slayer, and once I put a little distance between myself and all that *undeadness*, I was able to regain control.

But emotionally? I'm still shaky. After all, I just came perilously close to exposing what I am to my enemy. My *lethal* enemy. This supernatural shit just got very real.

And speaking of… It just dawned on me that I've been so caught up with my own internal battle that I haven't really stopped to think about Nick, about what he might be going through.

"I'm okay," I call through the door. "Wh-what about you?"

"Yeah," says Nick. "All good. Sorry about that."

"No need to apologize," I say. "I get it. Unnatural urges and all." I open the door a couple of inches and peer out at him. When I see his grim expression, I immediately want to cheer him up. "See?" I try, teasing. "I knew there must be something that's not your fault."

He gives me a small smile for my effort.

"So does this mean you want to attack me as badly as I want to attack you?" I ask.

Nick raises his eyebrows at me, and in the awkward silence that follows, I realize how sexually suggestive that must have just sounded.

"What I mean is…uh…"

"Relax. I know what you mean," he says, widening his grin. "And I think it's similar, but not exactly the same. I want blood, sure. But like I said, Zach has a connection at a blood bank, and he keeps me hooked up with a steady supply. As long as I don't let myself go too long without it, it's not really a problem. It's just, when you cut yourself…" He shakes his head. "That was like somebody waving a Snickers bar right in my face. Kind of hard to resist, you know? Even if you're not hungry."

"So you're comparing me to a Snickers?" I ask.

"A little nutty with a gooey center?" muses Nick. "Sounds about right to me."

There was a time when I would have gotten into it with him in a major way over "a little nutty." But thinking back on all those times I was so judgmental with Nick, such a hard-ass to him…

"You really think I have a gooey center?" I ask quietly.

He leans against the doorjamb and peers down at me through the narrow opening in the doorway, and my center most definitely turns to goo.

"I think you can be very hard to resist," he says. And now I'm pretty sure he's not talking about his bloodlust. I feel a tug of desire down low in my belly.

I start to open the door all the way when a burst of laughter erupts from the bar area, reminding me that we're both currently on the clock.

"We still have customers?" I ask, trying to rein in my not-safe-for-work—and possibly not-safe-for-*me*—impulses.

Picking up on my shift into business mode, Nick stands up straight and clears his throat, nods. "I just finished last call."

"And what about…uh…"

"Quentin?" says Nick. "He's not here anymore."

I open the door all the way. "So that was Quentin, huh?"

"That was Quentin," he says. "And before you ask, no, I didn't know he was going to stop by tonight."

Maybe not, I think. *But he did stop by, didn't he? And not to see you. Clearly, he was targeting me.*

If I hadn't cut my finger, I'm not sure I could have kept myself from exposing my supernatural side. Unlike Nick, I don't have a nonviolent way to satisfy my urges. I could have found myself in a slay-or-be-slain situation with Quentin tonight. And I don't know if I would have come out of it alive.

If I needed further proof that I've got to get the upper hand with my slayer—and fast—I guess I have it.

"You sure you're okay?" asks Nick.

"What?" I shake my head, trying to shake off my increasing fear.

"Yeah," I say. "I'm okay. I guess we both had unexpected visitors tonight," I add without thinking.

But I should have thought. I definitely should have thought. My offhand comment earns me a dark look from Nick.

"I better get back out front," he grumbles. And before I can say anything else, he's gone.

· · · · ·

A little later, Nick and I fall into what's become our regular nightly routine of closing the bar up together. But as we stack the chairs on the tables, neither of us says anything, and the vibe between us is kind of tense. Finally, I can't freaking take it anymore.

"Just so you know, I wasn't expecting my ex to stop by tonight," I say, breaking the silence. "I mean, my mother told me he was going to be in LA this weekend, but I totally forgot about it. Because even though my mom desperately wants us to get back together, I don't. I don't think about him that way anymore. Or any way, really."

"Then why did you get all dressed up tonight?" asks Nick.

Seriously? That's what he's hung up on?

"Oh my God," I blurt out, slamming a chair down onto a tabletop. "Why do you think?"

He blinks, unsure for a second. Then, gradually, he gets it. The corners of his mouth curl up ever so slightly, inviting his dimples out to play.

I stare across the room at him, and he stares back at me. The ambiance of the room changes. The chilly atmosphere between us lifts, and the air becomes sultry. It feels almost as if we're back on the beach, when we almost kissed.

We could easily pick up where we left off before we were interrupted.

But the surprise appearance of the other slayer last night stirred up doubts in me about Nick. And mixed in with all the swoony feelings I'm rocking right now, those doubts are still there.

Plus, I'm still reeling a little from my almost confrontation with Quentin.

Not to mention that hooking up in the workplace is simply not professional. Even if it is after hours.

"I mean, thanks to you, half my clothes don't even fit me anymore," I say, trying to back off my implicit admission that I got all dressed up for him. "And I need to wear something that hides these muscles." I realize none of this explains the makeup, and I think Nick realizes it too. He doesn't call me out on it though.

"Okay," he says, nodding. "Fair enough."

We go back to work, stacking the chairs in silence for a while. But this time, it's more of a comfortable silence. Companionable, even.

Out of the corner of my eye, I spy Nick pushing up the sleeves of his cardigan. That's when it occurs to me that, in the year or so that we've been coworkers, I've never seen him wear anything other than T-shirts.

Hmm...

I bite my bottom lip to suppress a smile. Maybe I wasn't the only one who got all dressed up tonight.

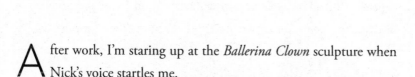

CHAPTER
14

After work, I'm staring up at the *Ballerina Clown* sculpture when Nick's voice startles me.

"Paying your respects to the patron saint of Venice?"

I turn and see him walking toward me from a little way up the block.

"Patron saint of Venice?" I ask.

He stops a couple of yards from me and points up at the sculpture. "I like to imagine it's watching over us," he says. "One misfit looking out for all the other misfits who live in Venice Beach."

"You're not a misfit," I tell him. "Aren't you the guy who gets along with everyone?"

"Not *everyone*," he says with a pointed look at me.

I grin. "Is that why you're standing so far away?" I ask.

He grins back. "I thought I'd keep my distance until we decide on a game plan for tonight."

"I was thinking about that," I say. In fact, I was pondering it the whole drive over. My mind kept going back to the marked difference between my knee-jerk, must-slay reaction to Quentin versus my more conflicted reaction to Nick. "And I think I have an idea."

"Do tell."

"I'm thinking I need to get to know you better," I say. "As a person."

"Just one problem with that," he says. "I'm not a person anymore. I'm a vampire."

"See, that's what my slayer thinks," I say. "That's why she wants to kill you. But here's what I'm thinking… If she gets the message that there's more to you than just the fangs and the…uh…blood drinking, it'll be harder for her to just blindly hate you and easier for me to control her. And if I can get control of her around you, I'm thinking it'll be easier for me to control her slayer butt around other vampires too." I sweep my arms out in front of me as if I'm indicating the proposal I've just laid out. "So what do you think?"

"Sounds like you want to play truth or dare without the dare part," says Nick.

"Oh please," I say. "You're a vampire and I'm a slayer. The dare part is understood. The dare part is playing the game at all." I cross my arms and give him a challenging look. "What do you say we take a little walk and have a little talk?"

. . . . .

Nick keeps his hands in his pockets, and I do the same. We maintain about a foot of space between us as we stroll together, side by side, toward the beach. My slayer is quiet but vigilant.

"So what do you want to know?" asks Nick.

At first, I don't know what to say. I'm not used to being the one asking the questions. With my parents, with casting directors, and sometimes even with my friends, I always seem to be the one who gets quizzed. The swing in the power dynamic feels strange but also…*nice.*

Since I don't really have a specific agenda, I decide to start with the basics. "Where did you grow up?" I ask.

"Pretty much all over Los Angeles," says Nick.

"Your family moved around a lot?" I ask.

He hesitates. "Actually, I moved families a lot."

I knit my brows, a little puzzled. "Because your parents were divorced?" I ask. "Remarried?"

He hesitates again. "Dead," he says. "They died in a car crash on the 101 when I was seven."

"Oh my God!" I stop walking, and so does he. "I'm so sorry. I didn't mean to—"

"It's okay," he says with a shake of his head. "You didn't know."

"But I shouldn't have pried like that. I should have asked you something less personal," I say. "Like your favorite color. Or your favorite food. Or your favorite band—"

"You think my favorite band isn't personal?" he teases.

I hate that after I've stupidly dredged up what's probably one of his worst memories ever, he feels like he needs to make *me* feel better.

I also really kind of like that about him.

"I'm so sorry, Nick," I say. Because honestly, I don't know what else *to* say.

"It's fine," he says. "I mean, it's not fine, obviously. It'll never be fine. But it happened almost twenty years ago. And I survived DCFS—"

"DCFS?" I ask.

"Department of Children and Family Services."

I take this in for a moment and look at him. Or maybe it's more like I *see* him. For the first time since I've known him, I really see him.

"How?" I ask softly.

"How what?" he asks.

"How did you survive DCFS?"

He looks back at me, and it's like he *sees* me too.

Maybe he always has.

He smiles a little sadly. "I guess I learned how to get along with everyone."

· · · · ·

We walk on in silence until we reach the beach. A few steps in, my platform sandals start to wobble and sink into the soft sand.

"Hold on a sec," I tell Nick.

I lift a foot to remove my shoe, but I begin to teeter. Quicker than my eyes can track the movement, Nick's hand is on my arm, steadying me. I feel his ice-cold touch through the sheer material of my blouse. It somehow warms me to the core.

Slowly, I peer up into his eyes. "Thanks."

He looks down at me. "No problem."

And suddenly, it's like my senses are just as amplified as his. I notice everything. His smile, his killer dimples. The pungent scent of the ocean air mixed with the musky scent of his cologne. The light, reassuring pressure of his hand still grasping my arm.

Unfortunately, my slayer is superattentive now too, alerted by the unexpected contact. Why can't she just mind her own goddamn business? Why can't she leave me—leave *us*—alone?

The piercing in Nick's eyebrow is catching the moonlight again, shining like a star. It makes me want to make a wish about Nick and me. A wish that, considering our natures—considering that we are supernatural freaking enemies programmed to annihilate each other—can't possibly come true.

But I go ahead and wish it anyway.

· · · · ·

"I went to the Musicians Institute, here in LA," says Nick.

Playing the getting-to-know-you game again, we're sitting together on the beach, watching the waves roll in as moonbeams reflect off the water. I dig my fingers and toes absently into the cold, damp sand.

"I inherited a little money on my eighteenth birthday," he continues. "Not a lot, but enough to cover the tuition."

I turn to him with an admiring smile. "So you're self-made," I say.

"Carrie," he says with a teasing grin back, "no vampire is *self*-made."

At the mention of the V word, my slayer pricks up her ears. I should probably change the subject, but what Nick has just said piques my curiosity too. Mentally tightening my reins on my alter ego, I ask, "But you wanted to be made, right? You wanted to become a vampire?"

"I did."

"Can I ask…*why*?"

Nick hesitates.

"Or is that too personal?" I ask quickly, not wanting to repeat my earlier mistake.

"No, it's just…a lot," he says.

He turns and looks out over the ocean. Then he picks up a shell and tosses it into the waves, thinking. Having apparently reached a decision, he turns back to me.

"You have to understand," he says, "I don't remember my parents much. And growing up, being shuffled around from one foster home to another, I never really felt like I belonged anywhere. But when I met Quentin and Zach and we started playing together, we just, I don't know… *clicked*. I felt like I was part of more than just a band. I felt like I was part of a family. So when they let me in on their secret? And they offered to punch my immortality card? I mean, I know it seems like it should have been this huge decision. But for me, it was a total no-brainer. When they offered me eternal belonging? Hell, I couldn't say yes fast enough."

It all makes sense. After everything he's told me—and after seeing the way Quentin looked out for him at the bar earlier tonight—it all tracks. All except for one little thing.

"So why risk it?" I ask, repeating the same question I asked a couple of nights ago. My eyes search his. "Why put your *eternal belonging* on the line just to help me?"

Nick's gaze doesn't waver from mine. "You know why," he says in a voice that makes my breath hitch and my belly do flips.

All at once, I do know why. Maybe I've known all along.

I'm not sure if he makes the first move or if I do. But there's one moment when I'm sitting here on the beach not kissing Nick, and then there's the next moment, when everything changes.

Nick's mouth presses against mine. Rationally, I know his icy lips should be cooling me down, not heating me up, but right now, there is no reason. There is only burning. And needing. And aching.

I deepen the kiss, or maybe he does? Not that it matters. All that matters is what his tongue is doing, what his fingers are doing as they thread through my hair, and oh God, what it's all doing to me!

My toes curl involuntarily, squishing wet sand between them. I lift my hand to touch Nick's face, and the damp granules sticking to my fingertips feel rough against his surprisingly soft, smooth skin.

It's like a movie kiss, or rather it's like you imagine a movie kiss would be if it were actually happening to you. It's like when the music swells, the focus gets a little fuzzy, the action starts to unfold in slow motion, and you get totally swept up and away. There's an unreality to what's going on between Nick and me, yet it's more real than anything else ever has been. Certainly, it's more real than any other kiss ever has been.

Obviously, this is not my first kiss. But honestly? It might as well be. I've never felt this way before, and right now, I can't fathom feeling this way with anyone else ever again. It's as if I'm unravelling, going mad in the best possible way, losing all control—

Wait.

Losing all control?

Suddenly, I'm aware of my slayer. She is subdued but not passive. Definitely *not* passive. And with a jolt, I realize that she's watching us, biding her time. Like a calculating understudy, she's waiting hungrily for her chance to step in and take over.

I break the kiss and shove Nick away from me.

"No," I say, breathless. "You have to stop."

Nick looks at me, also breathing heavily. His expression is all confusion. "I'm sorry," he says. "I thought you wanted this."

"I did," I say quickly. "I *do*. But you almost made me lose control."

Nick grins. "Isn't that a good thing?"

I shake my head slowly, sadly. "No," I say. "Not when you're a vampire and I've got a ruthless vampire slayer waiting in the wings."

CHAPTER
15

N o!" Liv slams her fork down on the table after I finish recounting how the previous night went down. "You and Nick can't be doomed lovers. You just can't be," she insists. "*Bar Wars* is supposed to be a sci-fi action-romance. Not a tragedy."

"You may need to take some artistic license with the story," I say glumly. I continue to push my egg-white breakfast burrito, no cheese or sour cream, around on my plate.

Liv, Heather, and I are in the middle of Saturday brunch at the Firehouse on Rose. The diner—most famous for being the place that Keanu Reeves patronizes just before all the drama with the bus in the movie *Speed*—is located in an actual refurbished firehouse. As I look around at the bright-red walls and the firefighting memorabilia hanging there, I desperately wish I had some foolproof way to fight this supernatural vampire-killing fire burning inside me. But as I realized last night, wishes don't always come true.

"But you've only been a slayer for like, what? A few days?" asks Heather.

I shrug.

"That's nothing," she says. "You can still get on top of this."

"Maybe enough to keep what I am hidden from the other vampires. Maybe enough to keep myself safe and alive," I say. "But not enough to ever be with Nick. Think about it. If I lose control with him—even for just a second—it gives my slayer an opening. And I could kill him. Literally *kill* him." I put my fork down. Shoving my plate away, I lean back in my chair with a sigh and shake my head. "No way can I risk that happening. I mean, I didn't even want that to happen before, when I thought I couldn't stand him. But now…"

"You like him," says Liv. I notice it's not a question anymore.

I shrug again. "It doesn't matter," I say. "We can't be together. It's too dangerous."

The three of us are quiet for a few moments.

"Okay, we need cocktails," says Heather, breaking the silence. She tries to flag down our server.

"I'm not sure cocktails will help," I say.

"Couldn't hurt," says Liv.

Just then, my phone *pings* with a text alert. I glance down at it.

"Oh crap!" I say.

"What now?" asks Heather.

"My ex," I say. "I totally forgot I'm supposed to meet with Jonathan today. He wants to *talk*."

My besties grimace in sympathy.

I don't want to deal with Jonathan right now. I really don't. My gut instinct is to text him back, say something's come up, and cancel.

But the problem is I never want to deal with him. When it comes to having the tough conversations like this, I'm a total freaking wuss. And that's why I'm in this awkward position with him now. For two years, instead of making a clean break of things, I've been giving him a string of maybes and let's-sees, hoping eventually he'd just get the message and move on.

I've been justifying my behavior by telling myself that I was sparing his feelings. That I was being kind. I mean, I do know how painful rejection can be. As an actor, I experience rejection on pretty much a daily basis.

But giving someone false hope is not kind. I see that now.

Sometimes wishes don't come true. Sometimes you can't have the person you want.

"Maybe it's karma," I say.

"What?" asks Heather.

"My situation with Nick," I say. "Maybe it's the universe paying me back for the way I've been treating Jonathan."

"I don't think that's how the universe operates," says Liv, pushing her glasses farther up on her nose.

I frown down at the text from my ex, thinking.

Regardless of how the universe operates, I need to change the way *I* operate. I need to find the strength to pull on my big-girl panties, set Jonathan straight, and set him free to move on.

Then maybe at least one of us can be happy.

Having caught Heather's signal, our server appears at our table. "Can I get you something else?" he asks.

I peer up at him, and I decide to chuck my mostly-stick-with-water rule right out the freaking Firehouse door. If I'm going to finally get real with my ex, I need something a little stronger. "Cocktails," I say. "Definitely cocktails."

• • • • •

Two hours and two mimosas later, I walk into the Starbucks on Main.

Jonathan is already here, sitting at a table with some big fancy iced coffee. When he sees me, he smiles and gets to his feet. He's wearing another one of his ultrapreppy outfits: madras shorts, white polo, and Adidas sneakers. He looks good, I guess. The same as he always does. In two years, he hasn't really changed.

"Carrie," he says.

I paste on a smile and cross over to him. "Hey, Jonathan."

He goes in for a kiss, which I clumsily manage to avoid. We end up in an awkward hug. As he wraps his arms around me, I feel his hands on my back stiffen. He pulls away in surprise.

"You've been working out," he says.

I'm dressed in another look styled by Heather. This time, she put it together with a few things she borrowed from the wardrobe closet at her work. The puffy-shouldered pin-tucked shirt does a good job of camouflaging my new upper body, while the stretchy, black denim capris minimize my lower-body bulk. But the illusion is purely visual, I realize. The hard swells and contours of my body are all too apparent to the touch.

"Yeah," I say, wriggling out of the embrace. "I've been...*training.*"

"Oh. That's cool I guess," says Jonathan. Although his lack of enthusiasm for my new muscles is clear.

And I have to say, it really kind of pisses me off. I mean, it's one thing for my agent, for casting directors, for Hollywood decision-makers to judge me based on my appearance, but it's another thing entirely to be judged by someone I know, someone I used to care for. Someone who claims to still care for me.

"I'm a lot stronger than I used to be," I tell him. "And I'm getting stronger all the time." And as I say it, I realize I'm not just talking about my physical strength. Maybe he hasn't changed, but I have. Or at least I'm trying to.

"Well, can I get you something?" he asks. "A coffee?"

I shake my head. "No thanks." I take a seat at his table, and he sits down opposite. "I just came from having brunch."

His dark-blond brows come together, and his forehead furrows. He scrutinizes me. "With that guy?" he asks.

"Guy?"

"The other bartender," he says. "The one with the piercing and the ink and the...*hair*." The disapproval in his tone is obvious, not to mention wholly offensive. Now it's like he's judging Nick based solely on the way *he* looks.

My anger starts to intensify.

"You don't know anything about Nick," I say evenly.

"I know he's not the guy for you."

"Then maybe you don't know me all that well."

"Carrie," he says, "of course I know you. I know you better than you think. Maybe even better than you know yourself."

I sit up straighter, and my irritation builds. Did he really just say that?

"Be careful," I tell him. "You're starting to sound like my mother. And just to be clear, that is *not* a compliment."

"Look," he says, totally oblivious to my mood, "I understand that you might want to rebel a little. Take a walk on the wild side. But come on. The low-paying job? The low-class boyfriend? That's not you."

"Oh my God," I say, barely containing my rage. "Do you even know what a snobby little shit you sound like right now?"

He sits back in his chair and blinks at me, clearly surprised by my uncharacteristic outburst. But quickly enough, he regains his composure and pegs me with a hard stare.

"What's happened to you?" he asks.

"Excuse me?"

"Why are you acting this way?" he asks.

For a moment, I'm struck speechless.

"I may have come to LA to be an actor," I say when I find my voice. "but I assure you, I am definitely not *acting* right now."

"Are you ever coming home?" he asks.

"I am home," I say.

"No," he says. "You're slumming."

And that's it. I am *so* done.

"You know what?" I say. "I came here knowing what I had to say to you but not knowing if I'd have the strength to say it. But as it turns out, you're making this pretty damn easy for me. You and me? We're not taking a break," I say. "We're broken up. And we're not getting back together. Ever. I'm sorry I wasn't clear about that two years ago," I continue. "I should have been. And that's on me. But you don't know me, Jonathan. And honestly? I don't think you ever really did. To you, I'm just that girl at the country club pool. I'm the girl from the right family with the right pedigree who went to the right schools, and ever since we met, you've just been filling in all the rest. And that? That's on you."

"Are you finished?" he asks quietly after a bit.

"*We're* finished," I say, standing up. "Goodbye, Jonathan. And good luck to you. Truly."

"Yeah? Well, good riddance to you," he practically spits at me. "Have fun with your fucking bartender."

For so long, I've been avoiding this conversation because I thought it would make me feel bad. Yet despite Jonathan's parting insult, I actually feel...*good*. Lighter. Like a weight I've been carrying around for more than two years has finally been lifted. They say that the truth will set you free, and what do you know? It's true. There's almost a skip in my step as I turn and head for the exit.

But as I push the door open and emerge onto Main Street, something else starts to drag me down. I remember that the bartender in question isn't actually mine.

And with things the way they are, he never freaking can be.

CHAPTER
16

Mentally, I'm still pretty deep in pity city when I arrive for my last night shift of the week at Pete's. By contrast, Nick is in great spirits. It makes me wonder if the terminally star-crossed nature of our romance hasn't completely hit him yet, or worse, if maybe he's already over it.

"So I've been thinking about things," says Nick. He's waiting by the register for me to finish ringing up my sale so he can ring up his. "And I have a plan for tonight."

I nod, frowning down at the keys. "For our training session," I say.

"For our *date*," he says.

My eyes shoot up to meet his. "Nick," I say. "We can't. You know we can't."

He gazes down at me, and his dark eyes seem to dance, shining even brighter than the barbell piercing in his eyebrow. "Or maybe we can," he says mysteriously.

$\bullet\ \bullet\ \bullet\ \bullet\ \bullet$

After work, I meet Nick under the *Ballerina Clown* with mixed emotions. I want to share his optimism about us. I do. The butterflies

I'm rocking right now at just the sight of him in his dark jeans and his Nirvana tee are proof enough of that. Except it feels to me like we're starting something that we can't finish. And that makes me question the wisdom of starting anything at all.

I turn in the direction of the beach, our usual destination, but Nick reaches out a hand to stop me.

"I thought we'd go this way tonight," he says. He gestures toward Abbot Kinney Boulevard, the main drag through Venice. "Cool with you?"

I shrug. As we cross the street, Nick shortens his stride so I don't have to rush to keep up, and we fall into an easy pace with each other. I only wish my slayer wasn't along for the stroll, looming between us like an unwelcome chaperone.

"Are we going someplace in particular?" I ask.

"You'll see," he says playfully.

We walk together in silence for a bit, past an assortment of art galleries, shops, and restaurants, most of which are dark.

"Looks like everything's closed," I say.

"Not everything," he says. He points up ahead at the one well-lit establishment on the block. It's a karaoke bar.

I slow my pace. "Karaoke?"

"I'd like to get to know you better too," says Nick, all smiles. "And I find that a person's choice of karaoke song says a lot about them."

I stop cold. My eyes go wide in horror. "You expect *me* to sing karaoke?"

Stopping too, Nick takes in my reaction. "Uh-oh," he says. "You say that like it's a bad thing."

"If I'm singing? Trust me, it's a *very* bad thing," I say.

We're just a few steps from the entrance to the Full Moon Karaoke Lounge.

"I just figured since you're an actor…"

"*Actor*," I say. "Definitely *not* a singer."

Nick frowns. "Is that a hard pass on karaoke?"

"If it is, do you hate me?" I ask with a little grimace as my compulsive people pleasing starts to rise to the surface.

"If it wasn't, would your song have been 'Wannabe' by the Spice Girls?" he asks.

"God no," I say.

"Then no, I don't hate you," says Nick. "So moving on to phase two of my plan for the night…" He takes a breath. "Would you like to come up?"

I blink at him, a little baffled. "Come up?" I ask. "Come up where?"

"To my place," he says, pointing to one of the windows above.

Now the pieces start to fit. "You live over the karaoke bar?"

Nick gives me a sheepish look as he combs his long fingers back through his hair. "My plan would have gone a lot smoother if we'd hit the lounge first," he says. "I could have plied you with fancy umbrella drinks and wooed you with a killer karaoke rendition of 'Wonderful Tonight' before I tried to get you upstairs." He grins. "Now you probably just think I'm a creeper."

I shake my head. "I don't think you're a creeper."

He broadens his grin. "You haven't been upstairs yet."

I laugh.

My slayer isn't laughing though. She's listening. Closely. And like the disapproving chaperone that she is, I know she'll intervene to separate us as soon as things get good. And she'll use lethal force to do it.

"I want what you want, Nick," I say. "But—"

"Shh," says Nick, placing his index finger lightly on my lips. The brief, icy touch sends a river of heat flowing through my body, washing away some of my doubts. "I might have a work-around for our little problem if you're up for it."

Talk about an understatement. I mean, what we have here isn't just a *little problem*. It's not even a big problem. It's literally life and death. And considering that Nick just chose immortal life? How can he be willing to court death just to be with me?

But knowing that he is? Well…

How can I possibly say no?

After a moment, I nod toward what I assume is the building's residential entrance. "Lead the way."

· · · · ·

I follow Nick past the row of mailboxes and up the narrow stairwell. The wall to my left reverberates with music from the karaoke lounge. I can't discern the exact song that's playing, but I can feel the bass pounding in my chest. Or maybe that's just my heart hammering in anticipation.

Nick unlocks the only door on the second-floor landing and pushes it open. Waving me in, he flicks on the lights. Just inside, there's a bike hanging on a whitewashed brick wall. A drywall divider separates the narrow entryway from the rest of the space.

He guides me around the divider and hits another light switch. Overheads illuminate an open loft space that stretches the full length of the building. Exposed air ducts and wooden support beams give the place an industrial feel. There are three large windows, but each is concealed by blackout shades pulled all the way down.

The loft is loosely arranged into three zones: first, a kitchen area; next, a living room/music room area; and finally, all the way at the back, a bedroom area.

"Meow!"

Startled by the noise, I look down and discover a small, short-haired black cat with white paws, bright green eyes, and a slightly crooked tail. He—or maybe she—begins to thread through Nick's legs.

"Who's this?" I ask.

"Eddie," says Nick.

"Eddie?"

"Short for Eddie Van Halen."

I smile. A he then.

I squat down on my haunches and give Eddie a scratch hello. He pushes his head into my hand, purring loudly.

"Fair warning," says Nick. "He's a shameless flirt."

"Takes after his owner, I guess," I say, grinning up at him.

"Ha!"

"You know, I wasn't expecting a cat." Much to Eddie Van Halen's disappointment, I get back up to my feet. "Aren't cats more of a witchy thing? Aren't vampires supposed to keep bats?" I tease.

"Well, if they follow me home one night, I'll take them in too," he jokes.

"Of course you will," I say after a moment. But I'm not joking.

Looking at Nick, I think about the little boy who lost his parents all those years ago, who never had a real home. Of course he would give a home to this homeless cat. I know that now, because I know *him*.

Earlier today, I got angry at Jonathan for judging Nick. But the fact is I judged Nick too. I made all kinds of assumptions about him based on what I saw or what I *thought* I saw. I did to him exactly what Hollywood does to me. What I *hate* that Hollywood does to me. I typecast him.

I am so stupid. So. Freaking. Stupid. If only I had gotten to know

Nick—the *real* Nick—sooner! Then I wouldn't have treated him like an enemy. I wouldn't have become his slayer. And we wouldn't find ourselves in this frustratingly impossible situation.

"Want something to drink?" asks Nick.

I blink. I didn't see him move to the refrigerator, but I don't think he used his vampire speed to get there. I think I just got a little lost in my own head.

He opens the fridge, and I see that it's stocked with a lot of the predictable single-guy fare: beer, Gatorade, water, an obscene amount of condiments, and several leftover take-out containers. But on top of the large cardboard pizza box, I also spy a pile of...*donor units of blood?*

I recoil.

My slayer doesn't like it either, but I suppress my revulsion and silently remind her—and me—that it's a good thing. It's evidence that Nick's *not* an evil predator. But if he starts drinking like a vampire— even if it's out of a plastic bag and not someone's vein—my alter ego is definitely going to need some wrangling. And right now, I'd really prefer to concentrate on other things.

"What are *you* drinking?" I ask warily.

He follows the direction of my gaze, then he turns back to me and smiles. "Beer," he says, amused. "Want one?"

· · · · ·

Nick opens a microbrew for himself, hands me a bottle of water, and makes sure Eddie Van Halen's food and water dishes are filled before he leads me to the middle zone of his place. Against one wall, there's a huge old sofa that Heather would absolutely deem "fugly." A functional but nondescript wooden coffee table sits in front of it. There's no TV,

I notice—something the actor in me would notice, of course. There is, however, a laptop, open on the table.

The opposite wall is clearly the heart of this place. It's a literal wall of sound. A turntable occupies the place of honor in the center of a massive shelving unit that houses hundreds—maybe even thousands—of vinyl albums. Three guitars—one acoustic, two electric—are propped up on a rack. I notice that the acoustic bears a strong resemblance to the tattoo on Nick's forearm.

A simple chair and a metal music stand crammed with handwritten pages curling at the corners are positioned near the guitars. A few papers and pencils litter the scuffed hardwood floor. Next to the chair, a dirty coffee cup rests atop a knee-high pile of well-used notebooks, apparently serving as a makeshift end table.

"What should we listen to?" asks Nick.

I survey the seemingly endless selection of music. "You choose," I say.

"Nope," he says. "You're the guest. You get to pick."

I turn to him and narrow my gaze. "Is this some kind of a test?" I ask. "Like the karaoke thing?"

"Okay, first off," he says, "the karaoke thing wasn't going to be a *test*. It was going to be a way to get to know you better. And this time," he continues, "there are no bad answers." He waves his arm across his substantial collection of vinyl. "I like it all."

I take a sip of my water, thinking. Then I nod, accepting the challenge, and cross over to the shelves.

I begin to run my index finger along the spines of the albums, scanning the titles. Nick's vinyl collection, like his T-shirt collection, is heavy on rock bands from the 1970s, '80s, and '90s, although it does span all decades and genres of music. The records aren't organized alphabetically, but I suspect they're organized nonetheless, arranged in some way that makes intuitive sense to their owner. As I continue to browse the titles, I get the feeling that I'm looking at more than just an extensive music library. It's like I'm peering straight into Nick's soul.

I get to the Eric Clapton section and stop. I remember that Nick's karaoke song—the one he planned to *woo* me with—was going to be "Wonderful Tonight." Taking my best guess, I pull one of the albums off the shelf and check the playlist on the back.

Score.

It's the second track.

I hold *Slowhand* out to Nick. "Let's listen to this."

"Nice choice," he says with a smile that tells me he knows the reasoning behind my selection. "I don't like a lot of what the guy says, but I can't fault his music." He takes the album from me, and heat— the good kind, not the slayer kind—begins to rise between us.

With a smile of my own, I go over to the sofa. Somehow, I feel both unsteady on my feet and like I'm walking on air. Then I sit down with my water and watch as Nick carefully removes the record from its sleeve and places it on the turntable. He hits the power switch and drops the needle, and the bluesy-rock guitar opening of "Cocaine" fills the loft.

Nick pauses, listening for a second or two—out of respect for the guitar work, no doubt—before he comes over and joins me on the sofa. "So," he says.

"So," I reply.

So, my slayer seems to echo. Damn her.

"Can I ask you something?" asks Nick.

"Uh, yeah. Sure."

"Why such an oh-hell-no on karaoke?"

"Oh," I say. I shake my head. "I just hate performing in front of people."

Nick gives me a funny look. "But you act," he says.

I drag a finger through the moisture gathering on the outside of my plastic water bottle, trying to figure out how to explain. "Acting is different," I say. "When you're really in a scene, really connecting with another actor? Using what's stored up inside you to create something good, something honest and true? There's nothing better in the world. But getting up in front of people? Being judged?" I shake my head again. "That's like an audition. And I'm terrible at auditions."

"But it's not an audition," says Nick. "It's karaoke. And almost everybody's terrible at it. That's half the fun. Nobody's judging you."

"Are you kidding? I feel like everybody's judging me," I say. "All the time. Like, my parents think I'm not successful enough. And my agent thinks I'm not pretty enough. Not to go up for the lead roles. And—"

"But you're beautiful," interrupts Nick.

I look at him, and the way he's looking back at me makes me genuinely speechless. I don't know what to say. And even if I did, I doubt I could say it. A lump the size of planet earth is rising in my throat.

Nick reaches over and runs his fingers lightly through my bangs, brushing them off my face. "The first time I met you, I thought you were the most beautiful thing I'd ever seen. Like a ray of light," he says. "And since we've been hanging out, you're even more beautiful to me than ever." He grins. "And not just because of my super-duper amped-up vampire vision."

Wow.

I mean…just…

As if on cue, the first song ends, and the slower, sexier opening strains of "Wonderful Tonight" surround us. The electric guitar licks are full of yearning—kind of like me right now. The soulful sound fuels the electricity already sparking in the air.

Nick takes my water and puts it on the coffee table along with his beer, and isn't he clever to think to free up our hands like that? As for me, I can barely think at all. My brain is turning to certified mush. My limbs are nothing but quivering slabs of jelly.

Moving carefully, like it's one of our training sessions, Nick scoots a little closer to me on the couch. "Is this okay?" he asks softly.

"Yes," I somehow manage to answer. My voice is so husky and deep, I almost can't recognize it.

Nick slides his hand around the back of my neck. His fingers slip up into my hair. "Still okay?" he asks as a delicious shiver zips straight through me.

"More than okay," I whisper.

He leans in toward me, and my body throbs. I want him so much I could weep for the longing.

"Still okay?" he asks again.

"Oh, for crying out loud," I say. I'm seriously about to explode. "Just kiss me already."

His dark eyes flash in amusement. "Bossy-pants," he says, teasing me.

"Slacker," I tease in return.

"Take that back," he says with a grin.

"Make me," I say.

And with a look that tells me he's more than up for the challenge, Nick goes to work.

CHAPTER
17

As Nick's lips touch mine for the second time, something deep within me stirs and breaks free, and I can't ignore the truth any longer. Nick isn't the only one on this couch who's had feelings for a while. Honestly? I think I've been attracted to him since he first walked into Pete's.

But before now, I just couldn't own it. I guess Hollywood did such a number on me that I couldn't see myself as his love interest. I figured that role belonged to someone much hipper, much cooler, much edgier than I am. So I told myself I wasn't his type. I typecast myself.

I locked my feelings away, just like he must have done. But tonight, here we are, like two actors coming together and tapping into all these unexpressed emotions. Only with us, there's no acting. What's happening is 100 percent real.

It's a lot—almost too much—but I don't want to miss a thing. So I try to savor each nuance. Like the way his mouth fits so nicely against mine. The way he tastes of beer and spearmint and something else, something that's uniquely Nick. The way his fingers press against my skin so carefully and deliberately. It's almost like he's playing a guitar, trying to coax a kind of music out of me.

My guttural moan isn't exactly melodious, but it seems to satisfy Nick. He gently pulls back and looks at me, grinning. "Still okay?"

I'm about to say yes. Miraculously, my slayer is still in check. But then I notice that Nick's vampire fangs have come out of hiding. And my freaking slayer notices it too.

In an instant, red bleeds across my field of vision. Desperate to maintain control, I shake my head.

Getting the message, Nick uses his lightning-quick speed to retreat from the sofa to the kitchen. He also seems to be struggling to regain some kind of control.

"I'm sorry," says Nick. "I should have warned you. The fangs come out when we're hungry, when we're threatened…and when we're *aroused*."

This is news to me—and to my slayer. While we both mull over this latest information, my vision clears and settles back to normal.

Nick is still trying to reel in his fangs. I guess I could take that as a compliment, but I'm way too depressed to be flattered. As "Wonderful Tonight" ends with the guitar practically weeping with emotion, I want to weep too. Me and Nick? It's just never going to work out.

I start to get up. "I–I should go," I say.

"No!" says Nick. "No, wait. Please."

"Why?" I ask. "We obviously can't do this, no matter how much we want to. With a vampire and a vampire slayer, there's no such thing as safe sex."

"Just wait," he says. His fangs have finally retracted. "We got a little ahead of ourselves. I didn't have a chance to tell you about my idea."

Right. Nick said he had a work-around, didn't he? For our *little problem*.

"All I'm asking is that you hear me out," he says. "Okay?"

I frown, thinking about this.

I should go. I mean, why prolong the inevitable? At best, sticking around will only lead to more disappointment and make it even harder to leave later. And at worst? One of us could get hurt, and I don't mean emotionally.

Nick is a vampire. And I'm a slayer. We're meant to be enemies, not lovers.

Except Nick is also *Nick*. And I'm also *Carrie*. And Nick and Carrie…

With a sigh, I sink back into the couch. "What's your idea?"

Nick disappears behind the dividing wall by the front door. While he's gone, I reach for my water and take a big swallow. Then I lean my head back against the sofa cushions, close my eyes, and listen to the music. We're into track three now, "Lay Down Sally." I realize that the lyrics are about a man trying to convince a woman to stay and spend the night with him. It could be Nick singing to me. I can't decide if that's funny or sad or just a really odd coincidence.

"Carrie?"

Hearing Nick's voice, I sit up straight and open my eyes. Nick is standing over me, holding out a chain wrapped in some kind of canvas with a combination lock on the end.

"What's that?" I ask.

"My idea," he says.

I just look up at him, confused.

"It's my bike lock," he explains.

"Okay," I say. Only his explanation hasn't really *explained* anything. I'm even more confused.

"Think about it," says Nick. "We want to be together, right?"

"Right," I say. No confusion there.

"But we can't," he says. "Because you're afraid of losing control, right?"

I feel the heat of a blush bloom on my cheeks. "Right."

"But if we restrain your sword arm with this," he says, holding up the bike lock, "then even if you lose control, you won't be able to slay me."

It takes a few moments before I fully understand what he's proposing.

"So you want to chain me up while we…uh…"

"Shit," he says. He runs a hand through his hair and gives me an embarrassed look. "Now you really do think I'm a creeper, don't you?"

Do I?

Up until now, I haven't been all that experimental in the bedroom. I've only ever slept with Jonathan, and sex between us was always pretty standard, I guess you would say. I mean, we were both young when we got together, and he was only slightly more experienced than I was. The two of us never engaged in any kind of kink. To be honest, I've never even fantasized about it.

But right now, looking at Nick holding the chain and lock, I get an ache deep and low inside me. My body feels warm, and my head fills with a whole anthology of steamy scenarios that I would love to act out.

I realize I want this with Nick. I'd want it even if we weren't paranormal foes. And if it really is a legitimate way for us to get around this supernatural stumbling block in our relationship? All the better.

"I don't think you're a creeper," I say with a grin. "Actually, I think you might have just solved our *little problem*. Big-time."

CHAPTER
18

Practically giddy with excitement and lust, I let Nick lead me back to the bedroom area of his loft. But once we get there, I start to feel a little shy about the *mechanics* of it all.

Nick picks up on my reticence. "You can trust me, you know," he tells me. "I promise I won't do anything you don't want me to do."

"I know," I say. "I trust you." And as I say it, I know it's true.

"So do you want to…um…" Nick looks down at the bike lock in his hands. Now he seems kind of shy too.

I laugh nervously. "Maybe I'll just…" I gesture at the bed.

"Good idea."

I sit on the mattress and slip my feet out of my shoes. Then, swinging my legs up onto the bed, I scoot across the dark-green comforter.

"I'm guessing you've never done anything like this before either?" I ask.

"Nope," says Nick. "You're my first slayer."

"Ha, ha," I say. "You know what I mean."

"Relax," says Nick with a smile. "We're two reasonably intelligent and very horny adults. Something tells me we'll be able to figure it out."

I grin back, and I do relax. It's Nick after all. As I look at him and stretch my right arm out toward the bed frame, it occurs to me that its black metal construction is actually pretty perfect for this sort of thing.

Nick takes my hand and starts to wrap the bike lock's chain around my wrist, and there's that dull ache again. I squirm, a little impatient, as wetness pools in my panties. But then he frowns and stops what he's doing.

"Stumped already?" I tease.

"It's just…do you want to take your shirt off first?"

I'm still wearing the puffy-shouldered blouse and the dark denim capris that Heather put together for me to hide my newly acquired bulk. The same outfit I wore to brunch, then to meet Jonathan.

I can't help recalling my ex's lackluster reaction when he felt the hard contours of the muscles underneath my shirt.

"Sorry," says Nick quickly. "I didn't mean to rush things."

"No," I say, dropping my arm. "It's not that. It's…"

Suddenly, I'm feeling self-conscious. And uncertain. Not about Nick—no, I definitely want to be with Nick, no question about that. It's just that lately, I've been struggling to get comfortable with my own body. So is it any wonder that I'm a little unsure about baring it all to Nick?

"Carrie?" he asks. "Everything okay?"

Just say it, Carrie. Just say it.

"You may not be attracted to my body," I blurt out.

Nick blinks at me. It feels like an eternity passes before he finally replies. "Of course I'll be attracted to your body," he says. "Because it's *your* body. And I'm attracted to *you*."

I want to believe that. I do. But if Nick ends up judging me because of my appearance, goddammit, I'll seriously want to slay myself.

"But you have to understand," I say. "You may not be able to tell because of the way I'm dressed, but my slayer body is different. It's… bigger. A lot bigger."

"My vampire body is different too," says Nick. "It's cold as ice, and it doesn't have a heartbeat." With that, he tosses the bike lock onto the bed and pulls his Nirvana band tee over his head, tossing it to the floor. "Are you still attracted to *me*?"

Am I attracted to him?

Oh. My. Freaking. God.

I confess, I've tried to imagine what Nick might look like shirtless, but I never imagined this. His broad torso is like a lesson in anatomy, the lean muscles all tight and perfectly defined. I mentally wipe the drool off my chin before I answer his question in a very decisive affirmative.

But even as I manage to croak out a yes, I know that I'm not attracted to Nick's body just because it's hot. I'm attracted to his body because it's *his*. This latest reveal is just another pixel in the total picture of the guy. And really, it's the total picture that's making the temperature of my own body boil, that's making the beating of my own heart accelerate.

I remind myself that I trust him. I trust Nick. So, dismissing my doubts the best I can, I remove my top. I'm not wearing a bra. With breasts this small, I don't really need the support, and since the shirt is opaque, there was no reason to put one on for modesty's sake. Completely naked from the waist up, I cast my shirt onto the floor with Nick's tee.

I brace myself.

I would say that Nick stares at me without judgment, but that's not exactly right. The way he takes me in, it's like he's a judge in a pie-baking contest, and I'm a fresh-from-the-oven slice of heaven on earth. He looks at me with hunger, as if he wants to devour me.

I feel my nipples tighten under his gaze.

"Nick," I say, "your fangs."

They've elongated, which yes, based on what he shared earlier, does confirm his attraction. Only problem is their sudden appearance also rouses my slayer.

Nick mutters a curse as we both do battle with our otherworldly natures.

But dammit all to hell, I am not going to let these instincts ruin things for us. Not when we've come so far. Not when we're so, so close.

With everything I have, I tell my alter ego to go screw herself. I mean, this is *my* body after all. Not hers. I should be able to do what I want with it. And right now, what I want is to get it together with Nick's body in as many ways as possible, as soon as possible.

Keeping a tight rein on my supernatural impulses, I recline on the mattress and extend my arm toward the bed frame again. "Chain me up," I say. "Now."

Probably not the smartest thing to say to a vampire who's trying to contain his sex drive. My provocative words—coupled with the desperation in my tone—seem to make his fangs grow even longer.

I close my eyes so my slayer can't see his response. Then I feel his cool hand on my wrist as he presses it against the metal frame. My pulse races under his touch. I'm aware of the weight of the fabric-covered chain as it wraps around me once. Twice.

I hear the snap of the lock, and my exhale of relief is part sigh, part moan. My eyelids flutter open, and my gaze lands on Nick.

"Okay?" he asks.

"Come here," I say. I lift my free hand up toward his face, and that's all the invitation he needs.

He joins me on the bed, and we pick up where we left off. But the energy between us has shifted a little. Before, even though we were moving cautiously, there was also an undercurrent of urgency. I think maybe we were both subconsciously playing beat the clock, trying to get as much of each other as we could before my slayer came between us. But now, with my sword arm restrained, it doesn't feel like we're trying to get away with something. It feels like we're really, truly starting something.

And as for the restraint? Well, I have to say, this practical solution to our *little problem* also adds another level of excitement. I'm surprised by how empowered it makes me feel. Even though I'm restrained, it's not like I'm giving up control. No, it's more like I'm taking control.

And I want more.

I drag my mouth away from Nick's so I can whisper in his ear. "Nick?"

"Hmm?" he murmurs into my hair.

"Maybe we should restrain my other arm too."

He pulls back a little to look at me. "The sword switches hands?" he asks.

"It hasn't yet, but…" I bite my lower lip and raise my brows at him suggestively. I know when he gets my meaning because his pupils dilate, and his dark eyes darken even more with desire.

"Well, we can't be too careful, can we?" he says, playing along with my little ruse.

"My thoughts exactly."

"But I don't have another bike lock," he says.

"We're two reasonably intelligent and very horny adults," I reply with a smile, using his words from a little while ago. "Something tells me we'll be able to figure it out."

He smiles back, and his dimples are so adorable I want to gobble them up. After a moment, his dark eyes seem to light up with an idea. He sits back on his heels, unfastens his belt, and pulls the leather strap out of the belt loops of his jeans. He holds it out for my inspection. "We could use this," he says.

The dull ache in my belly gets sharper.

I swallow, nod. "Works for me."

I stretch my free arm out toward the other side of the black metal bed frame, and Nick crawls over with the belt. The worn leather cuts lightly into my flesh as he secures the strap around my wrist.

"Too tight?" he asks.

I test it, then shake my head. "Nope. I'm good."

Nick is staring down at me, and I feel his gaze travel over my body, all splayed out for him. The body that lately, I've been trying so hard to hide.

"You're not just good," he says hoarsely. "You're incredible."

He continues to look at me, but I want to feel more than his eyes on me. I want to feel his hands, his mouth, his…everything.

"So are you going to make a move?" I ask. "Or what?"

With a sexy grin, he stretches out next to me. But then, with a glance up at my restraints, he turns my face so he can look directly into my eyes, and he gets a bit serious. "You're in charge here, all right?" he says. "You have to tell me what's okay and what's not okay. You have to tell me what you want."

And for once in my life, saying what I want is easy. So easy.

"I want you, Nick," I say simply. "I just want you."

In response, Nick kisses me long and slow and deep. Leaving me breathless, he starts to make his way down my length, exploring every last inch of me. I lie back against the pillows, writhing and reveling in the caress of his lips on my throat, the weight of his large hand cupping my small breast, the scrape of his teeth against my nipple.

Eventually, those talented fingers of his find their way to the fly of my denim capris. He tugs gently at the waistband. "Can I take these off?"

"Yes," I say. "Please." Because I'm really not thinking about my new shape anymore. I'm not thinking, period. I am nothing but soul-deep yearning. For Nick.

I arch up toward him, lifting my butt off the mattress, and he efficiently strips off my pants and panties in a single, swift movement. Fully naked and exposed, I watch him, waiting, thinking he's going to remove his pants as well. But instead he parts my legs, settles himself between them, and goes back to work on me. I swear, I will never call Nick a slacker ever, ever again.

He kisses his way down my stomach, down to my navel, down even lower. As I wriggle beneath him, his hands press against my hip bones, attempting to hold me still. When the flat of his tongue sweeps across the most intimate part of me, I gasp.

"Jesus," he says. "You even taste like sunshine."

His words make me liquefy. Honestly, I'm surprised I don't just dissolve right into the mattress.

His hands move to my thighs, parting me wider. Then there's his tongue again, the tip this time, circling and flicking, doing mad, wild things to my clit.

"Is this okay?" he asks, but I feel his words more than hear them, feel his voice vibrating against my skin and his breath blowing across the hot, damp folds of my flesh.

"Yes," I say. My voice is little more than a whimper.

His tongue pushes inside me, dipping in and out, and the pleasure is so intense it makes me squirm.

He lifts his head slightly, and his gaze is fire. "Is this okay?" he asks again.

"I—yes," I manage.

Grunting with satisfaction, Nick goes down on me again. It dawns on me that the music ended, probably a while ago. It's just the staticky scratch of the needle mixing with the sounds of Nick, the sounds of lapping and licking and sucking and groaning that could almost be a song of their own. There are other noises too, noises that are coming from me but don't sound like me at all.

Suddenly, Nick slides a finger into me. My body bucks, clenching on to him like a lifeline, even as he's making me drown.

"Is this okay?" he asks.

"Hmm…"

"Is that a yes?" he asks. He nips at the inside of my thigh.

"Mmm…"

"Carrie. Is that a yes?" he repeats. He curls his finger inside me and runs his thumb over my sex.

"Yes!" I practically shout. "Yes, God, yes!"

I grasp the bed frame and hold on tight, trying to anchor myself, but it's no use. Liquid heat is already rising inside me. Overflowing. Sweeping me up and away. And lying here, tethered to the bed, I become completely unmoored.

I ride the waves for moments that seem to stretch into hours. When things finally calm to a ripple, Nick withdraws from me and presses a kiss against my sticky, oversensitive skin, eliciting one last shudder.

He peers up the length of my body at me. My vision is still a little unfocused.

"Okay?" he asks with a raised eyebrow.

I have to laugh. "I think I left okay in the dust a while back."

He laughs too. "I meant your arms," he says, looking up at my restraints. "Do I need to undo them?"

"My arms are fine," I say. And even though I am thoroughly sated and so wrung out I can barely move, my gaze wanders down to the front of his jeans and the noticeable bulge there. I suck in my bottom lip. "But if you wanted to undo your pants…"

"Whatever you want," he says thickly.

Nick quickly sheds his remaining clothes, and now I have more evidence than just his long, hard fangs to tell me that he wants me as much as I want him.

"The vampire thing makes condoms unnecessary," he tells me. "But if you would be more comfortable—"

"No," I say, shaking my head. "No, I believe you."

Not bothering to hide his eagerness, he grasps his cock in a way that makes my breath catch. For a moment, I wish my wrists weren't bound so I could be the one wrapping my hands around him, guiding him inside me. But then again, the restraint also kind of increases my need, kicking my desire up to the next level.

I want to rise toward him, but my limbs are limp. Luckily Nick has enough stamina for the both of us. He hooks my leg around his other arm, lifting and opening me to get a better angle. As he rubs himself against my entrance, I seriously think I might pass out from the anticipation.

He pushes inside me, only I'm too wet and he's too anxious, and the combination makes him keep slipping out. But then, finally—

Yes.

God, yes.

We find our rhythm, slow and careful at first, just like everything else about this relationship of ours.

"Okay?" asks Nick.

"Just fuck me," I whisper.

He gives me a wicked grin that flashes his fangs. I'm vaguely aware of my slayer waking up and trying to get between us, but I silently tell her this isn't a freaking threesome.

Like Nick said, I'm in charge here. It's kind of thrilling, really, and it adds to the thrill of what's happening.

Nick cups my ass and lifts me higher, and his thrusts get faster, deeper. Before long, heat is building inside me, a heat that isn't about vampires and slayers. It's only about Nick and me.

"Fuck," says Nick. "I can't—I—"

"It's okay," I say. "It's okay."

And as I feel him lose control inside me, I let myself lose control again too.

· · · · ·

Nick has released my bonds, and we're lying in his bed, spooned together under his comforter. With the tip of my index finger, I absently trace the ink on the inside of his forearm.

"This looks like your guitar," I say. "The acoustic one."

"It is," he says into my ear. "Donna."

Donna?

I stop tracing the outline of the tattoo. "Wh-what?"

"My acoustic," he says softly. "Her name is Donna."

Is this a thing that musicians do? I wonder. *Name their guitars?*

About the last thing I want to hear right now is Nick whispering another woman's name in my ear. Even if it is just the name of his guitar.

Is it just the name of his guitar though?

I'm definitely not going to ask if the acoustic is named after someone. Nope. I am so not going to go there. After everything that's just passed between us, I definitely don't want to talk about some other—

"So is there a real Donna?" I ask. I try to keep my voice casual, but I can hear the edge in it, and I'm pretty sure Nick can too.

My heart goes as still as a vampire's as I wait for Nick's response. Then, after what feels like centuries, he finally says, "My mom."

My heart starts to beat again.

"You named your guitar after your mom?" I ask, rolling over to face him.

He nods. "It used to be hers," he says. "She was a musician too."

I smile. "I bet she'd be proud of you if she could see you now," I say. "Following in her footsteps like this."

He shrugs. "I like to believe that she'd be proud regardless. That she'd just want me to do whatever makes me happy."

What a concept, I think.

I'd like to believe that about my mother too. Only I know better.

But before I start going down that rabbit hole, I stop myself. I don't want to think about my mom or my family drama. I just want to think about Nick and me. That's what makes me happy.

I snuggle closer to him, and he hugs me tighter.

"It's almost sunrise," he says after a few minutes.

I glance at one of the tightly shielded windows. "How do you know?" I ask.

"I can sense it," he tells me.

A few days ago, this would have sounded strange, but in less than a week, so much has changed. I nod.

"When the sun comes up," he continues, "I'm going to fall asleep, and you won't be able to wake me up. It'll look like I'm dead, but I'm not. I'm—"

"Undead," I say.

"Undead," he says, suppressing a yawn.

I run my hand lightly along the line of his jaw. His eyes start to drift shut, but he fights to keep them open.

"You're welcome to stay as long as you want," he says sleepily.

I think about it, but then I shake my head. "I should probably go," I say. "If you're out cold, and I fall asleep, I don't know if I can trust my…"

"Slayer," he murmurs.

"Slayer," I echo.

We just look at each other for a moment or two longer.

"Tonight," he says finally, ending the silence, "was…"

Before he can finish his sentence, Nick rolls onto his back, and he's out. But considering the smile on his face—and the similar smile stretching across my own—I don't have any trouble filling in the blank.

Out of nowhere, Eddie Van Halen—the cat, that is—jumps up onto the mattress, startling me. His white paws pad across the comforter, and he climbs gingerly on top of Nick. After circling around a couple of times and kneading at the bedding with his claws, he settles in a ball on Nick's chest in a way that makes me think that this is their regular daily routine. I'm glad Nick won't be alone all day.

"Take care of him, Eddie," I say as I give the cat a little scratch behind the ears.

Then I smooth my hand over Nick's hair and gently kiss him goodbye before I get out of bed and locate my clothes.

Getting dressed is a bit of a challenge though, because I can barely stop myself from doing a little happy dance. There are no words to express my bliss. I feel like I'm floating.

The only thing that keeps me somewhat grounded is that, on my way out, I notice that the wall by the bedpost where my sword arm was restrained is ever so slightly singed.

CHAPTER
19

When I get home, Liv is still asleep. I try to sleep as well, but after my night with Nick, I'm way too wound up. So after tossing and turning for a bit, I decide to burn off some excess energy by going for a run.

I pull open my bottom dresser drawer and start to reach for a long-sleeved tee, but then I stop myself. I just saw the incapacitated state of a vampire during the daytime hours with my own eyes. Clearly I'm not in any danger of discovery by my undead enemies. Not until dusk anyway.

But more than that, after being with Nick, I don't feel like such a stranger in my own body anymore. I feel like I've taken ownership of this new shape, like it's...*me*. And honestly? If I want Hollywood to stop expecting me to look a certain way, I really need to accept myself as I am, however I am.

I grab a pair of running shorts and a tank and put them on.

· · · · ·

As I walk down Rose Avenue toward the beach, I feel the delicious warmth of the sun directly on my arms and legs for the first time in days. It makes me realize how much I've missed it, and I have to wonder if Nick misses it too. Does the fact that he's living an eternal life make up for it being a strictly nocturnal one?

It dawns on me then—no pun intended—that Nick and I can never be together in the sunshine. But if we can be together at all? And share more nights like last night? The no-day-dating thing seems like a small concession to make.

With an undeniable bounce in my step, I pass the CVS and peer up at the *Ballerina Clown* sculpture suspended above it. I look at the sad-clown head perched atop its tutu-clad body, and I want to tell it to cheer up. If I managed to find this kind of happiness despite my dual nature, dammit, you can too.

I get to the beach path and start to stretch. My muscles are still a little sore from last night's...*activities*, but I'm certainly not complaining. After a quick warm-up, I decide to head south into Venice.

Taking it easy at first, I follow the path along the Venice beachfront walk. It's pretty early on a Sunday morning, so aside from a few bikers, power walkers, and runners like me, the normally bustling venue is mostly quiet. The funky boutiques, T-shirt shops, and CBD purveyors are still closed, their graffiti-covered metal doors pulled down and locked tightly over their storefronts.

I jog by a lone smoothie stand that's open for business, then by a café where the workers are hosing off the outdoor dining area and setting up the tables and chairs.

Picking up my pace a little, I see a woman laying out macramé jewelry, displaying her handmade wares on a blanket spread out at the edge of the concrete walk. A few strides away, there's a caricature artist also setting up for the day.

Pushing a little harder, I approach the Muscle Beach outdoor gym. Like the *Ballerina Clown*, it's a true Venice landmark. For more than half a century, tourists have flocked to this open-air workout facility to watch some of the best bodybuilders in the world train.

At this early hour, there are no tourists. The metal bleachers around the gated gym are deserted. But the gym itself is buzzing with activity as a number of the facility's muscular members put the weight lifting equipment to good use.

As I get a little closer, I notice that several of these bodybuilders are women.

Intrigued, I slow down. Then I watch from outside the gate, a little in awe, as one woman bench-presses what looks like an astronomical amount of weight while another woman spots her. The weight lifter's muscles bulge, her tendons strain, and her skin glistens with sweat at the exertion. There's a real beauty to this show of strength, a beauty I guess I'd never really considered before. At least not in connection with my own gender.

My gaze sweeps across the gym, surveying some of the other female weight lifters. I'm filled with admiration, but I also feel a twinge of guilt. After all, these women came by their muscles honestly. They earned them through hard work and discipline. On the other hand, I just woke up with mine.

"Are you looking for a trainer?"

I turn in the direction of the voice. One of the women, the weight lifter who just pressed all that weight, has come over to the gate where I'm standing. Probably in her early thirties, she has short-cropped dark hair and piercing blue eyes. Her black sports bra and boy shorts reveal acres of tanned skin stretched taut over sculpted muscles.

Sculpted by training.

Feeling like a giant impostor, I aimlessly kick the toe of my running shoe against the ground.

"No," I say. "I can't really afford a gym membership."

I start to go.

"I'm not talking about that kind of training," she says to my back.

I stop, turn around again. Her penetrating eyes meet mine.

And suddenly, I *know*. I know this is the slayer who's been watching me, who took flight that night after observing Nick and me together on the beach.

"I'm Jenn," she says, extending her hand to me over the gate. "Jenn Muldoon."

"Carrie," I say. "Carrie Adams."

I shake her hand, and my head floods with question after question after question. Since the morning I woke up with inexplicable muscles and the uncanny ability to produce a flaming sword, I've been in the dark about, well, pretty much *everything*. But here, now, is someone who can shed a little light on things. Here, *finally*, is someone like me. Someone who can help me understand exactly what I am. And maybe give me some real tips for controlling it.

"Would you maybe have time to get a coffee or something?" I ask. "And talk?"

· · · · ·

My new acquaintance and I hit the open smoothie stand and get a couple of protein shakes. Then we grab some seats in the empty bleachers overlooking the Muscle Beach gym.

"So…Jenn," I say once we're settled. "I guess you're also a…you know…"

"Vampire slayer," she confirms.

"Right. Vampire slayer." I nod and take a sip of my drink. "And are there others like us?"

"There are others out there, for sure," she says. "But I don't know how many. I've only ever encountered one besides you. My mentor, James."

"Is James here?" I ask, looking around. "Can I meet him too?"

Jenn's expression turns grim. "No," she says. "He made the ultimate sacrifice."

It takes me a moment to get her meaning. "He died?"

She nods.

"I–I'm sorry," I say.

Jenn shrugs. "It's the risk we all live with."

I get a sick feeling in the pit of my stomach. This slay-or-be-slain thing really is no joke.

But I don't want to dwell on that, not while I have a source of actual, honest-to-God information. I give her loss a few respectful beats of silence. Then I indicate the bodybuilders—some male, some female—still working out in the gym. "So none of them are slayers?"

Jenn shakes her head. "No," she says. "They're all just human."

This touches on a subject that's been bothering me for a while. "What about us?" I ask. "Are we still *human* too?"

She frowns, thinking. "Yes and no," she says. "We're not immortal, not like *them*."

The way she says *them*, with such complete and utter contempt, makes me flinch a little. It must be her inner slayer breaking through. I drop a pin, figuring I'll come back to that later.

"Slayers aren't immune to aging or disease," she continues to explain. "We have a normal human life span. But we're not normal humans, obviously. I guess you could say we're superhuman."

Superhuman.

I take another draw on my straw and consider this.

"But you train here," I say. "Is that because we need to work out to maintain our…uh…" *Superhumanness?* "Muscles?" I finally land on.

Jenn shakes her head again. "No. We could lie around and eat ice cream all day, and we'd still be just as strong, just as powerful."

Her words give me pause. As someone who's been carefully counting calories and measuring servings to be a certain body type, the thought of not having to ever do that to maintain this kind of a physique is pretty mind-blowing.

"But I like the challenge of working out," says Jenn. "And the bodybuilding gives me a cover story. You know, a way to explain my muscles." She raises her brows at me and gives me an intent look. "How are you explaining yours?"

I shrug. "Mostly, I hide them under baggy clothes."

"But not today," she says.

"No," I say. I recall my night with Nick, remembering how wonderful it felt to have him look at my body, muscles and all. I can't help but smile. "Not today."

"Good," says Jenn with a nod of approval. "Then you're getting more comfortable with who you are."

"I guess I am," I say, still smiling.

"You're embracing your power."

I think about the way I stood up to my agent, to my ex. "I am," I say. "I really am." I take another sip of my protein shake.

"So you'll be slaying your vampire soon," she says.

I almost choke on my shake. I cough so hard it makes my eyes water.

Oh my God. Is she talking about killing *Nick?*

Just the thought has always been abhorrent to me, even before I got to know him. But now? After last night? It's positively unthinkable.

It's some time until I get the hacking under control and I'm able to breathe normally again.

"You okay?" asks Jenn.

I nod as I brush a stray tear away. "Yeah, I'm okay," I say. I decide it's time to revisit that pin I dropped. "But you kind of caught me off guard when you said that thing about my vampire. That was just your slayer talking, right?"

She gives me a confused look. "My slayer?"

"You know," I say. "The voices in your head, the fire in your gut. Your slayer."

"I don't *have* a slayer," she says slowly. "I *am* a slayer."

Uh-oh. I'm not getting a good feeling about this.

"You don't try to fight it?" I ask.

"Why would I?" She sits up straighter. "I save my fight for the ones who deserve it."

All I can see in my head is Nick. "But what if they *don't* deserve it?"

She peers at me, studying me for a bit. I watch as understanding dawns in her eyes. "Oh, I get it," she says. "The first kill is the hardest."

I gulp. *First* kill? As in more than one?

Am I sitting here casually drinking strawberry-banana smoothies with a multiple murderer?

"There won't be a body, if that's what you're worried about," she assures me.

I gape at her. "Excuse me?"

"There won't be any evidence to connect you to a crime. Not that killing something that's already dead is a crime. If your sword touches any part of them, they just dissolve into a pile of ash that you can sweep up and chuck in the dumpster. The universe has our backs."

Oh. My. God.

I think about the past few nights with Nick, about how close I've probably come to reducing him to the ash that Jenn has just so callously described. I feel the blood drain from my face, and I can't quite suppress my shudder.

"Jeez," says Jenn, eyeing me. "You really are a squeamish one, aren't you?"

Okay, so I guess I shouldn't really be so shocked. I mean, we are vampire slayers after all. And that pretty much sums it up: we're supposed to slay vampires. Plus, I know how compelling the impulses are. I know that once the fire of blind hatred starts to burn, it's almost impossible to contain it.

Except it *is* possible to contain it. I know that too.

I try to pull myself together. "I just want to live my *own* life," I tell her. "Not one that's been forced on me."

She shrugs. "You get used to it."

"You get used to being a vampire-killing machine?" I demand.

She blinks, a little taken aback.

"You must've had a life before all this," I say, pressing her. "Don't you want to find a way back to it?"

I see something flash in her eyes then, and it's not slayer rage. It comes and goes so quickly that it's almost like it wasn't there at all. But it *was* there. I know it was. And I'm pretty sure it was regret.

"I can't go back," says Jenn.

But honestly? I think there's a part of her that wishes she could.

So I resist my impulse to get the hell away from her. Maybe we can help each other. I can show her how I've been resisting my slayer, and she can fill me in on what else she knows.

Unfortunately, as she goes on talking, the wisdom she shares with me doesn't seem all that wise. "I have a new life now, and so do you," she insists. "And we both have an important job to do."

I frown doubtfully.

"If you find your courage wavering," she adds, "just remind yourself why you hate him."

"What?"

"Your vampire," she says. "You hated him before he became a soulless bloodsucker, right? Otherwise, you wouldn't have become his chosen slayer."

At least that confirms what Nick told me about the vampire-slayer connection.

I take a deep breath. "We had some issues," I say carefully. I'm thinking I should be prudent with what I reveal to her about our relationship.

"Well, now you don't just have *issues*," she shoots back, taking on the tone of a true believer. "You have a solemn duty to protect the world from undead scum. Starting with *him*."

She sounds exactly like my inner slayer now. She's spouting the same kind of hateful crap that I hear echoing inside my head.

I don't know about other vampires, but I do know about *my* vampire. I know that the slayer party line simply doesn't apply to Nick. Not to the Nick I've come to know and...*like*?

Maybe even more than like?

There was a time when I avoided confrontation, but now I know I have to speak up. For Nick's sake but for Jenn's too.

"What if he's not undead scum?" I ask.

"What?"

"You're talking like we're the Avengers or something, saving the world from evil," I say. "But if my vampire isn't hurting anyone, why should I hurt him?"

Jenn leans back and pegs me with that intense blue-eyed gaze of hers. "What exactly was going on down at the beach the other night?" she asks me.

I swallow. "What do you mean?"

"It almost looked like the two of you were about to kiss."

Her statement hangs suspended in the warm salt air between us. But before I can figure out how to respond, Jenn starts to laugh.

"What?" I ask, a little thrown. "What's so funny?"

"You," says Jenn. "You think this vampire of yours isn't a threat. But I've got news for you. He's a much bigger threat than you think."

I look at her blankly. "I don't understand."

"It's just like James warned me," she says.

"Warned you about what?" I ask.

"I'll bet your vampire is really turning on the old charm, right?" she says. "Running every play in the romance playbook. Pulling out all the stops to get you to fall for him?"

I freeze.

What she just said is kind of true, but I'm not going to admit that to her. So I don't say anything.

Still, I have the horrible feeling that my happiness is like a speeding car headed straight for a brick wall, and it's about to be totaled beyond recognition. I hold my breath, bracing for impact.

"He's trying to neutralize you," says Jenn. "Your vampire is trying to save himself and the rest of the bloodsuckers by taking away your power."

I crinkle my brow at her. "I still don't understand."

"According to James, the bond between a vampire and a slayer is forged by hate but broken by love." Jenn says it almost reverently, like she's reciting something sacred. "Don't you get it? Your vampire is manipulating you. He's deliberately trying to make you fall in love with him." She gives me a meaningful look. "Because if a slayer falls in love with a vampire, the slayer loses their power."

If a slayer falls in love with a vampire, the slayer loses their power?!

After hearing this, I hightailed it home and put out the 911 to Heather and Liv. It was time for an emergency girls' night.

A little later, Heather arrived at the door with an excessive amount of wine plus an overnight bag, indicating that she wasn't planning on staying sober enough to drive back to West Hollywood this evening. Liv dug through the fridge and found the cheese plate and assortment of sandwiches that she brought home the other night, leftovers from her job's catering table. I got the wineglasses, plates, and napkins. Then we carried everything through the sliding doors to the balcony, settled on the mismatched outdoor furniture, and kicked off this special edition of girls' night several hours before actual nightfall.

Over our first glass of wine, I filled my friends in on the latest. Since then, our conversation has been going around in circles, the circles getting wider and a little wonkier with each successive round of drinks.

"But you have to admit," I say, "the timing is a little sus." I take a sip of my…*pinot grigio? Sauvignon blanc?* At this point, I've kind of lost track of what we're drinking. "I worked side by side with Nick for a whole year, and he never once so much as flirted with me. But I become his slayer, and *boom*! He's all of a sudden interested?"

"Well, to be fair," says Heather, "I do think he was interested before."

"But he never acted on it before," I argue. "And then, when it looked like it was too dangerous for us to be together, *he* was the one who pushed it. *He* was the one who suddenly came up with the whole bondage thing."

"He may have been interested in that before too," says Liv.

"Come on," says Heather. "Do you really think he's just playing you?"

Do I?

When I left Nick a little past sunrise, my answer would have been an unequivocal *no*. Our night together felt magical—and not in a supernatural way. Magical in a *real* way. Magical in a this-could-be-the-one way.

But what Jenn told me earlier today has got me questioning everything. In the span of just a few short days—or should I say *nights*?—I've gone from wanting to kill Nick to just plain *wanting* him. And sure, I thought it was because I was finally getting to know him. But could it be that I still don't know him at all?

"I don't know," I say with a frown. "Ever since Nick told me what I was, I've been wondering why he'd want to help me. I finally let myself believe it was because he cared about me, but…maybe he's just been trying to get *me* to care about *him*." I take another sip of my wine, trying to take the edge off the pain of this possibility. "Maybe he really has just been trying to take my power away. Maybe that's been his plan all along."

"But he has a cat," says Liv through a mouthful of Gouda and prosciutto.

Heather and I give her a quizzical look.

Liv swallows, washing down the food with a big gulp of wine. "He took in a stray cat and named it Eddie Van Halen," she says, explaining her reasoning. "Does that sound like the kind of guy who would be playing you?"

It doesn't. But there's a problem with her logic. A problem Nick himself has alluded to more than once.

"He's not a guy though," I say. "He's a vampire, and I'm a slayer. There are other things at stake."

Heather bursts out laughing. Liv and I shoot her a look.

"*Stake*," she explains. "Sorry," she adds, reaching for a sandwich. "I'm a little tipsy."

I'm also tipsy, tipsy enough that it takes me a moment to make the stake-vampire-slayer connection. When I do, I don't find it funny though. Right now, I'm not sure I'd find anything funny.

"It's just…I really trusted him, you know?" I say glumly.

"And now you trust this Jenn person more?" asks Liv.

I shrug. "Why would she lie to me?"

"Oh, I don't know," says Heather. "Maybe because she's a fucking serial slayer? And she's saying whatever she can think of to turn you into a fucking serial slayer too?"

I swirl my wine around and think about this. I can't deny that Jenn does seem to want me to be a ruthless vampire killer. But I remember the sound of her voice as she shared this particular bit of slayer lore with me. Her tone wasn't full of bravado and rage, the way it was before. It was soft and reverential, like she was revealing one of the world's great mysteries. Like she was imparting something true, something passed down to her by her mentor. Her *slain* mentor.

I shake my head. "It didn't sound like she was making it up," I say. "Honestly? I don't think this is something she *could* make up. It's too…*poetic*, you know? That a bond created by hate could be undone by love. She didn't really strike me as much of a poet. Like you said, she's kind of a—"

"Fucking serial slayer," finishes Heather. She takes a big bite of her turkey and Swiss on a mini croissant.

"Well," says Liv, "maybe Jenn and Nick are both telling the truth. Maybe a slayer does lose their power if they fall for a vampire, but Nick doesn't know that. And maybe he's genuinely falling for you."

We're all quiet as we contemplate that for a bit.

"Let me ask you something," says Heather as the sun slips below the horizon. "Would it really be so terrible if you weren't a slayer anymore?"

The question takes me by surprise. I realize that as much as I've been struggling with my new slayer body and instincts, I haven't even considered what it would be like to be completely free of them. I didn't even know it was a possibility.

Would I like to go back to being just a plain old ordinary human being and not have vampires stalking me, out for my blood? Of course! Would I rather not be spending so much time and energy wrestling with this vampire killer inside me? Hell yes! Would I prefer to have full control over my own body again? Abso-freaking-lutely! But by controlling my alter ego, I've also started to get in touch with my own strength. I've found the courage to stand up for myself in situations where, before, I would have just rolled over. And I definitely don't want to lose that.

Really, it comes down to a question of will. To surrender my power freely, like I did last night with Nick, is one thing. That felt empowering in its own way. But the idea of having my power stripped away from me? Under false pretenses? That's something else entirely.

If it's my body, what happens to it should be my choice.

"I guess it wouldn't be the worst thing in the world if I fell in love with Nick and lost my power," I say slowly. "The worst thing would be finding out that he's been actively trying to take my power away. The worst thing would be if our relationship just turned out to be one big con." I pause for a moment. "The worst thing would be if I fell in love with Nick, but Nick didn't love me back."

Just then, my phone *pings*.

I check it, and I feel even more conflicted than before.

"It's a text from Nick," I tell my friends.

Heather glances up at the dusky sky. "He messaged you as soon as the sun set," she says. "As soon as he woke up."

"What does he have to say?" asks Liv.

I hesitate. Then I turn my phone so my friends can see the screen.

Hello, sunshine 😃 ☀️ 🖤

"Aww," they both say in unison.

"That doesn't sound like a guy who's playing you," Liv says quietly.

Except I remember Jenn's assertion that Nick was pulling out all the stops and running every play in the romance playbook.

"Or it sounds like a guy who's playing me really well," I say.

My phone *pings* again. It's a longer message this time. The alcohol is starting to do a number on my vision, so I have to squint to read it.

"He says he can't get together tonight," I say once I make out his text. "He has band practice. They haven't rehearsed in a while, so they need to prepare for their gig at the Whisky on Wednesday."

My phone *pings* once more.

Miss you 👰 🔒 😍

But does he? Does he really?

I start to type.

"What are you doing?" asks Liv.

"I'm texting him back," I say. "I need to ask him about—"

"No!" says Heather, snatching my phone out of my grasp.

"Hey!" I say. "Give that back."

"No," says Heather sternly. "No tipsy texting." She deletes what I started to write.

"But—"

"Heather's right," says Liv. "You don't want to get into this over a text chain. Especially not when you're…um…"

"Shit-faced," supplies Heather. She types a short message and hits Send.

"Heather!" I say. "Did you just text Nick from my phone?"

"Uh-huh."

"But you said no tipsy texting," I say.

"Exactly."

"You're just as tipsy as I am," I say.

Heather stops and thinks about this. Or thinks about it as much as her wine-muddled mind will allow. "True," she admits. "But in this situation, unlike you, I can be unemotional."

She hands me my mobile. I squint down at the screen and read the very *unemotional* response that my friend just sent Nick.

K. Later.

• • • • •

I wake up Monday morning with a screaming headache. My throat is like sandpaper, and my eyeballs hurt. When Jenn said slayers weren't immune to aging or disease, she left something else out. We're also not immune to the effects of way too much under-ten-dollars-a-bottle wine.

I crawl out of bed and stagger into the living room. Heather is there, folding the sheets that I vaguely remember us using to make up the sofa for her last night. Incredibly, she doesn't appear hungover at all. In fact, she looks the opposite of hungover. With a little help from cosmetics, her green eyes are bright and her complexion is fresh and rosy. Her long hair is expertly twisted into a stylishly messy topknot. And she's already dressed in a nautical-themed outfit of white jeans, a navy-and-white-striped tee, and green Top-Siders.

I sweep my hand from the top of her head to the toes of her Top-Siders. "How is that all possible?" I ask in a voice that practically croaks.

"Good morning to you too," she says with a grin. Then she reaches into her bag, withdraws a packet of something powdered, and tosses it over to me. By some miracle, I manage to catch it. It's strawberry flavored. "Mix it with twelve ounces of water," she tells me. "It'll give you triple the hydration. You'll be fine in no time."

Just then, Liv's bedroom door opens. My roommate stumbles out, minus her fuzzy slippers, in a mismatched ensemble of SpongeBob SquarePants pajama bottoms and a Scooby-Doo shirt. She has the imprint of sheet wrinkles on her left cheek, and both her ponytail and her glasses are lopsided. She looks exactly how I feel.

Liv catches sight of Heather, then reels back, covering her eyes like she just stared directly at the sun and burned her retinas. "Ugh! How is that possible?"

Heather laughs and digs out a second packet. "I have one for her too," she says, tossing it to me.

This time, I fumble the catch a little. Lemonade flavored.

"I need to get to work," says Heather.

As she gathers her stuff to leave, I send up a silent prayer of thanks that I'm not on the schedule at Pete's tonight.

"Let me know how everything shakes out with Nick," adds Heather. "Okay?"

Nick. Right.

As we say our goodbyes and the front door shuts behind my friend, I remember everything Jenn told me yesterday. I recall talking it all round and round with my besties although, I admit, there are a few fuzzy patches in my memory. But I know for sure that Heather at least stopped me before I got into it with Nick over a tipsy text.

Then I remember my friend's tipsy text.

"Uh-oh," I mutter.

I give Heather's parting gifts to Liv. "Here," I say. "Mix these up for us."

I go off and hunt around for my mobile. Eventually I find it out on the balcony, along with three empty wineglasses, too many empty wine bottles, and the leftover food that's quickly becoming ant fodder.

Making a mental note to clean up, I check my text messages. After Heather's short and not-so-sweet text back to Nick, there are no additional messages from him. I'm not sure if that's good or bad.

But before I can ponder that too much, I see that I have another text message, received earlier this morning. It's from a contact I hear from so infrequently that it takes me a moment to truly comprehend the identity of the sender.

I read the words. Then, just to be sure, I read them again. And again.

A little dazed, I head back into the apartment. I cross over to the kitchen, where Liv is busy at the sink.

"I got a text from my agent," I say in a voice that reflects the amazement I feel. "I have an audition for the new ADA role on *Robbery-Homicide Division* tomorrow."

Liv looks at me, and her bloodshot eyes brighten. A slow smile spreads across her face. She lifts up two tall glasses filled with pastel-colored liquid—one pink, one yellow—the product of Heather's hydration powders.

"It's not exactly champagne," says Liv.

"Not a problem," I say, taking the pink one. "I don't think I'm ever drinking alcohol again anyway."

"Then you will be absolutely no fun to watch when you accept your Golden Globe for Best Television Actress in a Drama Series on *Robbery-Homicide*." Liv clinks her glass against mine and broadens her grin. "Salud!"

CHAPTER
21

Between my good news and Heather's electrolyte-packed hangover cure, I start to feel much better. To shake off the last of the after-effects of girls' night, I decide to go for a run. But this time, when I arrive at the beach path, I hang a decisive right, toward Santa Monica, to avoid the Muscle Beach gym area. I want to be at 100 percent before I chance another encounter with Jenn.

Afterward, I shower and dress so I can swing by my agent's Beverly Hills office. Once again, for confidentiality reasons, I need to go in to sign a nondisclosure agreement and pick up my audition sides. *My audition sides for a series regular! A series freaking regular!*

The Rebecca Sloane Agency isn't physically big, just a small outer office with Rebecca's office behind it. But the framed movie posters on the walls—a mix of major studio blockbusters and critically acclaimed indies, all starring Rebecca's clients—speak to the agency's real size. Honestly, I'm lucky to have scored representation here.

Rebecca's door is closed, I see. No telling if she's in or not. But both assistant desks are manned. I walk over to the smaller one on the left.

"Hi, Kevin," I say, in person for a change. "I think you have something for me. Carrie Adams," I add, just in case he doesn't connect the dots.

"Hold, please," he says, which seems more than a little strange, considering I'm standing right here in front of him. But then I understand that he's talking into his headset. And I'll admit, it's a small comfort to learn that I'm not the only one he keeps waiting.

After putting the call on hold, Kevin finds an envelope with my name on it as well as a clipboard with a standard NDA clipped to it. "Here you—" He hesitates as his keen gaze finally takes me in. "—*go?*"

Crap, I think as I hear the confusion in his tone and see it in his eyes—and no wonder! When I visited the office about a week ago, my body looked decidedly different. It's only now that I realize I dressed carelessly after my shower, in cropped leggings and a tank, without any thought to camouflaging my newly acquired slayer physique. And now it's on full display for my agent's assistant.

So stupid of me.

Kevin has Rebecca's ear all day long. Even an offhand word from him about my bigger build could mean dire consequences for me.

So before he has a chance to give voice to the questions that are obviously running around in his head, I snatch everything out of his grasp. "Thanks," I say, quickly tucking the envelope under my arm and scribbling my signature on the NDA. "I know you're busy, so I'll get out of your way. Wish me luck!"

I make a hasty escape, and I can only hope that Kevin doesn't feel compelled to share any of his observations about me and my changed appearance with his boss.

· · · · ·

I force myself to wait until I get home to pull out the sides and read through them. Looks like I'll be reading for the role of ADA Cassidy Carmichael. After a quick first scan of the pages, I see that there are two scenes: one is set in a restaurant, where Carmichael is having lunch with the DA; the other is a courtroom scene, where she delivers a closing argument to the jury.

As I go back and read the content more closely, I feel a little thrill ripple through my body. Unable to contain my excitement, I have to get up and pace. I swear, it's like this role was written for me, like the writers on this show somehow peered into my soul and penned my personal truth as an episode of a procedural crime drama.

I have to land this part. I just *have* to.

· · · · ·

I spend the afternoon preparing for tomorrow's audition, and overall, I'm feeling pretty darn good. Except the closer it gets to sundown, the less I'm able to concentrate. Thoughts of Nick keep invading my brain.

If a slayer falls in love with a vampire, the slayer loses their power.

I need to talk to him about this. I know I do. I need to gather up some of my newfound strength, tell him what I've learned, and see what he has to say about it.

The problem is, if it turns out Nick really has just been leading me on, it will straight-up break my heart. And even worse? If it turns out his feelings are genuine and I tell him about my doubts, I could end up breaking his.

Seems like a real lose-lose to me.

So I'm scared. I'm scared of rocking the boat. I'm scared of learning the truth. I'm scared of losing what I have—or what I think I have— with Nick.

And it's not just that. I'm also scared that if I lose Nick, it'll get into my head and screw with my brain and make me tank the audition tomorrow. Then on top of losing him, I'll lose this amazing opportunity too.

So would it really be so terrible to push this conversation with him off for just one more day? Just twenty-four measly little hours?

I mean, Nick and I don't work on Mondays. And although we've agreed to nightly training sessions, we didn't make specific plans to see each other this evening. It's not as if I'd be canceling on him or anything.

And he had band practice last night. He should certainly understand if I want to take tonight off to practice my lines.

I wish I could talk this all through with Liv or Heather, but Liv's phone is going straight to voicemail. She probably had to turn it off because she's on set and they're filming. Heather isn't answering either.

I stare at my phone for a while, silently weighing my options as the daylight disappears and the room gradually goes dark all around me. Then, still not sure what I'm going to do, I text a tentative greeting to Nick.

Hey 😃

Then I wait. And wait. And wait some more. Maybe he's not awake yet? Or he hasn't checked his phone? Or—

Just then, the three little dots appear. Nick is typing. Stops typing. Types some more. I hold my breath, waiting for the message to—

Hey.

That's it? That's all I get? After all that three-little-dot action? Okay, I guess it's my turn. I type and hit Send.

> Good news. I have an audition
> tomorrow 🙌

I wait again, watching those three little dots. Did whoever created the little dots think they were doing us all a favor by letting us know that someone was in the process of messaging us? Or did they actually have a real sadistic side, knowing full well that the dots would become a prime source of emotional torture?

The dots disappear. Then—

> That's great.

No emojis, I notice. Last night, it was all hearts and smiley faces. But tonight? Nothing.

My index finger hovers above the keyboard on my touchscreen as I try to decide what to text next. I type, delete. Type some more. Delete that too. Now I wonder if Nick is watching the dots. I wonder what he's thinking. More than that, I wonder what he really thinks about me.

So I decide to ask him.

Tomorrow.

> Need to prepare. See you Tuesday?

The response comes almost immediately. He uses my words—or Heather's words, really—from last night.

> K. Later.

It's not the first time that one of us has jokingly echoed back what the other has said. Only this time, I can't tell if it's supposed to be funny or...*not*.

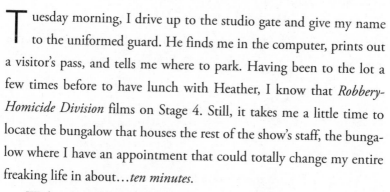

CHAPTER
22

Tuesday morning, I drive up to the studio gate and give my name to the uniformed guard. He finds me in the computer, prints out a visitor's pass, and tells me where to park. Having been to the lot a few times before to have lunch with Heather, I know that *Robbery-Homicide Division* films on Stage 4. Still, it takes me a little time to locate the bungalow that houses the rest of the show's staff, the bungalow where I have an appointment that could totally change my entire freaking life in about...*ten minutes*.

With a deep breath, I pull open the door to Bungalow 11 and step up to the front desk. "Hi," I say to the receptionist. "I'm here for the audition. Carrie Adams."

She looks up at me and smiles warmly. "Hi, Carrie, I'm Angela. Welcome."

I look around for the sign-in sheet, but I don't see one. "Uh, where do I sign in?" I ask.

Angela shakes her head. "No need," she says. "You can just have a seat, and I'll let them know you're here. Can I get you anything in the meantime? Water? Coffee?"

At first, I can't even respond. As an actor, I've gotten so used to being treated like a commodity, a type—barely a person at all—that her simple offer of hospitality is a little disconcerting.

After a moment, though, I manage to find my voice again. "No, thanks," I say. "I–I'm good."

She directs me around the corner to a waiting room—not a makeshift arrangement of folding chairs set up in a hallway but an actual permanent grouping of big leather chairs and sofas. I start to step across the threshold, but then I stop short. I blink. Look around. Blink again. There's no one else sitting here. No one else waiting to read. No doppelgängers. Not a single mini me in sight.

Well, this is a switch, I think.

I walk over to one of the chairs and sit, and I have to say, it's a little odd. With no one here to measure myself against, I don't know what to do. But then, gradually, I get my bearings. I use the time to find my center, to run my lines in my head, to remind myself that I've got this.

I've got this.

"Carrie?"

I look over to see a guy around my age in jeans and a gray Henley.

"Hi," he says. "I'm Rob." He extends his hand.

Getting to my feet, I shake it firmly. I can't help noting that this is the second person here who has introduced themselves to me by name.

"Do you need any water or anything before we go back?" Rob asks.

Again with the water?

"N-no," I say. "I'm all set. Thanks."

I follow him back to a large but comfortable office. There are more introductions. I meet the show's cocreators, a couple of the writer-producers, the director, and Josh Bateman, the TV veteran who plays DA Frank Fordham on the show. To tell the truth, it's all a bit overwhelming.

So when someone offers me water yet again, I accept. "I've never been to an audition where there was so much concern that I was getting my eight glasses a day," I say nervously.

They all laugh politely, and we actually chitchat a bit while I take a couple of swigs. My nerves start to ease up.

Then the director asks if I'm ready to get to it.

"Absolutely," I say, putting the water bottle aside.

"We'll start with the restaurant scene," says the director. "And Josh will read with you."

Josh Bateman will read with me?

The show's star gets up and stands next to me, pages in hand and ready to go.

That's when it hits me. This is the big leagues. The real deal. I'm not here to try out for some nameless character like Bartender or Nurse or Sports Fan #2. I'm auditioning to be a regular on a hit TV series.

You'd think that realization would make my anxiety spike. Only it doesn't. It actually helps to calm me down.

The fact that this isn't like any of the auditions I've had in the past is a good thing. It means these people aren't here to find out if I can perform on cue. Nope. They're here to find out if I can act, really *act*. And while I can't perform on cue very well, I actually *can* act. At least I think I can.

I also notice that there's no camcorder, and no one has asked me to do a 360-degree spin while they judge me from every freaking angle. This isn't about what I look like. This is about what I can do.

I'm still a little on edge, of course, but not in a debilitating way. Not in a way that will make me choke. Just the opposite. I feel like I can take this nervous energy and use it. I can channel it into my performance.

I can do this, I tell myself. *I can absolutely do this.*

The first scene is essentially a job interview, with Fordham feeling out Carmichael's qualifications to be an ADA—not too different from what's actually happening right here in this room. So I draw on all the feelings I'm experiencing right now, feelings of uneasiness and vulnerability but confidence and determination too. And since Carmichael's backstory isn't very far from my own, I dig into my extensive baggage as well. Maybe the cumulative trauma from my weekly family Zoom calls will turn out to be good for something after all.

"'Interior restaurant, day,'" reads the director. But he doesn't sound bored or detached. He sounds like he really cares, like he's really invested in what's happening here. "'Fordham sits at a table opposite a young woman, Cassidy Carmichael.'"

"Full disclosure," says Josh Bateman, only he's not Josh Bateman anymore. Before my eyes, he's somehow transformed into DA Frank Fordham. "I'm only meeting with you about the open ADA position because your father called me."

"You know my father?" I ask. Only I'm not me anymore either. Because Fordham isn't talking to me. He's talking to Carmichael.

"Our paths have crossed at a few bar association functions," he says. "And of course I know him by reputation. My team has lost more than a few cases to him. Your father is quite the defense attorney."

"Just so you know, I didn't ask him to recommend me."

"Oh, he didn't."

"Excuse me?"

"He didn't recommend you," says Josh as Fordham. "In fact, he called to ask me *not* to hire you."

I pause and take this in the way Carmichael would. She understands something about her father. The same thing I understand about mine. "He doesn't want me to get this job," I say. I'm in the perfect sweet spot for an actor, where I'm really not acting at all. "He wants me to join his firm."

"Excellent firm." Josh gives me his signature look, the one where he does that thing with his eyebrows that's pure Fordham. "And I'm betting they pay their associates a lot more than the DA's office."

"I'm sure that's true. But the world doesn't need another high-priced attorney to help criminals with deep pockets get away with murder. Literally."

"Then what does the world need?"

I take my time here. I think about what Carmichael wants to be in this world, obviously. But I also think about what I want to be, what I want to be to my own father and to everyone else in my life who wants to typecast me, pigeonhole me, force me into some kind of mold.

"Someone who's not afraid to stand up to them."

"'Fordham looks across the table at Carmichael for a beat, sizing her up,'" reads the director.

"Welcome to the DA's office, Ms. Carmichael."

The pleased reaction I express is Carmichael's, but it's mine too. Because for the first time ever, I feel like I really nailed an audition. *I freaking nailed it.*

To confirm this, something else happens. Something that's never happened before, not at any of those assembly-line casting sessions. The director gives Josh Bateman and me a few adjustments, and he asks us to do it again.

We take it one more time, from the top. Josh is an amazing scene partner, giving and taking and doing the work even though it's just an audition. When we finish the second run-through—which goes even better than the first—I let myself briefly fantasize what it would be like to do this every day.

Then it's time to move on to the courtroom scene.

"Ready?" asks the director.

It's a monologue, so I won't have a partner for this one. Josh is back in his seat, and it's all on me.

But I don't really feel like I'm alone. I look around, and for once, I feel like the whole audition room is rooting for me. The positive energy is palpable, and it energizes me.

Honestly? I've never felt more prepared for anything in my life.

I smile confidently. "Let's do it."

The director nods and starts to read. "'Interior courtroom, day. Carmichael approaches the jury box to deliver her closing argument.'"

"Good afternoon, ladies and gentlemen," I say, because I'm Carmichael addressing the jury.

I take a moment to focus. Then I launch into the scripted summation of a ripped-from-the-headlines case, pretty typical for the show.

"On January thirty-first of last year, the defendant, Gregory Porter, shot and killed Arthur Chen. This is not in dispute. Mr. Porter would like you to believe that he pulled the trigger in self-defense and that this was a justifiable homicide. However, the facts do not support this. Fact: Mr. Chen was unarmed. Fact: Mr. Chen was Asian. Fact: Mr. Porter was heard on more than one occasion spouting anti-Asian rhetoric and making blanket threats against the Asian community after losing his wife to a virus that originated in China."

I pause again. Because now, while I'm still Carmichael addressing the jury, I'm also me, addressing my inner slayer. And what's at the heart of this case isn't just something ripped from the headlines. It hits on a topic that feels extremely personal.

"And so," I say, "this was a killing motivated not by self-defense but by hatred, plain and simple. And that makes it not just a crime but the worst kind of crime. A hate crime." The passion of my delivery intensifies. "Hate—blind hate against someone simply because they belong to a particular community—is never justifiable." I stop, letting that idea land—not just with the room but with my alter ego too. I wait until I'm convinced that everyone—*everyone*—has heard me. "And that is why you *must* find Gregory Porter guilty of murder with special circumstances."

As I complete the scene, I feel a surge of power shoot through me, but I don't feel the need to squelch it. Because this power doesn't belong to my slayer. It's mine and mine alone.

· · · · ·

"So?" asks Heather through a mouthful of pins. She's working on altering a jacket on a dress form. "How did it go?"

She told me to come by when I was done with my audition, so here I am in the wardrobe department—although "department" is a bit of an overstatement. It's more of an oversize closet in a sectioned-off part of the stage, packed with racks upon racks of clothing, all labeled by character name.

"It was good, I think. Really good."

Heather takes the pins out of her mouth, puts her hands on her hips, and gives me a quick once-over. "Well, you look good," she proclaims.

I fidget a little with my sleeve. I opted for the same ensemble I wore to the J.Lo movie tryout: black leggings, black sweater, black suede booties. "You think? I'm wondering if maybe this should be my new go-to audition outfit."

Heather shakes her head. "No—I mean, sure. Yes. That's a good idea. It's a good look for you. But I'm not talking about the clothes. I'm talking about you." She smiles. "*You* look good. It's like, I don't know…you've got a glow."

"A glow?" I frown, trying to figure out what my slayer might be up to now. "Like a fiery glow? A radioactive glow?"

Heather laughs. "No. Like an I'm-at-the-top-of-my-fucking-game-and-I-know-it glow."

I relax, smiling. "It really did go well," I say. "I actually think I have a shot."

"Maybe we'll be working together again," says Heather.

"Shh!" I say. "Don't jinx it."

Heather eyes me with amusement. "Since when are you so superstitious?"

"Uh, I'm a freaking vampire slayer, remember?" I say. "If that's possible, I figure pretty much anything is."

"Fair point." Heather grabs a stool and motions for me to take a chair. "Speaking of… How's the other drama going? Did you talk to Nick?"

And just like that, I can feel whatever kind of a glow I've got going right now start to dim. "Not yet."

"Not yet?"

"Since you sent that text to Nick, things have been a little awkward," I say.

"Text?" asks Heather. She looks confused. "What text?"

At first, I think she might be joking, but from her expression, it's clear that she doesn't remember texting Nick from my phone. Not surprising. I mean, we were all pretty wasted that night.

I'm about to fill in the details, but I think better of it. After all, she was just trying to help. No reason to make her feel bad. And besides, this isn't her problem to deal with. It's mine.

"Never mind," I tell her with a shake of my head. "I know I need to talk to Nick. But I didn't want to do it last night. I was afraid it might not go well, and I just didn't want it messing with my head right before this audition."

"Okay," says Heather, nodding. "Okay, I can see that."

"But the audition's over now," I say. "And we're both working tonight. So…"

"So you'll talk to him tonight," says Heather. "And you'll figure it all out."

Right, I think. *Right.*

I just need to figure out how to ask my vampire boyfriend if he's really my vampire boyfriend or just my fake vampire boyfriend trying to strip me of my power to slay him.

Piece of cake.

CHAPTER

23

With hours of daylight to kill before my Tuesday-night shift at Pete's, I figure I'll go running. As usual, I do my stretches on the path first. Leaning into a lunge, I stare out over the familiar beach, what I've come to think of as *our* beach—Nick's and mine—although it looks different when it's not veiled in darkness.

Now, in the stark light of day, I think about everything that's passed between Nick and me over the last few nights. The talks, that first kiss, even the disagreements. It all felt so true to me. Is it possible that the curtain of night helped conceal Nick's deception? Is it possible that he was just acting all along? Is it possible that he's a better freaking actor than I am?

I try to shake off these doubts as I shake out my limbs to start my run. Then I take a deep breath and—

"I was hoping I'd run into you again," says someone coming up behind me.

As I recognize the voice, my body tenses and my shoulders hunch all the way up to my ears. So much for my warm-up.

Jenn. Or as Heather has dubbed her, the serial slayer.

I want to run away. Except I know she can run just as fast as I can.

Probably faster. Besides, this isn't something that I *can* run away from. I need to deal with her.

I try to keep my voice nonchalant as I turn to face her. "Jenn," I say. "Hi."

"How's it going?" she asks.

"Uh, pretty good," I say. "I might have a new job. I had a meeting this morning that went really well, so—"

"What about your slayer job?" she asks, interrupting my admittedly weak attempt at casual conversation. "How's *that* going?"

Crap.

I shift my weight from one running shoe to the other, trying to form a reply.

"You know, my offer still stands," she says, saving me the trouble of responding.

"What offer?" I ask.

"I can be your trainer," she says. "I can train you to kill your vampire."

Double crap.

"I can help you hone your skills and build your confidence," she continues, like she's selling herself as a life coach. "And then if you're still unsure, I can be your wingwoman. We can join forces and kill the bloodsucker together."

Okay, so not exactly a *life* coach. More of a *death* coach.

Triple crap.

No matter how things shake out between Nick and me, he certainly doesn't deserve a death sentence. I need to protect him from Jenn, and the only way I can see to do that is to protect Jenn from herself—or rather from her slayer self.

"Maybe I can help you get control over your impulses instead," I tell her. "Then nobody has to get hurt."

Jenn fixes me with her icy blue gaze, scrutinizing me. I brace for her to counter with another pitch for this one-on-one slayer boot camp of hers, where we become some kind of a deadly dynamic duo, like the Batman and Robin of vampire killing.

But then her hard stare softens, becoming more pensive.

"He broke your heart," she says quietly. "Didn't he?"

"Wh-what?" The question is so unexpected—and so unexpected from *her* especially—that I barely get the syllable out.

"Your vampire," she says. "Did he break your heart?"

"No, he didn't break my heart," I say a little defensively. I hold out my arms, displaying my spandex-clad body in full. "I mean, obviously not. I've still got my muscles, don't I? I've still got my power. It's not like he tricked me into falling in love with him just to take my slayer away."

Jenn shakes her head. "I don't mean now," she says. "I mean *before*."

Before?

I just stare at her in confusion.

She nods, mistaking my silence for confirmation. "I thought so," she says. "I thought we might be alike."

She takes a seat on the concrete bench at the edge of the path, and something happens. Jenn somehow appears smaller. It's not that her powerful physique changes. She's still just as ripped as ever. Only, I don't know… It's as if some of the boldness and bluster has drained out of her.

She motions for me to sit next to her. After a brief hesitation, I do.

"You asked me about my life before all this," she says. There's a look in her eyes—the same one I glimpsed the other day—but this time, it sticks around long enough for me to read it properly. It's regret, for sure. Sadness too, and…yes, heartbreak. These aren't sentiments I would normally wish on anyone. But in this case, since the alternative is murderous rage, I'll take it.

I nod, encouraging her to go on.

"Tom was my boyfriend," she says. "My *human* boyfriend. We were together for almost five years. We even talked about marriage and kids. I loved him, and I thought he loved me. But then he met *her*," she continues, anger building. "Fiona. One of *them*." Contempt creeps back into her tone, and rage starts to eclipse the more conflicted look in her eyes.

"Fiona was a vampire?"

"And Tom left me for her," says Jenn. "He left me for that blood-drinking bitch, and I seriously wanted to die."

My mind circles back to where this conversation started, and I make the connection. "He broke your heart."

"And I hated him for it," she tells me. "I *hated* him for hurting me so badly."

Oh. Ohhh.

All at once, I can see exactly where this story is going. "Fiona changed Tom?" I ask, although it's not really a question. "She made him a vampire."

Jenn nods. "And because I hated him so much, I became his slayer."

I feel a wave of empathy for the woman. I mean, I get where she's coming from. Like me, she was at odds with someone, and we were both unwittingly impacted by a choice that they—and they alone—made.

"I'm so sorry," I say, and I am. "But, Jenn, people get dumped. It sucks, but it happens. So you eat too much chocolate and drink too many margaritas. You binge a bunch of sappy rom-coms on the Hallmark Channel and have a good cry. You go on a shopping spree. You have rebound sex. And then you move on." I look at her. "You don't have to let Tom's betrayal dictate what you do with the rest of your life."

"After Tom's betrayal, I didn't have a life," she says. "I didn't have anything. At least being a slayer gives me a purpose."

Okay, maybe she's not just some motiveless villain. Or at least she didn't start out like that. As an actor, if I had to play her, I could certainly figure out how to connect with the role. I could find a way to justify her point of view, her actions. Still, that doesn't make them justifiable. She embraced her slayer, but I will never stop fighting mine.

Now, if I can just get her to start fighting hers.

"What purpose?" I demand. "Slaying innocent vampires?"

"*Innocent?*" Jenn sits up taller and stares back at me, and goddammit, everything about her is back to pure slayer. "You have no idea what they're really like, do you?"

"I know they're not all bad," I say, not giving up.

She narrows her gaze. "Is that your opinion?" she asks. "Or *theirs*?"

"What?"

"Did you know they can get into people's minds and influence their emotions?"

"*What?*"

"I'm pretty sure Fiona bewitched Tom," says Jenn. "That's why he left me."

Once again, I'm completely blindsided by this slayer.

"That's why they all need to be stopped," she adds.

I should argue that point. I know I should. But, at least for now, my campaign to turn her away from the dark side is derailed. I need to sit with this new information and think it through.

I already know something about vampire powers. Nick told me about his amped-up sense of smell and hearing and such. And I've seen his supernatural speed for myself, or I should say he moved so lightning-fast that my eyes couldn't keep up. But does he have other abilities? Other supernatural talents that he hasn't shared with me?

And if he does have the power to unnaturally influence emotions…

Has he been trying to influence mine?

No, that can't be right. Surely I know my own freaking feelings.

Don't I?

Suddenly, I picture Nick flirting with the customers, and I think about how he's always been able to charm everyone. Everyone except me.

But since he's become a vampire, it's like I've fallen under his spell too.

Oh my God! Am I literally under a spell? I wonder. *A spell to make me fall in love and lose my power?*

I mean, is vampire mind manipulation an actual thing? Has Nick been exerting some kind of magical influence over me, affecting how I feel about him? Is that why, in such a short span of time, he's gone from a guy I pretty much hated to a vampire I kind of—

Nope. I can't go there right now. I'm way too confused.

Jenn is watching me, clearly reading my thought process. Her mouth curves up in a small smile of satisfaction. "If I were you," she says, "instead of trying to control your urge to slay, I'd make sure your vampire isn't trying to control you."

· · · · ·

"So vampires are like Jedi knights?" asks Liv, her voice streaming out of my Bluetooth speaker as I drive my Prius along Melrose. She called to see how my audition went, but we quickly started discussing other things. "They know how to use mind control tricks?"

"I don't know," I say, and as I say it, I'm supremely frustrated. "I don't know" seems to be my answer to way too many questions these days, and I'm getting pretty damn sick of it. "That's what Jenn said anyway."

"Jenn the serial slayer?" asks Liv.

I let out a sigh. "She's extreme, for sure," I say. "But the story about her ex seemed real. And she clearly believes the mind control stuff. I don't think she's an actual liar."

"What about Nick?" asks Liv. "Is he a liar?"

I don't think so. But then again…

"I don't know," I say.

Uggghhh!

"Well, in *Bar Wars*," says Liv, "the slayer character would definitely give the vampire character the benefit of the doubt and not just believe everything Darth Slayer says. So maybe cut Nick a little slack when you see him, huh?"

I'm coming up on Pete's, so I start to look for a parking space. "I'll try," I tell her.

"Do. Or do not," says Liv in a froggy-sounding voice. "There is no try."

I smile. "Thanks, Yoda," I say. "I'll let you know what happens."

CHAPTER
24

I walk into Pete's and spy Nick behind the bar, and my heart freaking stops. In the two days since we've seen each other, I've let a whole lot of suspicions and misgivings get into my head. But in the process, I forgot something. I forgot *this*. The dizzy-in-my-head, lump-in-my-throat, ache-in-my-chest, fluttering-in-my-gut kind of feeling at just the sight of him.

They say that absence makes the heart grow fonder, but now I'm thinking it might also make the brain grow a little more impressionable. A tad more persuadable. I'm not going to say dumber, but at the moment, I'm not ruling it out either.

Oh, I'm not dismissing my questions. I still have them, and the two of us definitely need to talk. I've got to ask Nick what he knows about vampire mind tricks and whether a vampire-slayer love connection really negates a slayer's power. But we can discuss all that calmly. And Liv's right. Of course she's right. I should absolutely give Nick the benefit of the doubt.

Just then, he looks over at me, his gaze meets mine, and he…barely nods at me.

What?

And he just goes back to wiping down the bar counter.

What?!

Okay, what in the actual hell is going on here?

Admittedly, I would have put the big fat kibosh on any over-the-top PDA hanky-panky nonsense in our workplace. But since when does Nick give a crap about that? And since when is he so conscientious about cleaning the damn countertop?

I stomp through the bar, past the sparse Tuesday evening crowd, out to the back room to clock in. As I stash my belongings, I try to settle down and think about things from Nick's point of view. I mean, after the lukewarm texts that followed our steamy night of passion together, maybe he's just playing it cool?

Except the more I think about it, the more my anger rises. Not slayer anger. *My* anger. Because *come on.* Is this seriously the way you treat your new girlfriend the first time you see her after you've had slightly kinky, potentially lethal, knock-your-socks-off sex?

Nope. It definitely is *not.*

Which kind of begs a question.

Is what's been happening between Nick and me really real? I wonder. *Or just some kind of a vampire power play to take away my power?*

· · · · ·

By the time I get settled in my usual spot behind the bar, I want to scream at Nick. I want to smack that neutral and detached expression right off his stupid face. It's all I can do not to make a big scene in front of the customers.

Not that the customers would even notice. At this point, we have exactly three, and they're all otherwise occupied. My regular Tuesday-night drunk is only interested in his Johnnie Walker Black, and the man and woman seated at a table are only interested in each other. I watch them stare lovingly into each other's eyes, not at all concerned that their seemingly heartfelt feelings might be nothing more than the product of vampire shenanigans.

Irrationally, my anger intensifies.

I try to get a grip.

It's weird. Over the past week, I've gotten used to fighting against this kind of aggression from my slayer. But now my alter ego is totally quiet. There's not so much as a peep from her. All this emotion, all this rage, isn't coming from my supernatural side. It's coming from *me*.

Which makes it doubly weird. These kinds of negative feelings don't usually bubble straight up to the surface like this. Normally they're perfectly happy to stay buried, waiting for me to channel them into my acting.

"So how was your audition?" asks Nick. His tone, I note, is a little guarded. He's moved toward the cash register in the middle of the bar, but he's still staying squarely on his side of things.

Really? We're making small talk now?

My anger ratchets up another notch.

"Good," I say, determined to keep my head. I step toward the register too, but I stick to my side. "How was band practice?"

"Good," he says. "We worked on a new cover song to open the show."

"Good," I say. "So you're ready for tomorrow night?"

"I think so," he says. "What about you? Are *you* ready for tomorrow night?"

I look at him sharply. "What's that supposed to mean?"

He looks back at me a little funny. "You know what it means."

Okay. That's it. I'm done with the small talk.

"No," I say. "Actually I *don't* know what it means. Because I don't have the magical ability to get inside another person's head." I narrow my eyes and fix him with a hard stare. "Do you?"

Not the calm discussion I was hoping for, but there it is.

Suddenly, Nick's posture shifts. He lifts his arm, drags his hand through his shaggy black hair, and peers at me kind of sheepishly. And just like that, I *know*. I know it's true.

"Carrie," Nick begins.

"Oh my God," I interject, wide-eyed. "You do. You do have the magical ability to get inside another person's head."

I feel sick. Absolutely sick. All this time, while Nick was claiming to help me control my slayer, was he really controlling me?

He glances around a little nervously at the patrons. Then he steps closer and lowers his voice. "It's called influence."

"*Influence?*"

He nods. "It's a kind of, I don't know…vampire hypnosis, I guess."

"*Vampire hypnosis?*" I say, floored. "And you didn't think to mention this to me before?"

"I didn't mention it before because it's not relevant," he says.

"*Not relevant?*" I demand. I'm using all my willpower to keep my voice at an indoor level. "How can you think it's not relevant?"

"Because I've never used it," says Nick. "I would never use it. And I'd certainly never use it on you."

I frown, thinking about this. It's true, Nick has never exactly struck me as the control freak type. Actually, of the two of us, I guess I'm the one who best fits that bill.

Only things are different now. He's a vampire, and I'm his slayer.

"But how can I be sure?" I ask. "How do I know you're not using this *influence* on me right now?"

"Because you know me," Nick says. "You know I would never want to take away your free will. The other night, didn't I tell you that you were the one in charge?"

The other night?

Nick levels a dark, meaningful gaze at me, and my head floods with memories of our intimate time together. I see myself restrained but not powerless.

Because Nick gave all the power to me.

Crap.

My anger doesn't disappear, but it definitely comes down a few degrees. My brain feels a little scrambled, only I don't think it's because of any metaphysical mind manipulation.

"Okay," I say. "Maybe you're not playing supernatural head games with me. Still, you should have told me."

"Noted."

"Is there anything else?" I ask.

"What?"

"Is there anything else you know about vampires and slayers that you haven't told me?"

"I don't know," he says with a shrug and a shake of his head.

I stare at him, unconvinced.

"Okay, well," he stammers, "I'm…uh…strong."

At that, my eyes involuntarily drift down to his broad chest, to the long, muscular arms extending out of the short sleeves of his black band tee. It's Led Zeppelin tonight, although I'm not really thinking about the T-shirt. Now that Nick's brought up the topic of the other night, I can't help recalling the way he looked without his shirt, the way he gazed down at me, the way—

Nope. Can't go there. I need to get answers.

"Strong?" I ask, dragging my eyes back up to meet his. "What do you mean, strong?"

"Like, really strong," he says. "Superstrong? It's kind of like the speed."

I really shouldn't have all these images flashing through my brain, all these snapshots of him using this superstrength of his. Naked.

I remind myself that I'm still angry. And goddammit, I have every right to be. After all, Nick has been keeping something from me. Maybe he didn't use vampire influence on me, but he didn't tell me about it either.

And if he's been keeping that from me? Maybe he's been keeping other stuff from me too.

If a slayer falls in love with a vampire, the slayer loses their power.

Does he know this? And worse, has he been using it as a secret plot against me?

Is our budding romance not really a romance at all? Instead of *wooing* me, has he been trying to eliminate my slayer? Has he just been toying with my emotions as a way to keep himself and his vampire bandmates safe?

I need to know.

So I have to be superstrong too.

With my anger back on the boil, I take a deep breath. But before I can ask the question, an all-too-familiar slurring male voice calls out, "Hey, sweetheart! I'm ready for another round down here."

And boy, did that asshole just pick the wrooong time to disrespect me.

"I'm not your freaking sweetheart," I say as I march down the bar and unleash on my regular. "I'm your bartender," I tell him. "Or I was. I've had enough, and so have you. You're officially cut off." Then, to his astonishment, I snatch his glass away and go to the register to close out his tab.

While I'm ringing the guy up, I see Nick out of the corner of my eye. He's retreated all the way down to the other end of the bar, and he's watching me curiously.

I blow out a frustrated breath. Goddammit, I still don't know for sure if I'm *his* sweetheart.

· · · · ·

For the next hour or so, there's a slow but steady trickle of customers, and the place becomes just busy enough to prevent Nick and me from continuing our conversation. But finally we're left with only a handful of patrons, and no one seems to need anything. I make my way toward the center of the bar, and after a brief hesitation, Nick joins me.

"So what else?" I ask across the register. "What else haven't you told me?"

Nick narrows his dark eyes at me. "Where's all this coming from?" he asks. "Is there something that *you* aren't telling *me*?" Now that he's had a little time to think about my earlier interrogation, he sounds almost wounded.

Crap.

While I try to figure out what to say next, the door to Pete's opens, and a couple of new customers stroll in.

Double crap.

A middle-aged man and woman, dressed casually but tastefully and *very* expensively, approach my side of the bar.

I blink a couple of times. I must be imagining things, because the two of them look exactly like—

"Surprise!" they say in unison.

My parents.

Crap to the power of infinity.

"M-Mom?" I stammer. "Dad? What are you doing here?"

"There's a bar association conference in Los Angeles this week," explains my mother. "We weren't going to attend, but at the last minute, we thought, well, why not? Then we can see Carrie."

"Oh. Well…uh…" I'm totally at a loss here. "Can I get you a drink?"

"No time," says my father. "We have a dinner reservation up the street in fifteen minutes."

"Right. You should go. You don't want to be late." I start to relax a little. At least I'll have some time to compose myself and prepare while they're eating. "See you later?"

"We have a reservation for three," says my mother.

"Teri's with you?" I ask. I look around. "Where is she?"

"Of course Teri's not with us," says my mother. "She's at Harvard. Working on the law review. It'll just be the three of us."

It takes me a moment to grasp her meaning. "I–I can't have dinner with you right now," I say. "I'm working."

"Looks like you're just standing around," says my father.

"Well…"

"Surely," says Mom with a glance over at Nick, "your *friend* here can cover for the rest of the night."

And something about the way she says "friend" makes my spine go rigid. There's a scorn in her tone that reminds me of Jenn when she talks about vampires.

"I mean," she adds, looking around at the sparsely filled room, "it doesn't look as if it would be all that much work." And with that one offhand remark, my mother has somehow managed to belittle Nick, my place of employment, and me all at the same time.

"I'd be happy to cover," says Nick, stepping in.

"There!" says my mother. "See?"

I turn to Nick. "Uh…"

"Carrie," says my father, looking down at his designer watch. "We need to go." As if he and my mother haven't just sprung this on me. As if we've had plans all along and we're going to be late and it's all my freaking fault.

Uggghhh!

"It's okay. I'll see you tomorrow night," says Nick. As if there aren't still all these unanswered questions between us. As if tomorrow night is just another Wednesday night and not the Wednesday night of his concert—the Wednesday night where I either control my slayer in front of his vampire buddies or potentially die trying.

"Carrie," repeats my father.

Once again, the anger I feel is all mine.

Reining it in as best I can, I go in the back to retrieve my stuff and clock out.

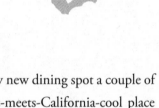

T urns out our reservation is at a trendy new dining spot a couple of
blocks up Melrose, an Italian-rustic-meets-California-cool place
that grows their own vegetables in the adjacent lot. My father has us
practically jogging to get there on time.

"I'm pretty sure they'll hold the table for at least fifteen minutes,"
I say.

Dad gives me one of his classic withering looks, total judgment in
his eyes. "Oh, is that how you do things in the service industry?" he asks.

I don't bother answering. I just roll my eyes and pick up my pace.

A few minutes later, we're seated at a table in a spacious room that's
all blond wood with black and white accents. And I have to admit, the
place smells absolutely delicious. The air is fragrant with garlic and
tomato and just-picked herbs. Our table even has a view of the open
kitchen, so we can see the staff making pasta from scratch. Dinner and
a show, I guess.

We order and our drinks arrive. Wine for my parents, just water
for me. My mother takes a sip of her chianti, then leans back in her
chair and aims a serious gaze across the table at me. "Sweetheart," she
says, "this isn't just a dinner. This is an intervention."

I almost burst out laughing. Not that interventions are a joke. They're actually quite serious business, I know, and in some cases, they can even be lifesaving. But in my case? Recent girls' night aside, I don't generally overimbibe. And do my folks really not see the perverse irony of conducting a supposed intervention while drinking alcohol themselves?

The two of them just continue to peer at me, somber and unsmiling. So I take the hint and keep my amusement to myself. I disguise my rising laugh with a cough and take a sip of water.

"Excuse me?" I ask.

"We're not just in town for a bar association conference," says my father. "We're here to see you, to conduct an intervention."

I'm flummoxed, to say the least. "I don't understand," I say, looking from one of them to the other. "I don't have a problem with alcohol."

"This isn't about a problem with alcohol," says my mother. "This is about a problem with your life choices."

Aaand there it is.

In retrospect, I should have seen this coming. After all, I'm not doing what they want me to do. I'm not pursuing the life they envision for me, and in over two years of weekly Zoom chats, they haven't been able to convince me to change my course. So now here they are, live and in-person, trying to disguise their controlling ways with this sick, twisted version of what's usually a selfless act of love and concern for someone's well-being.

Deep inside, my anger starts to simmer.

"No," I say evenly. "This is about *your* problem with my life choices."

"Can you blame us for having a problem?" asks my mother. "When we sent you to all the best schools in hopes that you'd join the bar, we certainly didn't mean Pete's. According to Jonathan—"

"Wait, what?" I interrupt. "Are you kidding me?" My anger levels up. Did Jonathan go back to Philadelphia and basically tattle on me to my mother? Is this his way of getting even with me for breaking things off with him? "So my whining, sniveling excuse for an ex-boyfriend went crying to you because I don't want to be with him?" I demand. "And now you're here taking his side?"

"This isn't about sides," says my mother. "We're all just very concerned about you, dear."

"Look at the evidence," interjects my father, shifting into lawyer mode. "You're barely scraping by, working a job that's far below your potential."

"I'm working a job that pays my bills and gives me enough flexibility to pursue an acting career," I counter.

"In over two years of trying," says my father, "you haven't booked a significant acting job."

"I just auditioned for a role on *Robbery-Homicide Division*," I shoot back. "A *lead* role. On a hit TV series. And it went really well."

My father blinks. He's not used to getting this kind of pushback. Not from me anyway.

"And what about this bartender person?" my mom chimes in.

"*Bartender person?*" I ask.

"I'm not advocating for Jonathan," she says. "If you don't want to be with Jonathan, fine. But do you really think that coworker of yours is an appropriate partner?"

My anger is like an express elevator shooting straight up to the penthouse.

Do I think Nick is an appropriate partner?

I certainly didn't at first, and now I have to wonder if that was partly because of my parents, because I let them get inside my head. I knew *they* wouldn't approve of him. And considering how hardwired I was to please them, maybe that's why *I* didn't approve of him. Maybe that's why, as Nick said, I was always on his case.

But the more I got to know Nick, the more I got to like him. The more I got to like *us*. And the more I could see the possibility of a real future for the two of us.

Except now, with all these questions between us...

"I don't know," I say, answering honestly. "But that's for me to decide. Not you."

"Are you using steroids?" asks my father.

For a moment, I just stare at him, speechless. "What?" I finally manage.

"Well, look at yourself," he says, gesturing across the table at me. I'm wearing another outfit that Heather put together to conceal my buff slayer bod, although it apparently hasn't fooled my dad's critical eye. Or did Jonathan go squealing to them about this as well?

"Sweetheart, your body didn't just change like this on its own," says my mother.

Oh no? I think. *That's how much you know.*

I have to bite the inside of my mouth to keep from saying it out loud.

"And steroid abuse can result in cognitive deterioration," adds my father. "It would explain all these poor decisions you've been making lately."

That's it. I've heard just about enough.

The server approaches with our food, but while the aroma of the pasta is mouthwatering, I simply don't have the appetite for any more of this BS. My anger is a burning fuse, ready to detonate. So before the guy can put the plates down on our table, I slide my chair back and get to my feet.

"I'm going to say this one more time," I say to my parents. "And I hope this time, you'll actually listen and hear me. I don't want to be a lawyer. I'm not going to law school. *Ever.* I only took the LSAT to make you happy. My whole life, I've only ever done what I thought would make you happy. But now I'm almost twenty-five years old. I'm an adult. And I need to do what makes *me* happy. So yes, right now, I'm working as a bartender. I'm sorry if you don't approve." I stop and consider what I just said. "You know what? I'm not sorry. I don't have anything to apologize for. I'm not robbing banks or stealing cars or running some shady internet scam. I'm tending bar while I try to get an acting career going. And okay, maybe that'll never happen. Maybe I'll be in the *service industry* for the rest of my life. But if I'm okay with that, then you have to be too. Because what I do with my life is *my* choice," I continue. "And who I date is *my* choice. And for the record, I'm not taking steroids. This isn't some kind of 'roid rage you're witnessing right now. This is just me finally—*finally*—being honest with you."

My parents are both looking at me, mouths agape, eyes practically popping out of their sockets. I don't think they could look any more surprised, not even if I whipped out my big flaming sword and took flight, crashing straight through the restaurant's skylight and disappearing into the Los Angeles night sky.

"Intervention's over," I tell them. "Enjoy your dinner."

As I walk toward the exit, the server—maybe an aspiring actor like me—catches my eye and gives me a discreet thumbs-up.

· · · · ·

I walk back down Melrose toward the bar. I feel strange, but at the same time, I also feel entirely like myself. Maybe that's what's so strange.

Usually I'm *not* entirely myself—especially not with my parents. But starting now, for better or worse, I'm done acting like the me that they want me to be. That's one role I really don't want to be playing. Not anymore.

As I get closer to Pete's, I entertain the idea of going back to work. Since I skipped out on dinner with my folks, there's still time to clock in again and finish out the rest of my shift. In retrospect, I do feel bad about ditching on Nick and leaving him to work the whole bar on his own, even if it is a slow night. Plus, maybe he and I could pick up our conversation where we left off.

I hesitate when I arrive at my car, still debating. Then, shoving my keys back in my pocket, I walk the last half block to the bar.

As I head for the door, I peer into Pete's front window, checking the crowd. If anything, it's even less busy than it was when my parents showed up to bully me into joining them for that outrageous sham of an intervention. Aside from a couple of occupied tables, there are only two people seated at the bar.

It's Heather. And *Quentin*.

So not two *people*. One person. One vampire.

Aaand cue my slayer.

My alter ego, quiet for most of the night, suddenly starts to stir. I become consumed with an overwhelming instinct to protect humans, only this time, it's different. It's stronger. Because now, it's *personal*.

What in the actual hell is going on in there? I wonder as I continue to watch the vampire with my friend through the glass.

Quentin must have expected me to be working tonight. I'm betting he came back to the bar to spy on me, to resume his quest to discover if I'm a slayer or not. After all, the last time he was here, his objective was interrupted. When I cut myself on that wineglass, he was forced to stop observing me and help Nick control his bloodlust. But since then, maybe he's started to wonder just how that glass broke in the first place, how an ordinary human woman could have shattered it with her bare hand.

What's not clear, though, is what Quentin is doing with Heather. Does the vampire know that she's my friend, my *good* friend? Is he trying to pump her for information about me? And to make her more forthcoming, is he perhaps using his *influence* on her?

I'm on the verge of seeing red as my hand wraps tightly around the door handle.

But I can't go in there like this. I'm already struggling with my slayer for control. If I put myself in the middle of all that vampire energy, I'll reveal what I am in a flash, and that'll be the end of that. And maybe the end of me.

But my slayer and I do agree on one thing: we need to make sure Heather is all right.

My eyes meet Nick's through the window.

We haven't exactly been connecting lately, but still, we've got a connection—partly supernatural but also partly *us*.

Jenn talked about the link between vampires and slayers as being *forged by hate but broken by love*. Assuming that's true, you'd think the further I got from hating Nick, the weaker that bond would get.

And I don't hate Nick. I don't. I'm not sure what I feel for him, but it's definitely not anything even close to hatred. Yet this connection between us seems to be more powerful than ever.

He's gotten through to my slayer before, usually by shouting. This time, though, he's able to pull me back from the brink with just a look. For a moment, I worry that this might be Nick using his vampire hypnosis on me. Logically, though, if I were under his influence, I probably wouldn't be worried about being under his influence, right? Besides, I don't feel like I'm being manipulated. As my slayer retreats, I once again feel entirely like myself.

And because I am entirely myself, I have to go in there. I have to make sure my friend is safe.

I decide to look at facing Quentin now as a way to test myself. It can be practice for tomorrow night at the Whisky. A kind of a dress rehearsal.

In the theater, there's a saying: *Bad dress rehearsal, good show.* Except I can't have a bad dress rehearsal. If I do, I might not even make it to the show.

With a deep breath, I strengthen my hold on my slayer and open the door.

CHAPTER
26

As I enter Pete's, the atmosphere is thick with vampire vibes.

Nick's eyes follow me as I walk up to the bar. "You're back?"

Since he saw me outside, struggling for control with my slayer, I know he's not just talking about my return from the restaurant.

"I am," I say with a firm nod.

"Carrie!" says Heather, smiling at me in greeting. "We were just talking about you."

My gaze darts from my friend to the vampire in the fringed suede jacket and multiple neck chains sitting cozily by her side. Does that mean that Quentin *has* been pumping Heather for info about me? And that Nick's just been standing around letting it happen?

My slayer starts to rise at that, but I immediately smack her down. Because honestly, I don't need her anger right now. I've got plenty of my own brewing. It's *my* rage that I need to rein in.

"You were talking about me?" I ask, trying to remain calm.

"Nick said you left to have dinner with your parents," says Heather. "I'm guessing there's a story there."

I digest this. Okay, so maybe things aren't quite as sinister here as I feared. But still…

"Nick also said he'd look after things here while I was gone," I say with an accusing stare at him.

"And that's exactly what I've been doing," he tells me evenly.

I glance at Heather, then train my gaze back on Nick. "Are you sure about that?" I ask pointedly.

"Everything's under control," he says. Then he turns to Quentin with a joking smile. "See?" he says, gesturing at me. "Didn't I tell you she's always on my case?"

I guess he's just trying to keep Quentin from noticing our subtext, but the jab annoys me all the same.

Cramming down my irritation, I try to play along. "Who's your friend, Nick?" I ask.

"Right," says Nick. "You haven't officially met my bandmate, Quentin." He turns to the vampire. "This is Carrie."

"*Enchanté*," says Quentin with a little bow at me.

"Pleasure."

I see the exact moment Heather puts it all together, when she realizes that she's sitting next to a vampire. One of the vampires bent on my destruction.

"The last time I was here, I saw you injure yourself," says Quentin easily. "I hope it wasn't serious?"

I shake my head. "It was just a cut," I say. "I'm fine."

"And everything's fine here," interjects Nick. "No need to stick around. Why don't you enjoy the night off?"

"What a good idea," says Heather, getting to her feet. "Let's go, Carrie."

"You're sure you won't stay, love?" asks Quentin, turning to Heather with disappointment. "Just for one *drink*?" The question is for my friend, although I'm almost positive that the way he says "drink" is meant to goad me, to see if it sparks any kind of a supernatural reaction. But as I said a few moments ago, I'm *fine*.

"Sorry," says Heather, hurrying over to my side. She grabs my arm and pulls me toward the door.

"Another time then," Quentin calls after us. It's an amiable enough invitation, but I can hear the underlying threat designed to poke my slayer. And my slayer hears it too.

But we're out of the bar now, on the sidewalk. And the farther Heather drags me away from Pete's, the more confident I feel.

"What the fuck is going on?" asks Heather when we're about a block away.

I hesitate, wondering where to even begin.

Then, deciding to start with the end, I smile. "I think I just had a really good dress rehearsal."

. . . . .

"But Heather's okay?" asks Liv. "Right?"

I nod. "She's Heather," I say. "Of course she's okay. She got the two of us out of there like a champ."

It's Wednesday morning, and Liv and I are seated at our kitchen island, clutching coffees while I give her the play-by-play of the previous night.

"You kept your slayer hidden in front of another vampire," says Liv. "That's huge."

"I guess," I say halfheartedly. "Except, with Quentin there, Nick and I didn't have a chance to finish our conversation."

Liv raises her brows. "Quentin was the only reason?"

"Yes," I say quickly. Although, given my track record of avoiding the tough stuff, I understand what she's getting at. "I fully intend to talk everything through with Nick. But there were too many interruptions last night. And since he can't do sunlight, I'll have to go another whole day without knowing where the two of us stand." I sigh. "And by tonight, it'll already be time for me to make *my* stand."

Talk about a problem wrapped in a difficulty inside a big freaking dilemma.

We're both quiet for a bit.

"Are you ready for that?" asks Liv, saying out loud what we're both obviously thinking. "Are you feeling ready for the concert at the Whisky tonight?"

It's not just a *concert*, and we both know it. It's my coming out party—or hopefully my *not* coming out party.

So am I feeling ready to keep my vampire slayer under wraps in a club full of vampires?

"Honestly? I think I am," I say. And I'm not just saying it to put my friend at ease. "Last night, as unsettled as things were between Nick and me, I really did feel like I had the upper hand on my slayer. And I did get through that trial run with his bandmate."

"And don't forget," says Liv, "you also stood up to your parents." She grins. "If you managed to do that, I'm betting you can do anything."

Reminded of the night's other face-off, I frown down into my hazelnut brew.

"Uh-oh," says Liv. "Did I say the wrong thing?"

I shake my head. "No, it's okay," I tell her. "It's just…with the vampires, if I can manage to get through tonight, it's done. You know? My problem with them should be basically over. But with my folks? I'm pretty sure last night was just round one. And now I have to wonder what their countermove is going to be."

"Countermove?"

"They're lawyers," I say. "They love a good fight, and they don't like to lose. So I don't think they're going to let this lie. What if they, I don't know…file a court motion to have me declared legally incapacitated? "

Liv laughs. "Oh please," she says. "If every actor-slash-bartender were deemed incapacitated, you couldn't get a drink anywhere in Los Angeles."

I smile. "True enough." But then my smile starts to fade. "But… do my folks maybe have a point?" I ask my roomie.

"What do you mean?"

"I mean being an actor in Hollywood is like being a drop of water in the Pacific. Or a grain of sand on Venice Beach," I say. "And with those odds…"

"Hey," says Liv. "Stop. You had a great audition yesterday. For a great role. Remember?"

With all the other drama going on, I've practically forgotten about the procedural crime drama. Was that audition really just *yesterday*?

"Have you heard anything?" asks Liv.

"Not yet," I say. "But I should probably call my agent this morning and check in."

My roomie gives me a look. "Probably?"

"I *should* call," I say, correcting myself. "I *will* call."

"Good girl," she says. She drinks the rest of her coffee. "I'll leave you to it." With a reassuring pat on my shoulder, she gets up, puts her mug in the sink, and walks over to the bathroom. At the door, she turns back. "You've got this, chica," she says with a wink before she closes herself inside.

As I find my phone, I hear Liv run the shower. I stare down at the touchscreen. I've got my agency's info pulled up on my contacts, but my thumb hovers tentatively over the Call icon.

Being hesitant about dialing my agent is nothing new for me. But this morning, it's...*different*. Usually when I check in after an audition, I'm expecting bad news. Mostly I'm just calling to confirm that it's a *no* and crossing my fingers that it's not a *no, and*. But this morning, for a refreshing change, I'm actually hopeful that it might be *good* news. So if it's not, the bad news will be that much more crushing.

But there are already way too many I-don't-knows in my life. And this, for better or worse, is at least something I can *know*.

I take a deep breath and press Call.

"The Rebecca Sloane Agency," says the assistant in his familiar businesslike tone.

"Good morning, Kevin," I say with all the positivity and confidence I can muster. "It's Carrie Adams. Is Rebecca available?"

"Hold, please."

Click.

I wait, bracing myself for his standard she's-not-available-I'll-tell-her-you-called response, already thinking about how to—

"Hello, Carrie."

For a moment, I'm too surprised to speak.

"Carrie? Are you there?"

"R-Rebecca?" I stammer, trying to get my head around the fact that my agent has actually accepted my call. "Y-yes. I'm here. Hi."

"You made quite an impression over there at Robbery-Homicide," she says.

"I–I did?" I barely squeak out.

"They're still seeing a few more people for the role, but you're definitely in the running."

I'm in the running?

Oh. My. God.

So it's not a *no*. Or a *no, and*.

It's a *maybe*!

"We should have an answer in a week or two," Rebecca continues. "So let's sit tight and see how this all plays out. If we get an offer, we'll talk that through. Otherwise, we'll discuss where we go from here."

Hearing this, I know I should be happy, elated, freaking over the moon with joy, and of course I am. But what I'm mostly feeling in this moment is…*relief*. In the process of being honest with my parents last night, I also had to be honest with myself. I had to face the fact that this chosen career path could turn out to be a long and winding road to nowhere.

Maybe I'll be in the service industry for the rest of my life, I told them. *But if I'm okay with that, then you have to be too.*

But now…

"Sound good?" asks my agent.

I smile. "Sounds great."

· · · · ·

I bask in my good news through most of the day, but as it gets closer to nightfall, my thoughts grow darker too. Can I really pull this off? Can I really keep my slayer concealed at the Whisky around Dracula's Army and their fanged fans? Or—

Nope. I can't start worst-case-scenario thinking. I've got to hang on to the confidence I was feeling earlier. I need to stay positive.

In my bedroom, I button the last button on the long-sleeved black jumpsuit Heather brought over for me to try on. Then I turn around to show her.

My friend gives me a quick head-to-toe and nods approvingly. "I like it."

I face the mirror to see for myself. "You're sure?" I ask, but it's not my style game I'm worried about. After all, tonight's not about looking good. It's about looking, well, *not* like a slayer.

Standing behind me, Heather meets my gaze in the glass. "Black is always minimizing, and the one piece gives you a nice, long line. Plus, the drop-shoulder seam deemphasizes your upper body." She flashes a grin. "Not to mention that jumpsuits are sexy as shit."

I frown, playing with the sleeves. "I'm not sure that matters."

"Of course that matters," she says.

"That only matters if I matter to Nick," I say.

"For what it's worth," says Heather, "I think you do matter to him. I think you matter a lot."

I stop fussing with my outfit and turn to look at her directly. "What makes you say that?"

"Well, last night?" she says. "With Quentin? Once I figured out what the fuck was going on, it seemed like Nick was being genuinely protective of you."

"It did?"

"It seemed like he had your back."

I think about this. And yes, I guess it kind of did.

"We still haven't really talked," I tell Heather. "Something always gets in the way."

Heather shoots me a challenging look. "*Something?*"

I'm about to rattle off the same list of excuses for the delay that I gave Liv this morning, but then I stop myself. Because, if I'm being honest, that's all they really are. Excuses.

"Or me," I confess, "Maybe *I* get in the way. My fear gets in the way."

Heather regards me curiously.

"What?" I ask.

"Get real, Pinocchio," she says. "You've had the guts to be straight with your parents, your agent, and even that creepy barfly at work. So you can definitely gather up enough girl power to hash it all out with Nick."

I let this sink in.

She's right of course. As unbelievable as it might have seemed just a week ago, I finally laid down the law, so to speak, with my parents. I asserted myself with Rebecca—a move that, if it hadn't gone well, could have lost me my agency representation. And even though I highly doubt Pete would fire me if he caught wind of me dressing down my regular Tuesday-night drunk, it wasn't exactly the most professional move in the world. It could have put my job in jeopardy.

But with Nick? What's at stake is somehow bigger. Bigger than my parents' approval or my acting career or my weekly paycheck. What's at stake is…*my heart*.

"You know that first night you learned what you were? Well, I meant what I said," says Heather.

I think back, trying to remember what she told me the night I found out I was a vampire slayer. "That Nick has epic dimples?" I ask.

"No—well, yes, I meant that too," she says with an offhand shrug and a wave. "But that's not what I'm talking about."

"Then what are you talking about?" I ask. "No offense, but I kind of had a lot running through my mind that night. I don't exactly remember our conversation word for word."

Heather looks me straight in the eye and gives me the kind of look you wish you could wrap up and stick in a drawer so you can pull it out every time you're feeling scared or lost or insecure. "I said it then and I'll say it again," she says. "You're a lot stronger than you think you are."

I smile back at her, and—

"Wait, wait, wait, wait, wait," says Liv, scurrying through the doorway. She has several rosary-type necklaces draped over her arm, each with a large cross dangling from it. "Time to accessorize." My roomie dumps the whole armload around my neck, then spins me toward the mirror. "What do you think?"

"I think Madonna called," says Heather. "She wants her eighties look back."

Peeking around my shoulder into the mirror, Liv talks to my reflection. "They were my grandmother's," she says. "She was very devout. Maybe they'll help you keep the vampires at bay."

"Thanks," I say with a grin. "But I don't think vampires are really afraid of crosses."

"And judging by Quentin's wardrobe," Heather says, "they're definitely not afraid of overaccessorizing."

I take the necklaces off and hand them back to Liv. "It was a good thought though."

Liv shrugs and starts to leave.

"Hang on," says Heather. "Maybe just one." She goes after Liv, sorts through the necklaces, and selects an amber-beaded strand with a large silver cross. She hangs it back around my neck, then steps back, admiring her handiwork. "Who's dressed to slay now?"

CHAPTER
27

That night, I leave my Prius at home and take an Uber to work. The plan is that Liv and Heather will swing by the bar to meet me at the end of my shift, and then we'll all drive to the Whisky together. Seated in the back of my driver Randall's red Honda Accord, dressed in the black jumpsuit with the single cross around my neck, I try to figure out how to resume my awkward conversation with Nick by running some lines in my head.

Is there anything else you haven't told me?

What's really going on between us?

Are we a thing? Or not really?

"Are you talking to me?" asks the driver. His reflection in the rearview mirror looks a little wary.

Oops. I guess some of the lines in my head managed to slip out of my mouth.

"No, sorry," I tell him, flustered. "I was just…uh—never mind."

I pull out my phone, open the Uber app, and bump Randall's tip up an extra 10 percent.

· · · · ·

At Pete's, I do a quick scan of the bar as I walk in. As is typical for a Wednesday night, the place is pretty empty. Fingers crossed, that means Nick and I will have a chance to finish our discussion.

But as my gaze shifts over to the bar, I stop. The guy at the register with his back to me is dressed like Nick, in jeans and a tee, and he's Nick's height, but he's nowhere near Nick's broad, muscular build. For a moment, I wonder if this slayer-vampire prophecy has somehow worked in reverse, if Nick has fallen in love with me and lost his vampire powers—but no, that's just wishful thinking. Unlike me, Nick had the big, buff bod long before he was turned. And the head full of thick, coarse gray hair definitely belongs to someone else.

"Pete?" I say, continuing up to the bar counter.

The deeply suntanned, sixty-something owner of the bar turns and gives me a welcoming smile that emphasizes the lines around his eyes and his mouth. "Carrie," he says warmly. "How are you?"

"What are you doing here?" I blurt out.

Crossing one long, denim-clad leg over the other and folding his arms across his chest, Pete leans back against the register and surveys me with amusement. "Well, it *is* my bar," he says.

"I know, but where's Nick?" I ask.

"He asked for the night off."

"He asked for the night off?" I ask.

Pete cocks his head and raises his bushy gray eyebrows at that. "He didn't mention it?"

"Nope," I say. "He most certainly did not."

· · · · ·

In the back room, I stow my belongings and close my locker, and my head is absolutely spinning. I don't know what in the actual hell is going on here. At first, I thought Nick and I might be the real deal. I really did. But then, after talking to Jenn, I started to worry that Nick might just be trying to trick me into having feelings for him to eliminate my slayer. Except then, after my dress rehearsal with Quentin and my subsequent conversation about it with Heather, I started to think that maybe Nick is in my corner after all.

But now? This unexpected absence of Nick—on tonight of all nights—is raising a whole fresh crop of concerns.

If Nick is *on* my side, wouldn't he be here, *by* my side, right now?

And since he's not? Maybe this past week really has been about romancing me to take away my power.

And since that hasn't been successful? Since I'm still a slayer? Maybe tonight is some kind of a nefarious backup plan. Maybe it has been all along. Maybe me walking into the Whisky will actually be me walking straight into a trap.

I know I could be letting my doubts get the best of me. But regardless, as my father would say, look at the evidence. Nick didn't mention that he wouldn't be at work tonight. It's yet another thing he didn't tell me. And goddammit, if that's the case…

How close can the two of us really be?

· · · · ·

Pete is at the beer taps, expertly scraping extra foam off a Sam Adams, when I take up my usual place behind the bar. He glances over at me, then does a double take. "You okay over there?"

I nod, a little embarrassed that my employer is seeing me all distracted and moody on the job like this. "Oh yeah," I tell him. I stand up straighter and try to put on a more professional expression. "I'm totally fine," I say, forcing a smile.

After studying me for a beat, he gives me a nod and walks off. I watch while he serves his customer the beer with the kind of easy smile and casual banter that's been perfected over decades of tending bar. Like Nick, the guy has some enviable people skills.

Eventually Pete leaves the patron alone with his drink and ambles back over to me. "You know, I think he's just nervous about tonight," he says.

"Wh-what?" I stammer.

"Nick," says Pete. "Said he needed the night off to prepare. This show at the Whisky is a big deal for him, you know. First major venue with the new band and all."

"Oh," I say, a little surprised that Nick would have gone into so much detail when he called Pete to bag out on his shift. "Yeah, I get it."

And I do. Considering how anxious I always am before I have to audition, I totally understand the nerves. But why would Nick tell Pete all this and not tell me anything?

Pete leans a little closer to me, and his tone gets softer. "I'm sure he meant to tell you," he says.

"What?" It's a little disconcerting that the guy seems to be able to read my thoughts.

"Probably just forgot to mention it," says Pete. "What with his jitters and all."

I'm starting to feel a little jittery myself. "Hey, no need for Nick to run his schedule by me," I say with a quick shrug. "I'm not his boss."

"No," says Pete. "From what I hear, you're a lot more than that."

What?

I'm so used to my father's cross-examinations that I immediately start to wonder if I might be stumbling into a trap with my employer.

"Is there some kind of a no-fraternization policy I don't know about?" I ask warily.

After a moment of silence, Pete bursts out laughing. "Hell no," he says. "I'm just glad that the two of you are finally together."

Muscles I didn't realize I was tensing start to relax, and—*bam!* That's when it hits me that Pete seems to know things about Nick and me. Things I certainly didn't tell him.

"So," I say, "do you and Nick talk…*often?*"

"Some," he says. "Especially since he's my tenant as well as my employee."

Now things start to snap into place.

"You own the loft?" I ask.

"I own the building," Pete says. "Nick used to DJ for me at the karaoke bar."

Nick's interest in karaoke makes a bit more sense.

"When he first started bartending, he used to still work an occasional afternoon shift there," continues Pete. "If I had a day booking for a private party or something."

I think back on all the times Nick showed up late for work, all the times I thought he was being lazy and irresponsible and just plain slacking off. Except it sounds like he was actually the opposite of a slacker, pulling down two back-to-back jobs.

"But he doesn't seem to be available during the day anymore," adds Pete.

No, I think. *He wouldn't be.*

And since Nick became a vampire, he's been on time for work every single night. Clearly I misjudged him on this count, but Nick's work ethic isn't really the thing I'm most interested in right now.

"And," I say tentatively, "Nick talks to you about…*me?*"

"Are you kidding?" asks Pete. "I couldn't get him to shut up about you if I tried. I swear, that boy was bonkers for you since the first time he laid eyes on you."

Hearing Pete say it, I remember Nick confessing something similar the night we spent together in his loft. I recall all the feelings his words ignited in me, and not one of them was doubt. I had no reason to doubt him then, and listening to Pete talk, I realize that I've had no real reason to doubt him since.

"For a year, I've been saying, 'Just tell her how you feel, Nick. Just tell her how you feel,'" says Pete. "But with the childhood he had, well, you can see how putting himself out there like that would be difficult."

Of course. Nick lost his family in a car accident. Then he pretty much relived that loss over and over again, being shuttled from one foster family to another. No wonder it's taken a year—and something as extreme as our current situation—to get him to declare his feelings.

"I'm just glad he finally got up the nerve to talk to you," says my boss, who apparently also doles out advice to the lovelorn.

"And he told you the two of us are together?" I ask, just to make sure I'm understanding correctly. "As in *together* together?"

"He did," says Pete with a warm smile. "And I must say, I'm very happy. For the both of you."

Something loosens in my chest, and for the first time in days—since the day I first met Jenn—I feel like I can breathe.

If a slayer falls in love with a vampire, the slayer loses their power.

Maybe it's true. And maybe Nick even knows it. We'll have to discuss it all eventually and clear the air. But regardless, that doesn't mean that what's going on between us isn't real or that Nick is acting out some devious plan to set me up and take me down.

I mean, Nick may have a motive to lie to me, his slayer, but he has absolutely no motive to lie to Pete. So if he told Pete that the two of us are together…

We're together, I think. *We really are together.*

I smile back at Pete. This time, the smile is real. "I'm happy too."

· · · · ·

"So Nick's been talking to Pete about you all this time?" asks Heather.

"Yup," I say.

"And Nick told him that he had a thing for you?" pipes in Liv.

"Yup."

"And he told him that the two of you are together?" asks Heather.

"Three for three," I say from the back seat of Heather's SUV. As promised, Liv and Heather showed up at the bar a little before closing, and Pete was kind enough to let me go early so I'd be sure not to miss any of Nick's set. "I think I can stop worrying about trusting Nick. Right?"

Heather nods as she steers onto Sunset Boulevard. "Nick has no reason to lie to Pete," she says, seeing things the same way I did. "And Pete has no reason to lie to you."

"See?" says Liv from the passenger seat. "I told you so. In *Bar Wars*, the vampire and the vampire slayer live happily ever after."

"Well, I'm not thinking about how this all ends," I say, sitting back with a smile. "I'm just glad to know that Nick and I really do seem to be starting something."

But as we approach the Sunset Strip, traffic slows to a crawl, and things in the interior of the SUV get quiet. The atmosphere starts to feel heavier, more serious. And suddenly, my offhand reference to "how this all ends" echoes eerily, taking on a more ominous meaning.

Heather is the first one to break the silence. "Are you sure you're up for this?" she asks me with a nervous glance over her shoulder. "I mean, I know I kind of teased you about the training sessions and all, but did they work?"

"Because if you're not ready for this," says Liv, "we can just do a U-ey and turn this car right around. As soon as we can get somebody to let us into the left lane."

With a sigh, I think about it for a moment.

Am I ready for this?

Well, I'm ready to stop looking over my shoulder at every turn and start looking ahead to the future—a future that seems to include Nick. And if controlling my slayer in front of a bunch of vampires will enable me to do that? Sign me up.

I suppose I could delay this confrontation until I'm feeling a little more secure in my ability to contain my alter ego. Except I don't think I want to do that. I've already spent too much of my life procrastinating, avoiding the hard stuff, putting off the tough conversations, and in retrospect, it's only ever made things worse. It's time to make things *better*.

In a way, tonight isn't just about conquering my slayer. It's about conquering all the worst aspects of myself.

And honestly? Over the past week, I've faced off against demons a whole lot scarier than my slayer. Or any vampire for that matter. And I've managed to come out on top.

"I'm ready," I say. "But…"

"But?" prods Liv.

Looking from one of my friends to the other, I suddenly start to have doubts. Not about me but about them. Or rather about the wisdom of them coming along.

"But maybe you should just drop me off at the Whisky," I say. "Maybe you shouldn't come inside with me."

"What?" says Heather.

"What are you talking about?" says Liv.

"It's just…we don't know what's going to happen."

"Exactly," says Heather. "Which is why we're going to have your back."

"We're your ride or die," says Liv.

"And I don't want the *die* part to become literal," I say. "If anything happened to either of you—"

"Stop," says Heather. She turns around in the driver's seat to face me—which sounds risky, but it's not like she needs to watch the road. The traffic has gotten so thick that we're at a total standstill. Three green lights have come and gone without us moving an inch. "Stop right there," she says. "Because however you're about to end that sentence? That's the way we feel about you too. So no way are we letting you face this alone."

"Friends don't let friends walk into a club full of vampires without backup," says Liv.

I could fight them on it, of course. But even with my supernatural sword of flames, I'm not sure I'd win this battle.

"Well, okay," I say slowly. "But I think we need to set some ground rules for tonight."

"Ground rules?" echoes Heather.

"Like what?" asks Liv.

I do a quick mental review of everything I've learned this past week.

"Once we get out of the car, we can't talk about slayers or vampires or anything like that," I say. "Vampires have supersensitive hearing, so they could be listening to anything we say. We don't want to blow my cover."

"What if we use code words?" ask Liv.

"Code words?" I ask.

"Instead of 'vampire,' we could say 'accountant,'" says Liv. "Or 'mechanic.' Or 'fishmonger.'"

"No," says Heather. "No code words."

"Hand gestures?" asks Liv.

Heather rolls her eyes at Liv and looks at me. "We'll watch what we say. What else?"

I think for a beat. "Remember, vampires also have something called *influence*. They can get into your head—literally. I don't know exactly how it works, but I'm thinking maybe we should avoid making eye contact with anyone but each other."

"I can do that," says Liv.

Heather shrugs. "Tonight, I've only got eyes for you two."

"And what else?" asks Liv.

I'm sure there are about a million other things I should be warning my friends about, but I can't think of any of them. All I can think is…

"You're the best," I say, trying not to choke up. "Really. Both of you."

"No, you are," says Liv. She makes a face to keep things from getting too weepy.

"No, you are," I return with a grin, grateful for her lighter vibe.

"If only flattery got you anywhere in LA traffic," grumbles Heather, turning back to the road.

CHAPTER
28

inally, we pull up at the valet stand outside Whisky a Go Go. Heather trades her keys for a numbered ticket, and we all pile out of the SUV. Standing on the sidewalk between Liv and Heather, I look up at the venerable old music venue, its exterior painted a vibrant red with black awnings. It strikes me that the Gothic color scheme is pretty perfect for the locale of a vampire band's gig.

Custom-illustrated signs featuring some of the legendary acts who've played the Whisky over the years decorate the exterior of the building. I notice there's a lot of overlap with Nick's collection of T-shirts and vinyl. What a thrill it must be for him to be performing here.

Over the entrance, there's an old-school marquee. Mismatched letters, yellowing with age, spell out the night's lineup:

WED NiTE

GO FiSH

BITTERSWEeT

DRACuLA'S ARMY

This is also the night of my big performance, the one I've spent this past week in training for. And while I'm definitely feeling a familiar fluttering in my stomach and shakiness in my limbs—not to mention an underlying current of absolute fear and dread—what I'm feeling mostly at this moment is...*pride*.

I'm so proud of Nick, so excited for him. So happy that he's reached this milestone in his musical career.

"Is it weird if I take a picture?" I ask my friends, pointing up at the marquee.

"Not weird at all," says Liv with a smile. "Sweet, actually."

"And Nick may not have thought to take one for himself," says Heather.

So before we go inside, I pull out my phone and snap a few quick photos. For Nick.

· · · · ·

"Which band are you here to see?" asks the woman at the door when my friends and I approach.

The question takes me by surprise. "Dracula's Army," I say. "We haven't missed them, have we?"

The woman shakes her head full of long, blond braids while she makes a note on her clipboard. "No," she says. "Go Fish just finished. But we keep a running tally of how many people each band draws. That's how we know who's worth booking again."

Sounds like the life of a struggling musician is every bit as brutal as that of a struggling actor. We really do have so much in common, Nick and I. If only I'd seen it sooner, before he became a vampire and I became his—but no. This is no time to be taking a stroll down the avenue of regrets. Tonight, it's about putting all that squarely in the rearview and moving forward.

We pay for our tickets. Even though it'll make things a little tougher for me, I can't help hoping that the vampires have turned out in a big way for Dracula's Army, in big enough numbers to earn the band a repeat booking. Because I just want things to be a little easier for Nick.

· · · · ·

Although I've lived in LA for more than two years and driven by the Whisky countless times, I've never actually been inside. Now that I'm here, I look around. I guess you could say this place is the music venue equivalent of Pete's. The stripped-down, no-frills interior stands in stark contrast to some of the newer, flashier clubs on the Sunset Strip. The lounge level is lined with huge, old-school booths upholstered in well-worn, tufted vinyl. The concert level is little more than a big, dark room—black walls, black floor—with an unadorned stage at one end. Roadies are setting up for the next band.

I glance around at the crowd, although "crowd" is being generous. The turnout tonight is pretty light—probably typical for a midweek show featuring a bill of local, mostly unknown bands.

"How you doing?" asks Heather. "All good?"

I use my slayer radar to scan the space, but I don't pick up on any vampires in the immediate vicinity. Still, I can tell that Nick is in the house. Along with others like him. They must all be backstage.

I turn to my friends and look from one to the other. "All good for now," I say with a reassuring nod. "Come on. Let's go find Nick."

The three of us head off in search of the VIP area, but we take a few wrong turns. We end up first at the restrooms, then at the emergency exit, before we finally arrive at a long, dark hallway blocked by a velvet rope. This time, the gatekeeper with the clipboard is a man—or, I should say, *was* a man. He's a vampire now, if my slayer senses are correct.

Here we go, I think.

Mentally, I put a box around my alter ego and lock it up tightly.

"We're with the band," says Liv. She turns to Heather and me, grinning. "I've always wanted to say that."

"Names?"

Automatically, I rattle them off.

The undead security worker checks his list. "I have Carrie Adams but not the other two."

"But we're all together," says Heather.

"Check again," says Liv. "Olivia Sanchez and Heather Mancini."

Except I now realize that it's no use. He can check that list a hundred times, and he won't ever find my friends' names on it. I never mentioned to Nick that my besties were coming with me tonight, never asked him to make sure they had backstage access too. Honestly, it never occurred to me that I had to.

As predicted, the vampire at the door shakes his head. "Sorry."

I have to say, deep down, I'm *not* sorry. Actually, I'm kind of thankful. While I know that Liv and Heather want to protect me, I also want to protect them. And keeping them far away from any potential conflict seems like the best way to do that.

"What if I flirt with you?" Liv asks the doorman, awkwardly twirling her ponytail.

The vampire laughs amiably. "I'd enjoy that, for sure," he says. "But I still can't let you back. Not unless you're on the list. I could lose my job."

"Ladies and gentlemen," says an amplified voice from the front of the house, "Whisky a Go Go is pleased to welcome to the stage... Bittersweet!"

As we hear cheers and applause and the opening chords of the band's first number, I turn to my two besties. "It's fine," I say. "Go watch the band. I'll meet you back out front in a bit."

Heather eyes me with worry. "I don't like it," she says. "I don't like leaving you all by yourself to walk into a den of—" She stops herself just in time. "—*musicians*," she finishes.

I guess we're using code words after all.

I look from one of my friends to the other, and it dawns on me that if things don't go well, this could be the last time I—no. Nope. Failure is *so* not an option.

I flash Liv and Heather a bright smile. "It's okay," I tell them. "Go. I'll see you out front." I use my index finger to draw an X over my heart. "Promise."

All at once, Liv launches herself at me, Heather follows, and before I know what's happening, the three of us are locked together in a big group hug. Part of me wants to stay in the warmth and safety of this embrace forever, but the rest of me knows I can't. It's showtime.

So with a final squeeze, I disentangle myself and pull free. When we all break, I see that everyone's a little weepy. Including me.

"Now get out of here," I say gruffly. "I've got this."

Liv and Heather look at me for a long moment. They don't say anything, but they don't need to. When they reluctantly turn away and I watch them go, I realize that the vampire has been taking the whole scene in. And now he's eyeing me curiously.

I blink back my tears and give him a shrug. "They just don't trust musicians," I tell him.

He gives me a friendly wink as he unhooks the velvet rope to let me pass. "Probably not a bad rule."

• • • • •

The VIP room isn't a room, exactly. It's more of a partially walled-off space behind the stage. As live music drifts up and over the heavy black curtain separating the backstage lounge area from the band that's onstage, I compose myself, step across the threshold, and—

Whoa.

There are a dozen or so VIPs gathered here, and I immediately know that most of them are vampires. Some are very old, older even than Quentin. And while advanced age makes humans physically weaker, it's clear that the opposite is true of vampires. The sheer power contained within this small space is so staggering it almost bowls me over.

I have the same reaction I had a week ago, the night of my face-off with Nick in the alley behind Pete's. Feelings of absolute hate and loathing flood through me. The same urges to confront, to attack, to *slay* overwhelm me.

Only I'm not the same as I was a week ago. I'm stronger. A lot stronger.

Oh, I'm not saying that it's easy to stand up to my slayer, to deny her the vengeance she so desperately wants. In fact, it's every bit as difficult as it's ever been. But now I'm not afraid of doing the hard thing. I don't need to take the path of least resistance and act in a way that pleases my alter ego—or anyone else, for that matter. Tonight I'm fighting for my *own* happiness.

Suppressing my slayer and everything she brings with her, I look around. I see that Jess, the so-called Dracula's Army groupie, is here, sitting on a couch with another vampire. But she's not the one I'm searching for.

Finally, my gaze finds Nick. He's standing in the corner, wearing jeans and a Rolling Stones band tee, talking with Quentin, and just like that, containing my slayer isn't so hard after all.

Since I had that conversation with Pete, I'm not confused anymore. I truly believe that Nick and I have the seeds of something real. And if we're going to keep it growing? I simply need to get through tonight.

Nick spots me and smiles uncertainly. With a confident nod, I grin back and cross over to him.

"You came," says Nick.

"Of course I came," I say. I give him a teasing look. "Did you think I was going to be a no-show like you were at work?"

"Sorry," he says. "I should have—"

"It's fine," I say quickly. "I talked to Pete. And I completely get it. You needed to focus."

"He needed to down a whole bottle of Pepto Bismol," interjects Quentin, clapping Nick on the shoulder.

I glance at Quentin, then turn back to Nick. "Nerves?" I ask.

"I would have called," he says sheepishly, "but I was…indisposed for a while."

I smile sympathetically.

"But I'm okay now," he says.

"Can I get you a drink, love?" Quentin asks me. His offer is all easy hospitality, but I can tell that my arrival put him a little off his guard. I don't think he was expecting me. And after a week of feeling me out, I can tell he still doesn't know what to make of me.

It's time to prove to him, once and for all, that I'm not a threat.

I shake my head. "No thanks," I say. "My friends are waiting out front. I just wanted to come back and wish you all luck."

"Have you met Zach?" asks Quentin. The question is casual, but I can detect the calculation behind it. "Our other bandmate?"

Okay. Here we go. Time to show all of Dracula's Army that they have nothing to fear from me.

"No, I haven't," I say with a glance up at Nick. "But I'd love to."

Quentin leads the way, and Nick and I follow.

"What about you?" asks Nick with raised eyebrows. His careful tone reminds me of our training sessions. "Are you doing okay?"

"I'm doing great," I say to reassure him about my slayer.

I also want to reassure him about me—about *us*—but this is hardly the time or the place for a real heart-to-heart. Still…

"And you know," I add quickly, "it was the same for me before my audition yesterday. I mean, I didn't have to hit the Pepto. But I did need a little time to myself."

He looks at me, eyes searching. "That's all it was?" he asks.

"That's all," I say. "Well, that and my own stupid insecurities. But we can talk about all that—"

"Zach!" says Quentin, slipping an arm around the waist of one of two vampires standing over by a small buffet table. "You haven't met Nick's coworker. This is *Carrie*." The way he says my name is heavy with meaning.

Zach is as fair as Quentin is dark, all blond hair and pale skin and delicate features. His build is taller than his partner's but slighter. And while Quentin seems to favor vintage clothing, Zach sports modern streetwear.

"Carrie," says Zach with a smile that reveals none of the suspicions I know he must be harboring. "I've heard so much about you."

"And none of it good, from what I understand," I say.

A little thrown, Zach looks questioningly from Quentin to Nick.

"I take it Nick basically describes me as his nagging work wife," I explain, trying to make a joke of it.

"Ah! So you're the one," says the vampire next to Zach, joining our conversation. He's older than the rest of us—in more ways than one. With strong, dignified features and dark hair just starting to go gray at the temples, he appears to be in his midforties or so. But considering the unbelievable amount of undead energy that's radiating off him, I'm guessing that millennia, not decades, would provide a more accurate measure of his age.

"Carrie," says Nick, "This is Arlo. Our friend from New York."

Arlo.

So this is the ancient Vampire Council member who flew in special for Nick's transformation, the one who brought The Book. The one who won't be leaving until the slayer issue is…*resolved.*

Okay, I think, reinforcing my hold on my slayer. *Let's resolve it right here and now.*

"Nice to meet you," I tell him.

"And you," says Arlo, giving me an appraising look. I admit, it's a little unnerving.

"How are you liking your time in Los Angeles?" I ask.

"To be honest," he says, "I prefer the nightlife in New York."

"But you can't beat the California sunshine." It's a supremely stupid thing to say, I know, but Arlo's attention is making me uneasy, and the words are out of my mouth before I realize they might sound hostile to vampire ears.

There's a change in the atmosphere, and it feels as if everyone is suddenly on alert.

Crap, I think.

Arlo eyes me suspiciously, but I try to act guileless, like the clueless human I used to be. I don't think I give anything away. "Alas," he says finally, "I burn quite easily."

"Sorry to hear that," I say.

Taking a step back, Arlo regards me from a different angle and takes a new tack. "Are you a fan of the band?"

Grateful for the change in topic, I smile. "I'm sure I will be," I say. "I've never actually heard Dracula's Army play before."

"We've never played a major house like this before," says Zach. "So it'll be a first for all of us."

"Oh!" Remembering my photos—and forgetting myself a little—I pull my phone out of my pocket. "I snapped a few pics of the marquee out front," I say, showing my screen to Nick. "Just in case you didn't. I figured you might want to have them."

He looks down as I flip quickly through the shots. "I didn't even think of it," he says, shaking his head.

I smile up at him. "Well, you've got a lot on your mind tonight."

"But you thought of it," he says, smiling.

And suddenly it's like it's just the two of us.

"Well, I get what a big deal this must be for you," I say. "It's your name up in lights." I pause. "Or the band's name anyway." I pause again. "In really old letters that don't match."

He laughs. "That's rock and roll," he says.

"I'll text them to you," I say. Quickly, I select the photos and send them to Nick.

"Thank you," he says. But the way he's staring at me says so much more.

I put my phone back in my pocket. "You're welcome."

"I have something for you too," he says.

"You do?" I ask. "What?"

"Remember when I said we were rehearsing a new cover song to open the show?"

I nod.

"It's something I picked just for you," he says. He reaches out and brushes his fingertips across my bangs. "And when I sing it, I'll be singing it to you."

Our eyes lock, my belly fills with heat, and I know what it means to fight fire with fire, because the burning I feel for Nick puts my slayer's blaze to shame. If I had any lingering doubts about Nick's feelings for me, they go straight up in smoke.

"Get a room, you two," says Zach, and the other vampires laugh.

Reminded that it's *not* just Nick and me, I look around, a little embarrassed. That's when I notice that the room has shifted again. The tension is gone. Slayer watch seems to be officially over.

Huh.

It's funny to think that after all the fear and worry, this was all it took. Somehow, by simply being my true self—and by letting my true feelings for Nick show through—I seem to have convinced them I'm not a danger.

My gaze finds its way back to Nick. His eyes are soft, his smile is relaxed, and his dimples are making their first appearance in days.

It's a perfect moment.

Until—

"Hello, Carrie."

At the sound of my name, my whole body seizes with dread. Everyone's attention swings in the direction of the voice. As I slowly turn that way too, I know that this perfect moment has just come to an end.

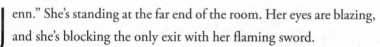

CHAPTER
29

J enn." She's standing at the far end of the room. Her eyes are blazing, and she's blocking the only exit with her flaming sword.

Nick's head snaps toward me at vampire speed. "*Jenn?*" he demands of me, his voice full of incredulity. "You *know* her? You *know* this slayer?"

I nod slowly, but I keep my attention on Jenn. "What are you doing here?" I ask.

"What you should be doing," she says.

"How did you get back here?" I ask her.

"I was very persuasive."

I think about that nice vampire at the backstage entrance. Did he get away? Or...

Bile rises in my throat, but I quickly swallow it back down. This is so not the time to be getting queasy.

This is the time to be strong.

I can't let Jenn do what she's come here to do.

I stretch out my arm and, like I did the morning I first woke up changed, I breathe. I focus. And I call to the superhero inside me.

In a flash, my own fiery blade appears. I hear the gasps behind me, and I know I've just outed myself, just marked myself as an enemy when I was so close to making friends. But sometimes you need to choose the hard thing.

Sometimes, you need to have the tough confrontations.

I display my weapon of fire, and it really is *my* weapon. I'm the one in control of it. Not my slayer. *Me.* Unlike Jenn, my vision is clear, no red filter clouding it. My mind is sharp, and I know the power is mine to wield as I see fit.

Jenn indicates my sword. "I hope that means you're joining me."

I shake my head. "Never."

"You're on the wrong side," she says.

"Why do there have to be sides?"

"Because there's good," she says. "And then there's evil."

"Oh, for crying out loud, look around," I tell her. I motion at Quentin and Zach, who have stepped up in front of Nick, ready to protect him from harm; at the other vampires here, who have abandoned their refreshments and their conversations to huddle together, trying to shield one another as well as their human friends from danger; at Arlo, who...*is hiding under the buffet table?* "Don't you see?" I continue. "Not all vampires are evil."

"What I see," Jenn says, eyeing me up and down, "is that not all slayers are cut out for the job."

"I don't know," I say. "It looks to me like you're the one who's shirking."

The fire in her eyes wavers slightly. "What's that supposed to mean?"

"Look at you. You're just sitting back and letting your slayer take the driver's seat," I say. "You're doing what's easy. And I get it, because I used to do what's easy too.

"But the first time I saw you, you were bench-pressing more than your own body weight. You don't even have to train to keep your muscles, but you do anyway." I shake my head. "You don't strike me as somebody who usually shies away from hard work. So I don't understand why you're not doing the hard work here."

The red blaze in her eyes wavers again, and I start to have hope that I might be able to reach her.

"The hard work isn't fighting vampires," I tell her. "It's fighting your own demons and getting past them." I pause. "And trust me, you'll never be happy unless you do."

No reply.

Still no reply.

We stand face-to-face, taking each other's measure. The room is silent except for the crackling of our twin flames.

Jenn's eyes dim a third time, and I dare to think I might've won her over.

"I'll never be happy anyway," she says.

So much for winning her over.

Her eyes flash, and she raises her sword, and that's when I know for sure that I've lost her.

"Step aside," says Jenn.

I don't budge. "I can't do that," I say. "You know I can't."

"I don't want to hurt you," she says.

"And I don't want to hurt you."

We continue our stare down. Then Jenn breaks eye contact. Looking past me, she raises her sword higher and tries to leap over my head, launching her attack on the vampires behind me. Instinctively, I lift my own blade and spring up to block her. With both of us suspended in midair, our fiery weapons collide.

A crash like thunder but more deafening explodes around us.

Sparks fly up from our interlocked blades, creating a kind of indoor fireworks show. I imagine that Bittersweet, the band that's currently playing, is treating its audience to an unexpected display of pyrotechnics.

"Back off!" shouts Jenn.

"You back off!"

Hovering up toward the ceiling, blades still clashing, we continue our struggle. Jenn's drive to slay vampires battles against my desire to stop such blind, senseless killing. Jenn is more experienced, but in this fight, I think I might have the edge. I'm not just acting out of compulsion. I have a real stake in this game. I need to protect Nick.

The sparks from our crossed swords grow more intense and more colorful, exploding more and more rapidly until—

With a sputter, both of our flames extinguish.

For a time, Jenn and I just hang, kind of like cartoon characters who haven't yet realized that they've run off the edge of a cliff. Then, all at once, we drop to the floor.

I land on my feet, but I stumble. Jenn, I see, is also trying to find her balance. When she does, she raises her sword arm again, but her blade doesn't emerge.

"Get her!" shouts Arlo, suddenly brave as he crawls out from underneath the buffet. "Get the slayer!"

He's pointing at Jenn, not me. Even though I've revealed my true nature, I suppose my actions have proven that I'm not a threat to his undead constituents. And I guess I could leave it at that.

Only I can't. I can't oppose such unthinking hatred one minute, then turn a blind eye to it the next. After all, for the last week, I've been living in fear of exactly this kind of a vampire assault. And just minutes ago, these same vampires might have attacked me—simply because of what *I* am.

No. The hate has to stop. Whether it's aimed at vampires or slayers, it simply must end.

Once again, I insert myself between the slayer and the vampires. Except now, it's the gathering of vampires I'm opposing. I can still feel that unnatural heat coursing through my body, but I know I'm unarmed too. At least temporarily, Jenn and I seem to have shorted out each other's circuits.

"No!" I say. "Wait!"

Arlo gets to his feet, and like many politicians, it's clear he'll have no problem striking at his opponents when they're down. "You think we shouldn't defend ourselves against slayers?"

I search my brain for a response, but I don't know what else to say. For a moment, I think I may choke the same way I've choked at way too many auditions.

But then I remember the one audition where I didn't choke. And suddenly, I have the words. So with a few embellishments of my own—and silent apologies to the writers of *Robbery-Homicide Division*—I launch into *my* closing argument.

"But what you're talking about isn't self-defense," I say. "It's killing motivated by hatred, plain and simple. And that makes it not just a crime but the worst kind of crime. A hate crime." I pause to look around the space. I have everyone's attention, but I can't tell if they're with me or not. "Blind hate against someone simply because they belong to a particular community—slayer or vampire—is never justifiable. Do you really want to live with that? Do you want to carry around the guilt of that…*forever*?"

Silence.

More silence.

Crap, I think.

Then there's the hiss of fire.

Double crap.

I turn. Jenn has recovered from our skirmish. Once again, she's flaunting her flaming blade. But the hatred burning in her eyes isn't quite as intense as before.

Maybe I got through after all?

She hesitates. For a moment, I'm not sure what she's going to do, and it looks like she doesn't know either.

I think about what *I'm* going to do. Honestly, there are no good options here. I'm not a killer, and I don't want to become one. But I also can't let Jenn go on a serial slaying spree.

Plus, I still don't know how my pretty little speech landed with the vampires behind me.

Talk about a rock and a hard place.

I look at Jenn, and that's the thing. For a couple of seconds, I'm looking at *Jenn*. Not the serial slayer.

She's fighting, I think. *She's doing it. She's doing the hard work.*

Then, instead of aiming her weapon at the undead gathering, she points it back the way she came. And in a blink, leaving a streak of fire behind her, the slayer is gone.

And then there was one.

Zach steps up to me.

I brace for what might be coming next.

"She's right, you know," says Zach, looking around at the vampire VIPs. I realize that he's arguing *my* case. "After all," he continues, "we're not the cold-blooded killers that slayers imagine us to be."

There are a few murmurs and nods of agreement.

"And not all slayers are the mindless assassins we imagine them to be," he adds with a glance over at me.

Then it dawns on me: we typecast each other. Slayers and vampires have been typecasting each other. For way too long.

"This slayer defended us against one of her own. I think it's clear she poses no threat to us. So," he says, eyes sweeping across the backstage gathering, "I see no threat here to eliminate."

Concurrence grows louder, stronger.

"But the laws," begins Arlo.

"Laws can be replaced with new laws," says Zach with a hard stare at the Vampire Council member. "Just like lawmakers can be replaced with new lawmakers."

At that, Arlo does a visual scan, reading the faces staring back at him. Then like the true politician he is, he says what he thinks everyone wants to hear. "Very well. I'll return to New York at nightfall tomorrow. And I'll report that the slayer issue is resolved."

There are a few cheers at that, and before long, the atmosphere in the VIP room becomes more relaxed. It doesn't exactly have the vibe it had before, but it feels like a party just the same. I guess you could say it's a celebration of sheer survival.

And boy oh boy, do I feel that.

I did it, I think. *I pulled it off.*

But no, that's not exactly right.

We did it, I think. *Nick and me.*

Without him, I could never have controlled my slayer. And I don't know if I would have discovered my own strength.

"Care for a drink now, love?" asks Quentin, offering me a beer.

I shake my head. All I want is to be with Nick. My eyes do a quick sweep, and I find him in the corner, all by himself, leaning against the wall.

And unlike everyone else here, Nick does not look happy.

I walk over to the scowling vampire and smile up at him tentatively. "Nick?" I ask. "What's wrong?"

"*What's wrong?*" he demands. "Are you kidding me?"

My smile fades. I honestly don't know how to answer.

"You've been hanging out with a vampire slayer. Behind my back," he says.

I've never seen Nick this angry.

"What? No, it's not—"

"You accused me of keeping things from you," he practically spits at me. "When all along, you've been keeping *this* from me?"

"No, no, no," I say. "It's not like that."

"How is it not like that?"

I search my brain and try to find the right words to explain. "I wanted to tell you. Really, I did. It's just, well, something Jenn said got into my head."

"What?" he asks. "What did she say?"

I take a deep breath. Time to come clean. "She told me that if a slayer falls in love with a vampire, the slayer loses their power," I tell him. Finally.

"What?"

From the look on his face, I can tell this is news to him. He didn't know. Of course he didn't know. There was never any kind of secret plot against me. It was just me foolishly keeping secrets from him.

"And once I heard that," I say, "I started to wonder if maybe us getting together wasn't real. I worried that maybe everything between us was just, I don't know…you trying to get me to fall for you so I wouldn't be a threat anymore."

"*What?*"

"It was stupid, I know," I say. Because now that I'm actually saying it all out loud to him, I realize how ridiculous it sounds. "I know that now."

"So you didn't trust me?" he asks, and mixed in with the anger, there's also hurt. "You didn't trust *us*?"

"I—"

"Carrie, I put my relationship with Zach and Quentin on the line to help you," he says. "I risked my *family* for you. The only family I have. And this is how you repay me?"

His words are like a stake to my heart. "Nick—"

"Dracula's Army to the stage," says a voice, crackling over a loudspeaker.

"I have to go," says Nick.

"But we'll talk later?"

"No."

The word sends a cold chill ripping through my body.

"No?"

He can't mean it. He just can't.

"What is there to talk about?" he asks.

"Us?" My voice breaks with emotion on the single syllable.

"*Us*? What *us*?!" he shouts. "You didn't trust me. And now I don't trust you. So there is no *us*. I'm beginning to think there never really was."

And with that, he stomps off to take the stage.

· · · · ·

A few minutes later, I locate Liv and Heather in the audience in the front of the house.

"Carrie, what's wrong?" asks Heather as soon as she sees my expression.

"Did you lose it in front of the vampires?" asks Liv.

"No," I say. "I–I lost Nick."

"Ladies and gentlemen," booms a voice over the club's sound system, "Whisky a Go Go is pleased to welcome to the stage…Dracula's Army!"

As the curtain goes up, my tears stream down.

"Let's go," I say.

"But—" starts Heather.

"I need to go!" I shout. "Now!"

My friends exchange a quick glance.

"Then, we're out of here," says Liv. "Vámonos."

Before she even gets the words out, I'm rushing on ahead, bawling so hard I can barely see. I push my way to the exit, bumping into people, jostling their drinks, probably aggravating quite a few along the way, but I don't care. I just need to leave.

Suddenly, I feel a small hand grab mine and start to pull me forward. And then there's an arm around my shoulders, holding on firmly, steering me through the crowd. With no more fight left in me, I relent and let my friends lead me toward the door.

My vision is clouded by tears, but there's nothing wrong with my hearing. I recognize the opening strains of a song that was playing just the other night. The night I spent with Nick. It's "Lay Down Sally."

I stop.

This must be the new cover song the band was rehearsing, the one they planned to open the show with. The one Nick said he'd be singing just for me. The last time I heard the lyrics about a man asking a woman to spend the night with him was the night I spent with Nick.

Blinking back my tears, I turn.

The stage is a blur, but I easily pick out the shape of Nick with one of his guitars. Something tells me that for the rest of my life, I'll always be able to pick out Nick.

He's at the microphone belting out those lyrics, and it dawns on me that I've never heard him sing before. His singing voice is like his speaking voice, but *more*. Deeper and more resonant. More emotional and raw. Pure rock and roll.

But while the original interpretation of this tune was playful and coaxing, Nick's is...*angry*. So angry. His delivery is laced with rage—a rage that I know I caused. And although the words are an invitation to stay, the message I'm getting is just the opposite.

I don't doubt that he's singing directly to me. Earlier tonight, that sounded like the most romantic thing in the world. But now the song just sounds like bitter regret. Every note says he's sorry he ever asked me to stay with him in the first place. Now, all he wants is for me to go.

I can't stay here and listen to any more of this. I just can't.

So with a heart that is somehow both full to bursting and completely bereft, I turn. And I go.

CHAPTER
30

The next day, I wake up to the aroma of Liv's French roast, which must mean I actually managed to fall asleep at some point. I rub my eyes and try to focus, but soon enough, I realize it's not just morning bleariness that's clouding my vision.

What with all the crying last night, things got so swollen and irritated that I had to remove my contacts. I'll pop in a fresh pair in a bit, after I get some caffeine in me. Then I'll be able to see clearly.

If only I'd been able to see clearly before. Before Jenn put all those stupid doubts in my head about Nick. Before my inability to talk straight to him basically pushed him away. Before I went and freaking ruined everything.

As I throw back the covers and swing my legs out of bed, I swallow down the lump in my throat that's already starting to rise again, blink back the tears that are already starting to well. Getting to my feet, I tell myself I should look on the bright side. At least I don't have a band of vampires out for my blood anymore. I can stop worrying about death threats and get on with my life. Only a life without Nick? Right now, that barely even seems like a life worth living.

I stagger out of the bedroom, putting one foot in front of the other. That's what I'll have to do now, I guess. Just keep putting one foot in front of the other. Then maybe I'll get to a place where it won't be so hard. Maybe one day, my whole body won't ache with emptiness because Nick isn't walking beside me.

"Hey," I say glumly to Liv. She's in her usual seat at our kitchen island, drinking her usual morning brew.

Hearing me, she puts down her mug. "Heyyy!" she says, her voice full of warm-and-fuzzy, whatever-you-need-I'm-here-for-you vibes as she turns to me. "How are…" She lets that sentence trail off, and her jaw goes slack. "…*you?*" she finally finishes.

Wow. I guess I must look every bit as bad as I feel. Maybe even worse.

"Sorry you have to see this first thing in the morning," I say, attempting a weak smile. "I'm still recovering from last night's ugly cry."

"It's not just that," says Liv softly.

"Yeah, I know," I say, rubbing at my eyes again. "I didn't sleep very well either."

I stumble past Liv, over to the Keurig. But as I grab a hazelnut pod and place it into the brewer, I feel my roommate's eyes on my back.

"Carrie," she says, "you're…*not* ripped."

I stop what I'm doing. Turn. "What?"

"Your muscles," says Liv. "They're gone."

"*What?*" I demand.

Liv pushes her glasses farther up on the bridge of her nose and smiles uncertainly at me. "I don't think you're a vampire slayer anymore."

For a moment, I can't move. I can't breathe. I can't even think.

I look down at myself, but without my contacts, all that's in focus is my feet. Heart pounding, I hurry past Liv, back into my bedroom. I head for the full-length mirror in the far corner of the room, but then I remember that I need my glasses.

Backtracking to the nightstand, I grab the black cat's-eye frames out of the top drawer. I put on them on as I skitter to a stop in front of the glass.

I stare at my reflection.

I barely recognize what I see from the neck up. My fair complexion is red and splotchy. My eyes are bloodshot and swollen and rimmed with red. My dark circles have dark circles. And my hair is matted and clumped together, sticking up and out at odd angles—the product of too many salty tears streaming into it followed by too much tossing and turning.

But from the neck down? I'm…*me*. Or the me I used to be anyway. No more massive shoulders or wildly buff arms. No more bodybuilder-caliber calves and thighs sticking out from my pink-striped boxers. And my white tank top, stretched out by my formerly overdeveloped lats and delts, now hangs loosely around my narrow torso.

Liv comes up behind me, and my eyes find hers in the mirror.

"How did this happen?" I ask. Even though I know how. We both do.

"You love him," says Liv with a smile. "You love Nick."

If a slayer falls in love with a vampire, the slayer loses their power.

"So it was true," I whisper. Tears are streaming down my face, but I don't bother wiping them away. "What Jenn told me was true."

"It sure looks that way."

"I'm not a slayer anymore," I say. "Because I love Nick."

Well, of course I love Nick. I've been falling for him all along—and not just over this past week. But I didn't fully realize it until last night, until I lost him for good. Once again, when it comes to the two of us, the timing is complete and utter shit.

"So what are you going to do about it?" asks Liv.

I shrug my bony little shoulders that now reveal the deepest secrets of my heart to the world. Or to everyone who knows the secrets of that *other* world. "I don't know," I say. "What *can* I do about it?"

"Well," says Liv, "I guess you can pretend it didn't happen. You can get Heather to dress you in layers that make you look a little bigger. And you can keep this from Nick just like you kept your encounters with Jenn from him. Just like you thought he was keeping things from you. Or," continues Liv, "you can dig in and fight. You can be honest with Nick, and you can fight for what you guys had. You can fight for love. Just because you're not a slayer anymore doesn't mean you can't fight."

Fight?

I've never been much of a fighter. Yet as I think back on the last week, I've certainly had my share of battles and confrontations and difficult conversations. I've found the strength to stand up for myself in ways I never could have imagined.

And Liv's right. Just because I've lost my slayer power, that doesn't mean I have to give up *my* power.

Still…

"What if I fight and I don't win?"

My roomie reaches a hand out and turns me away from the mirror so she can look at me face-to-face. "Can you really live with not knowing?"

It's a fair thing to ask. Especially since lately, I've been beyond frustrated with all the not knowing. I guess the final-round, all-in, big-money bonus question is *would it be worse to know for sure that Nick doesn't love me? Or to never know that he does?*

"What would happen in *Bar Wars*?" I ask.

"Oh please. You know what would happen in *Bar Wars*," says Liv.

"But *Bar Wars* is my story. This is your story." She gives me a tough look. "So you tell me. What happens tonight at Pete's on Melrose?"

. . . . .

I realize it's Thursday. 9:00 a.m. here. Noon back east. Time for the Adams family weekly touch base on Zoom, but that is *so* not happening today. No way am I dialing in to *that*. I'm still way too angry about the other night's ambush. I mean, I love my parents and all, but I really don't *like* them very much right now, and I don't want to get into another fight. I need to save my fight for something bigger. Something more important.

Because of course I need to know if Nick loves me. I have to know if the two of us have a chance. Which means I've got to talk to Nick. Tonight.

So instead of logging on for the latest inquisition, I decide to go for a run. I figure I'll use the time to sort things out in my head and start to think through what I want to say to him.

I stretch out my muscles—or lack of muscles, I should say—in my usual spot down by the beach, near the border of Santa Monica and Venice. I'm about to go right, into Santa Monica, but no. After last night, I need to go left, down along the Venice beachfront walk.

There are a lot of things I don't miss about my slayer. I don't miss the hate in my head all the time, the violent antivampire urges. I don't miss the fear that I might accidentally set something—or someone—on fire. And I sure don't miss the wrestling matches for control of my own mind. But as I take off down the path at what's become the normal pace for me, I do kind of miss the physical stamina. By the time I reach the outdoor gym at Muscle Beach, I'm tired, drenched with sweat, and practically wheezing.

Grabbing the top of the gate with both hands, I lean over and try to catch my breath. After a few moments, someone approaches, blocking out the sun.

"I see you're in love," says a familiar female voice.

I lift my head and peer up to see Jenn on the other side of the gate, standing there, her well-muscled vampire slayer physique silhouetted against the horizon. Since I'm still panting and puffing, I just nod in response.

"You fell in love with one of *them*." Maybe it's just wishful thinking, but the way she says "them" doesn't sound quite as contemptuous as it used to.

"Nick," I huff out. "His name is Nick."

"I hope he doesn't break your heart," she says.

"I hope so too," I say, lungs still struggling.

She watches me trying to recover. "Looks like you need a trainer."

I look sharply at her.

"A *fitness* trainer," she clarifies.

I shake my head. "Like I said before, I can't afford a gym membership."

"Well," she says, "maybe we could arrange a trade."

Now that my breathing has become a little more regulated, I stand up straight to look across the barrier at her. "What kind of trade are you proposing?" I ask.

"I could help you build back some muscle," she says. "And... maybe you could help me learn to control my slayer?"

My eyebrows shoot up. "You'll let *me* train *you*?" I ask. "Really?"

After a beat, she nods.

"What changed your mind?"

She takes a deep breath and looks up at the sky, thinking. Then she levels her blue-eyed gaze back at me. "When Tom first broke up with me, I was miserable. I thought I'd never be happy again. But once I became a slayer, well…I thought getting vengeance would make me happy."

"But it didn't."

"No," she says. "It didn't. I kept telling myself that it did, that I was serving some greater purpose, but…" She shakes her head and lets her voice trail off.

"That wasn't you talking," I say. "That was your slayer."

She lets out a small rueful laugh. "Before you came along, I didn't know there was a difference," she says. "Maybe I didn't want to know. But if I really do have a choice—"

"You always have a choice."

"Then I choose to fight this," she says. "I choose to see if maybe there's a way to be happy again."

I smile. "It's hard work."

She smiles back. "Please. I'm not afraid of a little hard work." Her icy blue eyes take in my slight frame. "Are you?"

I laugh. "Definitely not." I reach into the side pocket of my leggings for my phone, unlock it, and hand it over. "Give me your number," I say. "We'll make a plan."

CHAPTER
31

That night, I lock up my Prius. As I walk toward Pete's, I run lines in my head. I practice all the things I want to say to Nick, all the things I want him to know.

Since my run, I've been prepping for tonight like it's an audition. It was my way of keeping calm, staying focused—and not getting scared and wussing out. But this is so much more than a casting call. What's on the line isn't just some role on a TV show or in a movie. What's on the line is my future.

Our future.

Assuming we even have one, that is—but no. I really cannot go there. Right now, my head needs to be a no-negativity zone. Only positive thoughts allowed.

With a deep, bracing breath, I open the door and enter the bar.

It's Thursday night, one of our busier nights, and the place is already pretty packed. My gaze goes immediately to Nick's end of the bar, but he's not there. In his usual place, Sara is clearing a few dirty glasses off the counter.

I don't have a supernatural connection with Nick anymore, so I don't know if he's here, on his way, or maybe not coming at all.

Wrangling my growing panic, I weave my way through the tables, up to the bar. "Hey, Sara," I say. "Wh-where's Nick?"

She glances up at me. "Oh, hi, Carrie." She nods toward the back of the bar. "He's in the storeroom, finishing up inventory."

My whole body sighs with relief. "Gotcha," I say. "Thanks."

· · · · ·

I step into the back room, and I find Nick kneeling on the floor in front of several cartons of liquor, counting the bottles. His back is toward me, so I can't tell what tonight's band tee is. But his shoulders look tense, and it breaks my heart that his anger at me might be the cause.

I take a deep breath.

"Nick?"

Hearing my voice, he flinches. He doesn't turn around. "I'm busy here," he says without looking at me. He makes a note on the inventory sheet on a clipboard, then turns his attention back to the boxes.

He's not going to make this easy.

But that's okay. I came prepared.

This is my moment. This is what I've been rehearsing for. In a way, it's like my whole life up until now has been just one big rehearsal, leading me here.

This is where I tell Nick everything I've done wrong to try to make it all right. This is where I confess what I'm feeling for him and hope against hope that he might feel something similar for me.

Only I blank. My mind is a total. Freaking. Blank.

I stand here, mouth open, but nothing comes out. All my careful, well-chosen phrases elude me, and I'm left with nothing but my emotions.

Goddammit, am I really choking *now*? Am I seriously tanking *this*?

I close my eyes and remind myself that this isn't an audition. I don't need scripted lines. Hopefully, my emotions will be enough. I just need to speak from my heart.

I open my eyes.

"Nick, I'm so sorry," I say to his back. "I should have told you about Jenn."

No reply. He continues with the inventory.

"I meant to tell you," I say, pressing on. "Really, I did. Except there was always something getting in the way." I'm about to leave it there, but deep down, I know that won't cut it. I need to come totally clean. "Mostly, I guess *I* was getting in the way," I confess. "Me and my stupid fear of having the tough conversations."

Nick doesn't say anything. He still hasn't turned to face me, but he has stopped counting the bottles. I think he's listening.

"I let Jenn put all these questions about you in my head," I say. "But really, I had no reason to question you. I know that now."

Slowly, he sits back on his heels and puts the clipboard down. The muscles in his shoulders don't seem quite so taut anymore. Maybe he's *hearing* me?

"I thought you just changed your mind," says Nick quietly. He's talking to me, but he's still looking at the liquor bottles.

"Changed my mind?" I ask.

I watch from the back as Nick nods, his long dark hair grazing the neck of his tee. "As a foster kid, I bounced around a lot. And it always seemed like, just when I'd start to get comfortable, just when I'd let my guard down and begin to think that a temporary situation might become permanent, something would happen. There'd be some reason why they couldn't keep me, why I'd have to go. And I'd find myself right back in the system." He shrugs. "So after we got together, when you started acting so distant, I figured something like that was happening all over again."

"So you put your guard up?" I ask.

"I put my guard up," he confirms. "And I pulled back too."

It's basically what Pete told me. But hearing it from Nick, it's so much sadder. And while this certainly explains why Nick got all distant with me, why he seemed to shut down, it totally shreds me up inside to think that I caused him even a moment of pain. And that I brought back such painful memories.

"And when you pulled back, it just put even more questions in my head. It made me doubt you more. It made me doubt *us* more." I shake my head. "I'm so sorry, Nick," I say again. "I should have trusted you. I *do* trust you. I—"

I can't take it anymore. Playing this scene without a face-to-face partner is torture.

"Goddammit, Nick, don't keep your guard up now," I say. "Please. Look at me."

He doesn't move.

"*Look at me*," I repeat.

With a sigh, Nick gets to his feet. Keeping his eyes down, he shoves his hands into the pockets of his jeans and turns around.

Van Halen, I see. Tonight's band tee is Van Halen.

I wait for Nick to stop staring at the floor.

Finally, he lifts his eyes and looks at me.

At first, I can't read his expression. But soon, he starts to squint at me in confusion.

Gradually, I see the light of understanding dawn in his gaze, and I understand what must be going through his head.

I didn't dress in a way to deliberately expose my new build—or rather my *old* build—but I didn't try to hide it either. And Nick, who knows every inch of my body so well, clearly knows that there's been a change.

And since my confession to him last night, he knows the one thing that could have caused such a change.

Slowly, a smile stretches across his face, and I've never been so happy to see his dimples.

"I love you too, Carrie," he says.

All at once, he's closing the space between us, scooping me up in his strong arms, swinging me off my feet. I feel such a rush of relief and joy and love—God, so much love—that all I can do is laugh.

When he silences my laughter with a kiss, I totally forget we're at work. All I care about is that Nick loves me. *He loves me!* And I love him.

· · · · ·

I'm not sure whose night it is to close up Pete's, but it doesn't matter anymore. Nick and I are a team now. We've just finished stacking the chairs on the tabletops, and we're starting to upend the stools on the bar. As I work from my end and he works from his, I still can't believe I'm forgiven.

"I never should have doubted you," I tell Nick.

"And I never should have shut down on you," he says. "I should have been more open about my feelings."

"And I should have been stronger," I say. "And from here on in, I promise I *will* be stronger. Even without all my slayer muscles."

"Well, if you ask me, you're already pretty strong," he says. "Strong enough to take on a VIP room full of vampires and another slayer to boot."

"Maybe," I say. As much as the compliment from Nick pleases me, I know I haven't entirely earned the praise. "But I almost wasn't strong enough to come in here tonight and tell you I love you."

With a *plunk-plunk*, Nick and I stack the last two stools on the counter, coming together at the center of the bar.

"What was that?" asks Nick, grinning down at me. "What was that you just said?"

That's when I realize that I haven't actually said it yet. I haven't told him how I feel. Based on my new appearance, Nick was able to surmise it, of course. But I haven't said the words out loud.

And I definitely don't want him making judgments about me just because of how I look. Especially when it comes to something as important as this.

So I peer up at him, grinning back. "I love you, Nick," I tell him. "I absolutely freaking love you."

EPILOGUE

TWO WEEKS LATER

W hat do you think?" asks Nick.

I take a step back to assess our handiwork. We've just finished repainting my bedroom wall, the one with the fire damage, although the bedroom won't be mine for too much longer. I'm moving in with Nick.

But I'll be staying until Liv can find a new roommate. When it comes to rent, I don't want to leave her in the lurch.

"Looks good," I say with an approving nod. "Looks like a slayer never slept here at all."

Nick frowns at me. "I'm sorry," he says.

"For what?" I ask.

"You know what."

I sigh. I do know. Poor Nick. First he felt guilty about unwittingly turning me into a vampire slayer, and now he's been feeling equally torn up for unknowingly undoing the change.

I put down my paint roller and walk closer to him so I can thread my arms around his waist. "All you did was make me realize how much I love you," I tell him, peering up at him. "You don't ever have to apologize for that."

"I can turn you, you know," he says. "Just say the word, and we can get Arlo and The Book on a plane right back here."

I smile. We've talked about this before, but I'm not ready to take that step just yet.

It's not that I have any doubts about Nick. I am *so* done with the doubts. I know with absolute certainty that I want to spend the rest of my life with him. And if that life is an immortal one? So much the better.

And it's not that I'm squeamish about him biting me. Full disclosure? He already has. Since our initial foray into the world of light bondage with the bike lock, I've become a lot more sexually curious. I guess that's what happens when you have a partner you trust implicitly. And let's just say that I understand *exactly* why someone would want to be a vampire's blood donor.

But for now, after all the supernatural chaos, I'm happy just to be human again for a while. I'm happy just to be me.

And honestly? Being me has never been better. I mean, I'm moving in with my soulmate. I've got the best friends anyone could ever have. And I just gave my notice at Pete's because, in another two weeks— drum roll, please—I start my absolute dream job playing ADA Cassidy Carmichael on *Robbery-Homicide Division*.

I'm not sure how I'll explain the obvious change in my size when I show up for my first day of work. Then again, maybe I won't have to. After all, Heather will be handling my wardrobe. Besides, I know I didn't land this part because of what I look like. I got the role because of what I can *do*.

"Someday," I tell Nick. "Someday I'll ask you to turn me. But not today."

The truth is, as amazing as things are between Nick and me, I still have a fair bit of work to do repairing some of the other relationships in my life. I mean, I'm pretty sure my ex Jonathan hates my guts. And I don't think my parents are exactly thrilled with me at the moment either. So before I choose to become a vampire, I want to make sure there's no one out there who could be negatively impacted by my choice. Nick didn't know about the consequences, but I do. I don't want to be responsible for turning anyone into a slayer without them choosing it for themselves.

Plus, it might be a couple of years before I have enough Hollywood clout to demand that all my shoots be *night* shoots. But that's a problem for later.

In the win column, Jenn is trying to control her slayer. And she's making progress. Good thing too, because I know at least one vampire I very much want to keep *un*dead.

Nick wraps an arm around me. He uses his other hand to tip my chin up higher to better meet his gaze. "You really don't miss the power?" he asks. "The power that came with being a vampire slayer?"

It's a funny question, really. Because the power I had as a slayer never felt quite right. It wasn't a good kind of power. It was power that was rooted in hate.

It was only by fighting that power that I found my own power. A good kind of power. The *best* kind of power.

I move my hands up Nick's torso and over his shoulders, looping my arms around his neck. "Nick," I say, rising up onto my tiptoes and angling my face for a kiss. "How could I miss my slayer powers? I have you. I have love. True love. And that's the greatest power of all."

Nick grins, flashing epic dimples that, even if I do live forever, I will never get tired of looking at.

"You still slay me, you know that?" he says as his mouth homes in on mine. "You absolutely slay me."

ACKNOWLEDGMENTS

This is my second novel, and it was an absolute joy to write it—mostly because I had so many wonderful people supporting me along the way.

Thanks to my agent, Maria Napolitano, at KT Literary. I couldn't have a better advocate for my work. I'm grateful for all the gut checks, and I'm excited that we're embarking on the next phase of this journey together.

Thanks also to Flavia and the team at Bookcase Literary Agency. I wouldn't be where I am without you.

Thanks to everyone at Sourcebooks Casablanca and especially to my editor, Mary Altman. Working with you on my first book was like taking a master class in novel writing. If I delivered this second book in good shape, it's only because I could hear your voice in my head as I was writing it. And once again, your edit notes made all the difference. I'm a better writer because of you.

Thanks to my friend, Mara, who was an early reader. Your input on the acting storyline and your suggestions for ways to add dashes of Liv's Hispanic culture were invaluable.

Thanks to my friend and biggest cheerleader, Diana. You are the best hype woman ever.

Thanks to my BFF, Joan. Your unwavering love and encouragement, as always, mean the world to me.

And finally, thanks to all the aspiring actors, musicians, and other creators I met during my own time in Los Angeles. As I was writing Carrie and Nick's story, it was so much fun to think back to those early days when we were young and idealistic and had our whole lives ahead of us. There's a little bit of all of you in this book.

ABOUT THE AUTHOR

Gloria Duke is a pen name for Gloria Ketterer, a WGA award–winning radio writer, TV sitcom writer, and brand advertising copywriter. *Vampires Never Say Die* is her second novel.

Instagram: @gloriadukehea